"I reckon the two of you will have to run the paper together until the judge comes to town."

"Run it together?" Mary Lou's protest was incredulous.

"I have no intention of sharing my inheritance with a perfect stranger." Jared wouldn't give up the last claim he had to a family connection.

"It's not your inheritance." Mary Lou took a step toward him. "It's mine. You may be blood kin, but I was the only family Jacob Ivy had for the last eight years."

The sheriff opened the door. "The two of you can argue all you want. I won't dispossess either of you. The judge should be through town between Thanksgiving and Christmas. Learn to work together until then."

"He can't stay here!" Mary Lou was indignant.

"Sheriff, you have the authority to evict her." Jared made another attempt to settle the matter today.

"I do, but I won't be the one to throw an orphaned girl into the street without the judge's say-so." He tipped his hat to Mary Lou. "Good day to you both."

And he was gone.

Angel Moore fell in love with romance in elementary school when she read the story of Robin Hood and Maid Marian. Who doesn't want to escape to a happily-ever-after world? Married to her best friend, she has two wonderful sons, a lovely daughter-in-law and three grandkids. She loves sharing her faith and the hope she knows is real because of God's goodness to her. Find her at www.angelmoorebooks.com.

Books by Angel Moore

Love Inspired Historical

Conveniently Wed
The Marriage Bargain
The Rightful Heir

Visit the Author Profile page at Harlequin.com.

ANGEL MOORE

The Rightful Heir

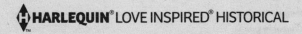

Recycling programs
for this product may
not exist in your area.

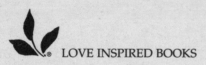

® LOVE INSPIRED BOOKS

ISBN-13: 978-0-373-28381-1

The Rightful Heir

Copyright © 2016 by Angelissa J. Moore

All rights reserved. Except for use in any review, the reproduction or utilization of this work in whole or in part in any form by any electronic, mechanical or other means, now known or hereinafter invented, including xerography, photocopying and recording, or in any information storage or retrieval system, is forbidden without the written permission of the editorial office, Love Inspired Books, 195 Broadway, New York, NY 10007 U.S.A.

This is a work of fiction. Names, characters, places and incidents are either the product of the author's imagination or are used fictitiously, and any resemblance to actual persons, living or dead, business establishments, events or locales is entirely coincidental.

This edition published by arrangement with Love Inspired Books.

® and TM are trademarks of Love Inspired Books, used under license. Trademarks indicated with ® are registered in the United States Patent and Trademark Office, the Canadian Intellectual Property Office and in other countries.

www.Harlequin.com

Printed in U.S.A.

A good man leaveth an inheritance
to his children's children: and the
wealth of the sinner is laid up for the just.
—*Proverbs* 13:22

In loving memory of Ashley Bailey

The light and joy of a niece
who celebrated everyone is sorely missed.

To my editor, Dina Davis,
for her support and expertise.

To Belle Calhoune, my fellow Love Inspired author
and accountability partner, for the
encouragement and laughs along the way.

To the readers, who join me for the story.

To Austin, for his continued sacrifice and wisdom.

To my sweet Maria, Melody, Asher and Judah.
God has blessed me beyond measure.

Having these wonderful people in my life
motivates me every day.

To Bob, my best friend.

And to God, for His mercy and constant help.

Chapter One

"I'll be right with you." Mary Lou Ellison was on her knees behind the press. A gust of wind from the opening door had caught her story notes and floated them under the edge of the beast of a machine.

A deep voice refused to wait. "I'm looking for the owner."

Mary Lou caught the edge of the paper and pulled it free. The notes on the harvest celebration were the most interesting she'd had in weeks. She wouldn't disappoint the townsfolk by not covering the festivities for the next edition of the *Pine Haven Record*.

She stood straight and looked at the intruder across the top of the press. "I'm the owner."

As expected, the man's eyes opened wide in apparent disbelief. The raised brows and confused expression were normal to her now. No one entering the office for the first time expected a woman to own a newspaper. Much less a young woman. At twenty-two, she was considered young by businessmen and old by most any man in search of a wife. Not that she wanted a husband. She could take care of herself.

"That's not possible." The handsome face rejected her claim. If she weren't a journalist, she would scold herself for noticing his strong jaw, thick hair and cautious blue eyes. Since details were her business, she allowed herself to take in the cowboy's lean build. Strong arms were encased in a suede coat. A leather vest covered his chest over a shirt of gray. Boots showing signs of hard work shifted on her floor. A Stetson swung in his hands.

"It is possible." She put the notes on her desk and placed the magnifying glass on top of them. The wind wouldn't send her on another merry chase. "And it's true. Has been for the last two months." She blew the hair out of her eyes and asked, "What can I do for you?"

He turned and looked at the words on the glass window. Taking one finger and underlining the backward lettering, he read out loud, "'Jacob Ivy, Publisher.' That's who I'm looking for."

The pain of her grief had eased into hollowness. Jacob's death was the only reason she owned the paper. He'd been her mentor and teacher but mostly her only true friend. She sniffed and answered. "Mr. Ivy passed just two months ago. I'm the owner now."

"Grump is dead?" He shook his head.

She saw it then. The breadth of his forehead and shape of his nose. He was Mr. Ivy—forty years younger.

Why was he here? Why, after all the years his grandfather had reached out to him, had he come now? When it was too late.

"Jared Ivy?"

"How did you know my name?"

Mary Lou pointed to a frame on the wall near the front door. It held a tiny photograph of two men and a small boy. "That's you and your father with Mr. Ivy."

The only man who could take away the life she'd built in Pine Haven followed her direction to study the photograph. Could Jared Ivy really disrupt her situation now? The deed to the building was locked in the drawer of the heavy desk Mr. Ivy had worked at for all the years she'd known him.

"I've never seen a photograph of my father." He lifted a hand and wiped the dust from the frame.

Mary Lou's heart ached for him. As much as his appearance was a mystery—one that could be upsetting to her future—she knew what it was like to be without any knowledge of her father.

"Mr. Ivy told me about the accident that took your father's life when you were a small child."

"He did?" Jared Ivy turned back to her. "Perhaps you could tell me."

"You don't know?" Why wouldn't a grown man know the circumstances of his father's death?

"My mother refused to speak about him. She said it would cause me unnecessary pain as a child. Then, when I became an adult, she didn't speak much about anything." He said the words without judgment.

"He and your grandfather started the newspaper together as a family business. Your father was killed while working to construct this building. He fell from the top of the wall when the wood was being pulled up to put on the roof."

Jared Ivy didn't flinch or blink. Somehow he absorbed the death of his grandfather and the details of his father's death without an outward reaction.

"What happened to Grump?"

"Doc Willis said his heart gave out." She dealt in facts all day long, every day. Some people accused her of being cold, but direct was the only way she knew to be. Years of condensing a tragedy into a few paragraphs, or a big event into a couple of sentences, had taught her to be concise. She smiled at the memory of Mr. Ivy telling her it made her a good newspaper woman. Having loved Mr. Ivy like she did, it hurt to tell his story in so few words.

"I see." He reached into the pocket of his vest. "If you'd be so kind as to direct me to the land office."

"Do you intend to stay in town? I thought you came to see your grandfather."

"I did come to see him." He pulled a watch from the pocket, opened it to check the time and slid it back into its place. "But as that is not possible, I have other business to attend."

Did she dare to probe beyond his vague answer? "I wonder you have other business in town. You must have arrived on the train today."

"I did."

The way he ignored her veiled query gave her cause for concern. What purpose did he have in Pine Haven with no living relatives here? "The land office is most likely closed this late on a Saturday."

"Nevertheless, I need to know where it is." He put a hand on the door latch. "If you've no wish to tell me, I'll ask at the hotel."

"It's beyond the hotel, on the opposite side of the street."

He thanked her and left. The Stetson went back on his head before he closed the door behind him.

Jared Ivy was nothing like his grandfather had imagined. More than once, Jacob Ivy had talked about how like his father the young Jared had been. The years since the man's death had left the young Mr. Ivy with no hint of the warm and caring family she'd grown to love through his grandfather's stories.

A looming deadline for the paper to be ready to print pushed the handsome man out of her thoughts. He could go to the land office, but he wouldn't find Mr. Little there.

She only had a short amount of time to put the words of her last story for the coming edition on paper. Almost everyone in town had attended the harvest celebration on the previous evening. The festivities had been pleasant and the food good. The annual affair warranted a spot at the top of the page. First she'd pen the words and then the tedious task of setting the type for the press would begin. She hoped she'd left enough space to do the story justice.

Her words had formed numerous articles for several years, but the town was judging her differently as the owner. As a reporter with Jacob Ivy looking over her shoulder, she'd done well. His years in the paper business had built a reputation of truth and integrity for the *Pine Haven Record*. Building the trust of the community now that she was the publisher was another story indeed.

Her heart ached anew at the loss of Mr. Ivy. He'd been the only true father figure in her life. She wouldn't let his grandson do anything to tarnish that memory.

Jared left the hotel and walked in the direction of the land office.

Grump was dead.

In the almost twenty years since his father had passed, it never occurred to Jared that his grandfather would die before he returned to Pine Haven. Jared had vague snatches of memories in which he sat on the edge of Grump's desk while the man scratched a pencil across the page to tell a story.

Grump had told his last story and Jared hadn't been here to read it.

When he found the land office closed, he went in search of the sheriff. The little sprite of a young woman at the paper office had proclaimed herself the new owner. The papers he'd retrieved from his luggage at the hotel said different. This piece of business could be settled before nightfall. He persuaded the sheriff to go with him to his grandfather's office and explain the situation to Mary Lou Ellison.

When he opened the door this time she had her back to the entrance. She turned and he was struck again by her confidence. Nothing about her spoke of the cowering fear he'd seen in his mother.

She wore a white blouse with the sleeves pushed up near the elbows. Black bands held them out of her way while she worked to gather the letters that would shape the stories she'd written. An ink-stained apron covered the front of her clothes. Her brown hair had been kissed by the sun and shone lighter around her face. A smudge of ink peeked from behind the tresses that escaped their pins and hung loose on her forehead. Green eyes met his again. The wariness he'd detected earlier came back with a vengeance.

"Miss Ellison, I've brought the sheriff with me to show you something." He knew the best way to deal with unexpected or unpleasant news was to get right to it.

"Let's not get in a rush now, Mr. Ivy." Sheriff Collins spoke up. The man's disheveled clothes and tired face made Jared wonder how well he could be protecting the citizens of Pine Haven. He looked like he needed a fresh shave and a good night's rest.

Jared wouldn't wait. Best to handle things immediately. "I see no need to dawdle."

Sheriff Collins looked him up and down. "I don't know how I feel about a cowboy who talks like a schoolteacher."

Mary Lou Ellison chuckled. "I'm not sure what to make of him, either, Sheriff." She put down the letters she was sorting and came to stand in front of the press. "He says he's Mr. Ivy's grandson, but he's nothing like the way his grandpa described him."

"He hadn't seen me in almost twenty years." Jared was losing patience with these two.

"That's what troubles me." Mary Lou pointed at him. "Why didn't you come see him in all that time?"

The sheriff ran his hand over the stubble on his chin. "That's a good question."

"My business is not the business of either of you." Jared watched the sheriff stand a bit straighter at his rebuff.

"Mr. Ivy, if you want my help in solving this situation, you're gonna need to hold your words a bit."

Mary Lou spoke up. "What situation, Sheriff?" Her eyes darted from the sheriff to him.

"Seems Mr. Ivy here has a will from Jacob Ivy saying the paper belongs to him."

Her face blanched at the sheriff's announcement. Jared hated to cause her pain, but Grump and his father had wanted him to have the paper. He'd let his grandfather down his whole life. He wouldn't deny the man the legacy he'd earned by building the *Pine Haven Record* to what it was today. His mother had prevented contact with Grump since his father had died. Without her presence to hinder him—*God rest her soul*—he would follow through with his father and Grump's wishes now.

Mary Lou turned to the sheriff. "The paper is mine. You were there the day Mr. Little gave me the deed."

Sheriff Collins nodded in agreement. "I remember, Mary Lou. It's just that you didn't have a real will. All we had was your word saying what Mr. Ivy had told you."

"So that's how you got the paper." He wondered if

she'd swindled Grump in his old age. Had Grump lost his reasoning? Did she hoodwink him?

Her wary eyes became daggers. "Don't you dare accuse me of swindling Jacob Ivy." The level tone of her voice spoke of controlled rage. Was she guilty and trying to cover it, or had she really cared about his grandfather? "He was like a father to me."

"He wasn't *like* a grandfather to me. He *was* my grandfather." It was best to say it and put everything out in the open. He reached into his vest for the will. "See for yourself."

Mary Lou took the will from his hand and unfolded the aged document. Her eyes skimmed the page. She folded it and gave it back.

"It says the land and the paper are mine." He tucked the will away.

"I read it." She turned to the sheriff. "Sheriff, you know Mr. Ivy wanted me to have the paper. You know how close we were. How he taught me about the newspaper business. Even if Jared Ivy is his grandson, does that mean he can come in and take away what was given to me?"

Sheriff Collins looked at Mary Lou and then at Jared. "She's right. The old man loved her. He took her in years ago."

"I'm glad to hear he had people in his life who loved him." Jared patted his vest pocket. "But his wishes are plain. I found this will in my mother's things after she died. Grump must have sent it to her when I was a boy."

Sheriff Collins asked, "Did you come here just to make your claim to the paper?"

Jared shook his head. "I came here to see my grandfather. I didn't know he'd passed." To his surprise, Mary Lou validated his words.

"That's true. He came in asking for Mr. Ivy." It seemed she was a person of integrity. If she'd chosen to lie about that, there would be nothing he could do to prove her wrong.

"Don't see why you brung the will then." The sheriff seemed to be doubting his word.

"I brought everything I own with me. My intent is to settle in Pine Haven." Jared glanced at Mary Lou. "I had hoped for the opportunity to spend time with Grump."

Sheriff Collins grunted and looked at both of them. "Only thing I know to do is make you sell it and split the profit."

"No!" Mary Lou stomped her foot as she said the word.

Jared agreed with her on this point. "The paper is not for sale."

She persisted. "I'd never sell. Mr. Ivy worked too hard to build the *Record* to what it is today."

He seized on her words. "And you said yourself, he built it for my family."

She glared at him then. "And *you* didn't want it!" The vehemence in her words was palpable.

"I didn't know about it."

She scoffed. "How could you not know? He wrote you every week. Page after page. He even included a copy of the paper hoping you'd use the schooling he paid for to help him make it better."

"I'm going to do just that." His words were as forceful as hers.

Grump had paid for his schooling? He didn't have the heart to tell this angry woman and the sheriff that he hadn't known about the letters. That his mother had confessed to burning them without telling him of their existence. Her deathbed confessions about so many things had driven him to return to Pine Haven and finally connect with the only relative he had left. Only now Grump was gone, too. Resentment of his mother's secretive silence about his father's family, and the revelation that she'd hidden them from him for the whole of his life, had instilled in him a deep mistrust of women. Mary Lou's quick move to take ownership of the paper without contacting him echoed his mother's furtive actions and reinforced that mistrust.

The sheriff twisted his brow in a frown. "Don't know exactly what to do." He rubbed the stubble on his chin with one hand. "I reckon the two of you will have to run the paper together until the judge comes to town. He'll have to sort it out for you."

"Run it together?" Mary Lou's protest was incredulous.

"I have no intention of sharing my inheritance with a perfect stranger." Jared wouldn't give up the last claim he had to a family connection. He had no living relatives and wouldn't let what was rightly his slip away from him to pacify a small-town sheriff or placate a woman who had entrenched herself in his grandfather's life. Possibly for the sole purpose of gaining his fortune at his death.

"It's not your inheritance." Mary Lou took a step toward him. "It's mine. You may be blood kin, but I was the only family Jacob Ivy had for the last eight years."

The sheriff opened the door. "The two of you can argue all you want. I won't dispossess either of you. The judge should be through town between Thanksgiving and Christmas. Learn to work together until then." He stepped through the doorway. "Mr. Ivy, I'd recommend you stay in the rooms upstairs that your grandfather used. Mary Lou lives in the quarters attached to the back of the building."

"He can't stay here!" Mary Lou was indignant.

"Sheriff, you have the authority to evict her." Jared made another attempt to settle the matter today.

"I do, but I won't be the one to throw an orphaned girl into the street without the judge's say-so." He tipped his hat to Mary Lou. "Good day to you both." And he was gone.

An orphan? Mary Lou was a grown woman. One who could take care of herself. It wasn't his responsibility to provide her with a home. No self-respecting woman would allow a man to take care of her in such a fashion.

"Oooo, the nerve of that man! He is forever taking the easy road as sheriff." She stood with her back straight and her fists clenched at her sides. The wrath of Mary Lou Ellison seemed to be a force to be reckoned with.

How would he endure one month with this fiery creature? Much less two?

He'd try a different approach. Perhaps he could reason with her. "Miss Ellison, I appreciate that you were close to Grump. I'm sure he loved you a great deal."

"He did. And I can tell you he wouldn't cotton to the way you're trying to put me out on the street." She turned on one heel and went back to the work she'd been doing when he'd arrived.

"I'm not trying to put you out on the street. I can give you a handsome sum so you can set yourself up in a nice room somewhere. Enough to get you through until you find work."

"A few measly dollars so I'll give you my paper? I am not interested, Mr. Ivy." She fished through the tray in search of another letter. Nimble fingers slid it into place beside the others.

"It's not measly. It will be more than a judge will give you when he comes to town and sees the paper is rightfully mine. He could even require you to pay me for the time you refuse to leave."

"Pay you? I earn my way here. Don't be surprised when the deed I bring to the judge has him sending you on your merry way. You *and* your will. A man's actions speak to who he is. A fair judge will see you as a grandson who only wanted an inheritance. This entire region knows I've worked on this paper since I was a schoolgirl. My time under your grandfather's tutelage will show how close we were."

"You've been here since you were a girl?" Why would Grump take in a young girl?

"Mr. Ivy knew my uncle well. When he got sick, I didn't know what would happen to me. Before he died,

Mr. Ivy promised that he'd take care of me. I've been here ever since."

Was she right? Surely a judge would consider blood kinship when deciding a man's claim. His grandfather was dead. No other living soul shared his blood. Jared was the end of the Ivy line.

"I'm sorry for your loss." He dipped his head to emphasize the sincerity of his words. He found it difficult to be alone in the world. It must be harder on a woman. Though he'd seen no sign of weakness in this one.

She nodded in response. "Thank you. Losing Mr. Ivy has been the hardest thing I've ever faced."

His head shot up. "Losing Grump? What about your own kin?"

Mary Lou shook her head. "My own kin didn't want me or love me. Not like Mr. Ivy did."

"But you said he knew your uncle well."

"He did. He knew well how little my uncle wanted me in the first place." She fingered the letter she held in her hand and stared at it as if seeking an answer. "No one ever understood me or was kind to me like your grandfather. It's a loss I'll not soon forget." She cleared her throat and slid the letter into place. "Now, if you don't mind, I've got work to finish to get the paper ready to print."

"I'll need you to show me how to set up the paper." He took off his coat and hung it on the coat tree near the door. He dropped his hat over the coat and pushed up his sleeves. The sound of tiny letters hitting the floor and scattering caused him to turn around.

"Look what you made me do." Mary Lou went down on her hands and knees to gather the errant letters.

Jared bent to pick up the composing stick she'd been using to set the letters for the story she was working on. He turned it over in his hand and put it back on the table. "How long will it take to redo this?" He got down on his knees to help her.

"Maybe an hour." She scooped up more letters and sat back on her heels. "Unless someone causes another delay."

He put his hands up in a defensive posture. "I only volunteered to help. I'm sorry you dropped this, but I can't think it was my doing."

The air went out of her in a huff. "You're right. I'm sorry for being rude."

"An apology? I'll admit you have surprised me, Miss Ellison."

She reached for another stray letter. "No more than you surprised me, Mr. Ivy."

How did she feel? What would it be like to have your business and home taken from you by a stranger? He was sorry for her, but at the same time it was his business. His home. It hadn't been hers to take in the first place. He'd be civil with her, but he wouldn't allow himself to be sympathetic to her plight to the point of giving up the only thing he had left of his family legacy. He must remind himself that, whatever her intention, she stole that from him. And he would get it back, no matter what.

Gunfire erupted in the street behind him. He took cover under the desk as Mary Lou scurried to her feet, reached for a pad and pencil, and headed for the door.

Chapter Two

Mary Lou let out a yelp when Jared reached from under the desk and caught her by the arm.

"You can't go out there! It's not safe!"

She jerked her elbow from his grasp. "It's my job." She left him, mouth agape, and went to the front window. She could see several people spilling out of the swinging doors at Winston's Grand Saloon on the opposite side of Pine Street. Someone she didn't recognize ran up the sidewalk in her direction. He had a pistol in one hand and a man lay prone in the street behind him.

"Lord, help me." She didn't realize she'd spoken out loud as she pulled the door open and stepped into the path of the fleeing gunman. The man tried to avoid her and ran headlong into a post on her porch. As he tripped and landed on his back, the gun he held flew across the ground and skidded into the middle of the dirt street.

"What are you doing?" Jared came out of the newspaper office behind her. "You could be hurt."

Mary Lou skipped down the steps and kicked the gun away as the gunman rolled over to get up.

She barked at Jared. "If you don't stay out of my way, you could get me killed." She turned to see Sheriff Collins emerge from the crowd around the victim. "Glad you could join us, Sheriff."

The man in the street made a last effort to get away, but the sheriff grabbed his arm and twisted it behind his back. "Whoa, there. Ain't no need in making me have to work harder. It'll just make me less pleasant when you're sitting in my jail."

Mary Lou held her pencil at the ready. "What's your name? Do you know the man you shot?"

The man protested. "Let me go. I didn't do anything."

The sheriff grunted. "That's what everyone who ends up in my jail says."

Mary Lou took a step closer. "Why did you shoot him?"

The man twisted against the sheriff's hold but was no match for the lawman's strength. "I didn't!" There was something in the tone of his declaration that made her think he could be telling the truth.

"Then why run away?"

"I didn't want to get shot."

Sheriff Collins held up one hand. "Let me get him to the jail, Mary Lou. I'll even give you first crack at talking to him, seeing how you helped me out when you kicked away his gun."

"Thanks, Sheriff." She hurried in the direction of the crowd in front of the saloon. "I'll be by as soon as I've talked to the witnesses."

The sheriff's voice bellowed behind her. "Let me do my job, Mary Lou."

She ignored him. If she waited for him to get back from putting the shooter in jail, most of the crowd would have dispersed.

She stopped short. The man on his way to jail might not be the shooter. She'd assumed so because he'd run away from the scene so quickly. What if he was another intended victim? Mr. Ivy would scold her for such assumptions. He'd say it was a poor journalist who lost their objectivity.

She approached the owner of the general store. "Mr. Croft, did you see what happened?"

"No, ma'am." The older man brushed his sleeves to remove the dust of the street. "I was just heading back to the store after getting my hair cut. Next thing I know, I'm lying in the street next to some fella who just got shot." He frowned and looked at her. "It's a sad day when a man can't walk through the middle of town without such an incident."

Mary Lou agreed with Mr. Croft, but she didn't have time for his commiserations today. "Thank you, Mr. Croft."

She pushed her way between the gawkers and tried to get a good look at the victim. He was a stranger. Most of the people who got into trouble at the saloon weren't from around Pine Haven. They were usually passengers from the train stopping over for business or cowboys on their way farther west who stopped into town for a rest from their travels.

Doc Willis pushed through the other side of the gathering. "Back up, folks. Let me see if I can help the man."

People pushed back just enough to let the doctor inside the tight circle of the curious. The man groaned and became combative when the doctor touched the bleeding wound on his leg.

A deep, rich voice spoke from beside her. "You'll only make it worse if you don't hold still." Jared leaned in close, causing her to shift and regain her footing. Mary Lou bristled at his intrusion.

The victim grunted and the doctor pushed the man's shoulder back against the dirt. "He's right. All that straining isn't doing you a bit of good." The doctor reached into his bag and pulled out a strip of white bandaging cloth.

Mary Lou wouldn't be pushed aside by Jared Ivy. As far as she was concerned, he was a newcomer who threatened her paper. "How bad is it, Doc?"

"He'll live, but he's gonna have a whopper of a limp for a while."

Jared's next words surprised her. "Did anyone see who shot him?"

Mary Lou jerked her head around to face him. "I was just about to ask that." Jared's eyes seemed to laugh at her when two men spoke up.

"I saw the whole thing." This man was another stranger. His words were slurred with liquor. From experience, Mary Lou knew nothing he said would prove helpful.

Winston Ledford, the owner of the saloon, spoke next. "Who's asking?" Mr. Ledford was known for being a shrewd businessman. Most of the town hadn't wanted a saloon, but he'd built it anyway. And the success of his business was a trial to them all. The violence of fist fights and the occasional shootings were punctuation to the endless raucous laughter and noise that never ceased to escape the doors of his establishment.

"Jared Ivy. I'm the owner of the *Pine Haven Record*."

Silence fell across the scene. Doc Willis looked up from tending his patient. "Mary Lou is the owner of the *Record*."

Mary Lou broke into the conversation. "Did you see what happened, Mr. Ledford?"

He shook his head. "I was in my office when I heard the commotion. It appears to me that this man was shot in the street, not in my establishment." He nodded to Mary Lou. "I see no reason for my presence here." He turned and walked away. The doors of the saloon swooshed behind him as he disappeared into the dark interior.

She decided to go straight to the heart of the matter. Leaning in as the doctor sat the shooting victim up, she asked, "Sir, do you know the man who shot you?"

"I do." His words were weak and he slumped against the doctor.

Jared interrupted again. "Who was it?"

The victim laughed. "I shot myself. My pa warned me that gun had a hair trigger. Went off in my lap when I reached to pull my winnings from the middle of the table." He suddenly looked around the circle of bystanders, very concerned. "Hey! Who got my money?"

Mary Lou sighed and backed away from the group. She knew without looking behind her that the crowd was dispersing. One man's careless actions had caused

quite a stir. The gamblers who took his money had probably tossed him into the street. End of story.

Jared caught up to her as she stepped onto the porch
in front of the paper. "Are you just walking away without finding out what happened?"

She stopped and turned on her heel. "There is no
story. It was an accident."

Jared spread his arms wide, palms up. "No story?
What about the man sitting in the jail this minute? He
probably has a story to tell."

"He was a victim of the commotion. The sheriff will
release him as soon as he knows the victim shot himself.
The man said he didn't do it before he was taken to jail."

"I'm not so sure." His eyes narrowed. "Not so sure
at all." He lifted a hand in parting. "I'll be back as soon
as I can."

She went into the paper and dropped her notebook
on the desk. Picking up the composing stick and beginning to reassemble the work she'd dropped onto the
floor earlier, she wasn't surprised when Jared didn't
follow her inside. He may be off on a fool's errand, but
she had a paper to print.

Jared turned the corner on Main Street and headed
for the sheriff's office. Why would a man run away
from a shooting with his gun drawn if he didn't have
anything to do with it? Something didn't sit right in
Jared's craw about this presumed-innocent stranger.

He opened the door of the sheriff's office and
stepped inside.

"What is it now, Ivy? Can't you see I'm a busy man?"

Sheriff Collins pulled the large key from the lock on the cell door at the back of his office. He hung the ring on a nail on the wall behind his desk. The man he'd hauled away from the scene minutes earlier declared his innocence from behind the bars.

"Hush up!" the sheriff warned the alleged criminal in the cell. He put the man's gun in the top drawer of his desk, locked it, dropped that key into the pocket of his leather vest and patted it. "You've caused enough trouble here today. Sit down and be quiet."

Jared watched the man who had appeared guilty after his attempt to leave the scene. What had really happened in the saloon? "Sheriff, the fellow with the bullet in his leg says he shot himself."

The prisoner rattled the door of the cell. "I told you I didn't shoot him!"

Sheriff Collins pinned the man with a stare. "I won't tell you again to be quiet." He asked Jared, "How did he say it happened?"

"Said his gun had a hair trigger and went off when he reached to pull the pot he'd won from the middle of the table. His only complaint is not knowing where his money went."

The sheriff looked from Jared to the occupant of the cell. "How much money you got on you?"

"What?" The man was outraged. "First I'm a gunman, now I'm a thief?"

Jared studied the man. He didn't yet know what to think about the events of the last hour. "Why did you run?"

The man almost snorted at him. "Ever been in a saloon when gunfire erupts? Everybody runs."

The sheriff pulled his lips in under the heavy mustache he wore and leaned his head to one side before shaking it. "No. Everybody doesn't."

Jared noticed the clothes the man wore. He looked familiar. "Who are you?"

"I'll ask the questions, Mr. Ivy." The sheriff didn't seem pleased to have someone horn in on his territory, but Jared's innate curiosity had his mind full of questions.

The prisoner pointed through the bars at Jared. "He just told you that man shot himself. You got no reason to hold me here."

"I'll be the one decidin' if there's a reason to hold you." The sheriff leaned against the side of his desk and folded his arms across his chest. "I'd like to know the same thing Mr. Ivy is asking. Who are you?"

"Name's Elmer Finch. I'm a newsagent on the train."

"That's where I saw you." Jared knew he'd seen that face recently.

"Well, I'll just go around to the depot and speak to the station master then." The sheriff straightened and headed for the door.

Elmer Finch spoke up. "The station master probably won't know me. Today is my first day with the line. You'll have to speak to someone on the train. I'd appreciate it if you're quick about it. The train had a long stop so some repairs could be made. I've only got a half hour before I'm supposed to be back on the job."

Sheriff Collins banged the door behind him as he left.

Jared walked to the cell. "What were you doing in the saloon?"

Mr. Finch didn't meet his eye. A sure sign to Jared that he wasn't being honest. "I was having supper."

"Hmm…" It wouldn't be productive to question someone who was lying. He decided to follow the sheriff and see what they could learn at the depot.

"You can mutter all you want. I'm telling you the truth." Elmer Finch's words rang out behind him as Jared closed the door to the sheriff's office.

Something wasn't right and Jared was determined to find out what it was.

After a trip to the depot and the doctor's office, Jared headed back to the paper. It might be his first day in town, but he was already stirring with anticipation about putting his first story in the paper. He opened the door and stopped short as a young man hung a copy of the paper to dry. Mary Lou loaded the next sheet of paper for printing. Several copies hung along the outer edge of the office.

"Why did you start printing the paper before I got back?"

"We always print on Saturday when we can. I don't like to work on the Lord's Day or wait until Monday morning. It gives overnight for the papers to dry, and you never know when you might have a problem with the press. It's best to get it printed as soon as the stories are complete." She nodded to the young man. "Andrew Nobleson, this is Jared Ivy. He claims he owns the paper, and Sheriff Collins says I've got to put up with him until the judge comes through town again. Maybe a month or two."

"How do you do, sir?" Andrew offered his hand and

pulled it back at the last second when he realized how much ink was on it.

"Hello, Andrew."

"Andrew is my apprentice. He helps with many of the odd jobs involved in putting out the paper."

Jared looked at Mary Lou, carefully inking the press for another copy. "I told you I thought there was more to the story."

She didn't even look up; just put the ink roller down while Andrew loaded the next sheet of paper. He cranked it under the press and pulled the lever to print the page.

"Was there?" She looked doubtful as she helped Andrew remove the paper and grabbed the ink roller again.

"I'm not exactly sure." He leaned against the desk. "Something about the man doesn't fit."

Mary Lou continued to work with Andrew. Jared watched them move with motions seemingly synchronized by the experience of having worked together for a long time.

"Then I'm glad I didn't hold the press for you. I won't print something that's vague or unfounded."

"It's not unfounded. And I've got equal say about what gets printed."

"Equal say? That's not how I heard the sheriff." She argued without missing a lick at the work she and Andrew did.

"He said we have to work together."

"That's fine. You can start where everyone else who ever worked here started. You can sweep up, and I'll teach you how to clean the press when we're finished printing. Next week you should be able to clean it on your own."

"What?" How dare she speak to him like a subordinate? "I'm not a hired hand or apprentice. I'm the owner. And I won't be ordered about by you or anyone else." She had nerve. That much was clear. He'd have to hold a tight line with her or she'd find a way to send him packing before the judge ever came to town.

"I'm just telling you what Jacob Ivy would have told you." She motioned for Andrew to move a stack of blank paper closer. "No one puts a word in a story of the *Pine Haven Record* until they've proved themselves. I'm quite certain he'd have made no exception for you."

The thought of Grump making her sweep the floors and clean the press made him smile. "Is that how you started?"

"It is." She lowered the paper into place and Andrew cranked to move it under the press.

The teenager nodded. "Me, too. I've only been allowed to work on the press since about a year ago when Mr. Ivy started slowing down and passing the work load to Miss Ellison."

Jared wasn't surprised at Grump's methods. It made sense. "How long have you worked here, Andrew?"

"Two years, sir." He pulled the lever and the press lowered again. The two of them were efficient.

"Andrew's very smart, though. Don't expect to move up as quickly as he did." Mary Lou let a tiny grin show at her words.

"I'll try to keep up." Jared laughed. So she was sarcastic, too. He appreciated her refusal to back down from controversy. Under different circumstances—like him not being the cause of the controversy—Jared might be attracted to a woman like Mary Lou Ellison.

She pushed the thought out of his mind with a smirk. "See that you do."

He sobered and stood his ground on the matter. "I want to learn every aspect of the business. But I won't be pushed to the side like I'm not the owner."

Mary Lou stopped her work. "What exactly do you want me to do?"

"Consider what I've learned about Elmer Finch." He pushed off his resting place against the desk and paced the front of the office.

"Who is Elmer Finch?" She drummed her fingers on the edge of the press as if she itched to get back to work.

"He's the man the sheriff arrested. The newsagent for the railroad. But why was he running away when you opened the door?"

She raised her eyebrows. "Perhaps to avoid being caught up in the gunfire?"

"But his gun was drawn. Most people run without stopping to draw their weapon. And if he was going to return fire, wouldn't he have taken cover inside the saloon?"

"Wait." She creased her brow. "He said he's the newsagent? I've never seen him before. The newsagent is an older man, slight-framed, with a mustache."

Jared shook his head. "He said it's his first day with the railroad."

The whistle sounded, signaling the departure of the

train. "He convinced the sheriff to release him, so he wouldn't miss the train."

"Hmm…" She tapped her finger on the top of her lip just below her nose. Her mouth was a straight line as she thought. "If he's the newsagent, he'll be back. The same man has ridden this route since the train came to Pine Haven last year. I have no objection if you feel pressed to pursue an answer to your questions." She inked the plate again and set the roller aside. "But I won't be willing to print anything that isn't verified."

He reached for a newspaper and pulled it from where it hung to dry. The headline jumped off the page: Jacob Ivy's Grandson Seeks Ownership of *Record*. He lowered the paper and looked at her. "I see you added the latest news. Dare I read the content of the article? Am I a villain in your story?"

"I hold myself to the same high standards I told you about. There is nothing in the story of bias or opinion. Merely a statement of facts."

He moved behind the desk and gestured at the chair. "May I?"

"I'm not sure I have a choice in the matter." She turned back to the press.

The article was just as she'd said. Clear. Concise. Without bias or conjecture.

It was a surprise after the way she'd resisted his arrival and insisted the paper was solely hers. He hoped she'd maintain that approach after the judge declared him to be the rightful owner.

He looked over the top of the paper at her. "You left

out the part about me coming here after being a ranch hand for several years."

She kept working without looking at him. "Humph. If you had come back to the office, instead of traipsing all over town, I'd have had time for a proper interview. I was only able to include the limited knowledge I have of you."

He raised the paper to finish reading. She wasn't one to be backed down. He could see that.

Watching her work today, and reading her story, gave him insight into why Grump had taken her on. Would it be lunacy to ask her to stay on once the paper was his? That depended on whether or not she'd only befriended his grandfather for the inheritance.

He hated to be so suspicious, but the lies his mother had told him all his life had left him skittish. Even when Momma hadn't lied, she'd avoided the truth. And he hadn't seen that truth until she'd confessed it all on her deathbed. He couldn't settle what he'd learned against the long-held belief that she was an upright Christian. How could he have been so wrong about someone so close to him? He didn't know if he'd ever trust his instincts again.

Suspicion was one trait he hoped would work to his advantage in the newspaper business.

Mary Lou studied Jared as he read the article. She didn't let him see her, but she watched every expression and waited for a response. As hard as it had been to write, she felt the town deserved to know the truth. After the way he'd announced it in the middle of town a few hours earlier, she hadn't seen another option. Best to get it out in the open to keep the gossipers at bay. The last thing she wanted was a man muddying up her life. Men had a way of intruding on her dreams and leaving her to pick up the pieces after they left.

Jared hadn't said a word after he'd read the entire paper. Andrew hung the last one to dry and reached for a rag to start the cleaning process. Mary Lou shook her head. "I've got it tonight. You go on home."

"Are you sure, Miss Ellison? I don't mind staying. I need to work all I can. Feed and board for Midnight is costing me a pretty penny." He looked eager to stay, but she didn't know how Jared's arrival would affect the finances of the paper. Best be conservative until they had a chance to talk it out.

"I think Mr. Warren may be looking to take on some more help at the hotel. Why don't you stop by there on your way home?"

Andrew's face lit up. "Thanks, Miss Ellison! I'll go right away." He snatched his hat from the coat tree by the door and was gone.

The banging of the door brought Jared from his reverie.

Mary Lou tossed him a rag. "Are you ready to learn to clean the press?"

He shook his head as if she'd dragged him back from far away. "Sure." He hung his coat on the rack by the door and pushed up his sleeves. "Do you have extra sleeve garters?"

She pointed to a shelf. "You can wear Andrew's."

They set to work amiably enough. She'd been prepared for him to argue at every point and was surprised when he didn't. He caught on to things quickly and didn't shy away from the dirty tasks. She was pleased by how soon they finished.

"Well, Mr. Ivy, I must say I'm impressed. I'd have figured you to quit before we were half done."

He pulled his coat on. "That's not very fair of you, Miss Ellison. You don't know me."

She nodded. "I guess you're right. The things your grandfather told me are from long ago. Change was inevitable."

He agreed. "We're all a result of many things. Who we are born to, but also the influences in our lives as we grow. I trust you'll learn to approve of me. Even if you never like me."

Mary Lou gasped. "Mr. Ivy, I never said I didn't like you."

"It was in your eyes, ma'am. A woman has a hard time hiding dislike."

"You don't seem to have taken a shine to me, either."

"Let's just say that for the time being we're at the same place, but on different sides of the situation."

"On that, we can agree."

He took his hat from the coat tree. "As to being in the same place, I already paid for the room at the hotel for the night. I'll move my things in tomorrow after services. If you'd be so kind as to show me where the rooms are."

Mary Lou looked out the front window. The sun had set. If they stayed any later, she'd have to light the lamps. "It's getting very late. I can show you after lunch tomorrow."

He nodded as a grin crossed his face. "Don't want the town to see me here after dark?"

"My reputation in this town was earned over years of guarding it. I'm not interested in marring it for your convenience when tomorrow will suit."

"I see." He put his hat on and opened the door.

She followed him onto the front porch. "Please don't think me rude. I just don't want anyone to get the wrong idea about our relationship."

"You've no cause for concern. I assure you, the only thing we will ever have in common is the paper. And I expect that to end as soon as the judge arrives." He tipped his hat. "Good evening." He stepped onto the street and turned toward the center of town.

"Ahhh. Another point of agreement. I expect the judge to send you on your merry way."

She heard his chuckle as he walked into the twilight.

Mary Lou went inside and closed the door. She lowered the shades and headed through to the back door. She was bone-weary. How had the beautiful day that promised a lovely story about the harvest celebration turned into a nightmare that might cost her everything?

Prayer and a restless night awaited her at home. It was a task she'd take on with zeal. Surely, God would not take away the life He'd only given her weeks ago.

Chapter Three

Mary Lou sang along for the closing hymn at Pine Haven Church on Sunday morning. The words of praise and the reminder that all her blessings flowed from God brought much-needed comfort. She'd struggled to concentrate during the service. Reverend Dismuke would not approve if he'd known how her mind had wandered while he spoke.

The tall man two rows ahead of her was a distraction she hadn't counted on. His baritone voice carried to her. Perhaps, because he was a man of faith, she should be more kind while they were forced to work together.

The thought wasn't in keeping with the faith she professed. Her kindness wasn't meant to extend only to others of faith. She should count her blessings that he wasn't an unscrupulous businessman who ranted about until he got his way.

The final prayer was said and she made her way out into the crisp October air. The preacher stood at the bottom of the church steps, greeting everyone as they left. She spoke to him just as Jared Ivy walked up behind her.

Jared's voice came over the top of her head. "Would you introduce us, Miss Ellison?"

She took a step away from him. "Reverend Dismuke, this is Jared Ivy. He's Jacob Ivy's grandson."

Jared gave a hearty handshake. "How do you do, Reverend? That was a fine talk you gave this morning. You'll have me studying on the words until I can come again next Sunday."

"It's good to meet you, Mr. Ivy. I'm sorry for the loss of your grandfather. I know Jacob would be proud you've come back to Pine Haven."

Mary Lou watched Jared as he spoke. "Did you know Grump well?"

Reverend Dismuke chuckled. "Well enough to know that's the name you gave him as a boy. Said it was something about the way he talked."

"Most times he barked more than he talked." Jared's eyes lit up at the memory. "I knew from the start it was just his way. He was a good man."

Reverend Dismuke agreed. "Yes, he was. He told me you'd be back one day. Said I could count on it."

Jared spoke to the minister but turned and smiled at Mary Lou. "The reasons I stayed away so long make for quite a story. Not one for the paper, but a story nonetheless."

What was the story? As a newspaper woman she wanted all the details. Somehow, looking at Jared now, she didn't think he'd be willing to share them with her.

* * *

Jared carried his saddlebags up the steps of the newspaper office. He looked again at the lettering on the door. How he wished he'd known to come earlier. Why had God let Grump die before he could get here?

He wanted more of the man than the vague memories he had as a young boy. The snatches of moments when Grump would laugh out loud, or even scold him, were all he had.

Opening the door he called out, "Are you here, Miss Ellison?"

She came through a doorway that led to a back room. "Yes."

"I brought a few things, but Andrew will be bringing the rest in a while. My saddle and valise."

"Oh, good. He must have gotten the job I told him about." Her pleasure at the news lit her face.

"Andrew must be very important to you." He set the saddlebags on the floor near the door and propped his rifle against the wall.

"He is. Reminds me of myself at that age."

"How is that?"

Mary Lou shrugged her shoulders. "Young. Alone in the world. But he's also determined to make something of himself."

Jared sank into a chair near the door. "Is that how you ended up with Grump? Set out to make something of yourself?"

She shook her head. Brown tendrils fell loose from the pins and swung to brush her cheek. "When I came to stay here, all I had were the clothes on my back and my momma's Bible." There was a sadness in her words that belied her bravado. "The determination was a gift from your grandfather. He taught me to believe in myself."

What had Jared missed in not knowing Grump like Mary Lou had? Grump had become the family she hadn't had. Ironic, because he was Jared's family, but Jared had been denied his association by a mother who'd let the pain of life harden her. Perhaps harden was too harsh a judgment. Maybe she wasn't hard but numbed by the sorrow of so much loss in her own life.

"So where does Andrew live?"

"Jim Robbins lets him sleep in the loft of the livery in exchange for chores."

Jared had worked hard much of his life and believed strength of character grew from honest labor. "Then he works here and now at the hotel. Is he able to do all that well?" He could almost see her bristle.

"Andrew doesn't have much choice. He has to earn his own way. He's as fine a young man as you'll ever meet. I dare say, when you've had the chance to work alongside him, you'll learn that soon enough."

Jared gave a curt nod. "I'm sure I will."

Mary Lou brushed her hands down the sides of her skirts. "All right then. Would you like to see the rooms? It's possible it's not as fancy as you're accustomed to." She walked toward the staircase in the back room.

He stood and picked up his belongings. "What makes you think I'm accustomed to fancy things?" His childhood had been spent in the comfort of his mother's small home with her feminine touches on all the furnishings. But his adult years had passed in a bunkhouse with ranch hands. "Fancy" was not a word to describe that place.

She stopped and turned, gesturing to his vest pocket. "That watch, for one thing. And you may wear a ranch hand's coat and boots, but you talk like a gentleman."

"Ah, so you're judging me by the way I look and speak? Didn't Grump teach you better than that?" He almost laughed when she let out a tiny huff of air.

"Mr. Ivy taught me a lot of things. Most important among them was to observe details."

"He should also have taught you that situations and people are not always as they present themselves."

"That's precisely what I'm saying. You, Jared Ivy, are a contradiction in every way."

That did cause him to chuckle. "I will tell you the reason I speak as I do, but only because we have to work together. My mother became a schoolteacher when we moved back to her hometown after my father died. She required more of me than the other students. She insisted that her work would be judged by my upbringing. Her efforts were successful—except for my spelling. I never did master it like she wanted. I think the more she pushed me to conquer it, the less my mind absorbed."

"I see. That's understandable. But what about the watch?"

Jared gave a slight tilt of his head. "The watch is a personal matter."

Mary Lou blinked and said, "Oh. Please forgive the intrusion." She turned back to the stairs and led the way to Grump's old rooms. Was she truly sorry or was her sarcastic bent peeking through her words?

At the top of the stairs a small landing stopped in front of a plain door. She opened it and stepped aside for him to enter first.

"Everything is just as Mr. Ivy left it. I've dusted and swept up, but I didn't have the heart to move any of his belongings." She sniffed and he caught a glimpse of her catching a tear before it fell from her lashes. "Leaving everything made me feel closer to him."

"Thank you." He set his things down near the door and wandered deeper into the space. A woodstove sat in one corner with a pipe leading through the ceiling. A large rocker stood on a rag rug by the window on the same wall.

Mary Lou cleared her throat. "He didn't cook much, but there are basic utensils here." She pointed to a shelf along the back wall over the cupboard. "The bedroom is through that door." She indicated the far wall.

Jared tried to imagine Grump sitting in the rocker or leaning over a plate of beans at the small table with two chairs. Grump's Bible sat on the same table with a lamp.

"We used to talk for hours about the Bible or the next big article we were going to print." Mary Lou's voice was soft and reverent. The look on her face as she stared at the table let him know her mind was visiting a dear memory.

"I hope you'll share some of those stories with me in the course of time." Emotion he hadn't expected clogged his throat.

"Oh, most of those conversations wouldn't interest anyone but me or Mr. Ivy." She twisted her hands together.

"All the same, I came here to find Grump. I'll have little to piece together except the memories of others."

She looked up then and met his gaze. An open love for his grandfather shone in her eyes. "When you say it like that, I don't see how I can refuse you." She backed up. "I'll leave you to settle in."

"I guess I'll see you in the morning." He followed her to the door.

Standing on the landing, she paused. "I've got a stew simmering on the stove next door. I'll be glad to bring you a bowl for your supper in a bit. It being a Sunday, I didn't think you'd have much chance to prepare anything for yourself."

"That's very kind of you." Her generosity was unexpected, given how she must despise the purpose for his presence. "What time do you open the office?"

"I'm always in early on Monday. Andrew comes to help distribute the papers."

A rap on the door downstairs drew their attention. It must be Andrew with the rest of Jared's belongings.

He stepped onto the landing with Mary Lou. It suddenly felt very small. Mary Lou Ellison was beautiful. Not in the traditional way a man defined beauty. Other women may have finer features but there was a strength in her that drew him. They stood so close he could see the black ring around the green of her eyes. He knew her skin would be as soft as a moonlit whisper. In other circumstances he might be tempted to give in to the emotional draw he felt for her.

She was close enough to touch. But the ownership of the paper stood between them like a gulf.

The door below opened and Andrew called, "Miss Ellison? Mr. Ivy?"

Jared took a step back and bumped into the door to his new residence.

Mary Lou blinked again and cleared her throat. She didn't take her eyes from his as she answered, "We're coming down now, Andrew. I was just showing Mr. Ivy his rooms."

"After you." Jared waited for her to descend several treads before he followed. He'd best keep a good distance between him and Mary Lou. He wouldn't let his heart sway him away from his mission to honor Grump's legacy by insuring the future of the *Pine Haven Record*. Not even for someone his grandfather had approved of to the point that she carried on for him in the void left by his death.

Monday morning dawned with the memory of life's new challenges. Mary Lou checked her reflection in the mirror in her room before heading downstairs.

Jared Ivy's presence had been awkward yesterday. She'd called up the stairs when she'd brought his stew and found the door to his rooms open. He'd asked her to leave the food on the tread at the bottom of the steps without coming to the doorway to acknowledge her. It had taken prayer and several deep breaths to keep her from taking the food back to her kitchen in the face of his perceived ingratitude.

"Well, if he thinks I'll be cooking and cleaning for him, he'll have to think again. I am my own woman now. A businesswoman. I don't have the time or the inclination to tend to a man who is perfectly capable of tending to his own needs." She pulled the bottom of her jacket down with more than the needed force and had to straighten it again before she left for work.

She entered the paper through the back entrance and found Jared Ivy at his grandfather's desk. Her desk.

Lord, please let it still be my desk after the judge comes to town.

Jared looked up from something he was writing. "Good morning, Miss Ellison."

"Mr. Ivy." She heard the tightness in her voice and hated it. She needed to conduct herself as a business owner, not a woman who was out of sorts because a man had dared to enter her domain.

He nodded to the clean bowl on the corner of the desk. "That was a fine stew. Thank you."

"I wasn't sure you were going to eat it when I brought it last night."

Jared continued writing for a moment then stopped. "Why wouldn't I eat it?" He was distracted by whatever was on the page.

Mary Lou was accustomed to his grandfather ignoring her, or only half listening, but he'd been her boss. Jared wasn't her boss. Or even her colleague. She had no intention of continuing a one-sided conversation. She began to pull down the papers from where they'd been hung to dry and stack them neatly. Andrew would arrive momentarily to help distribute them.

She jumped when Jared reached over her shoulder to take down the next paper. "What are you doing?" She put a hand to her chest and took a deep breath.

"Helping?" He added the paper to the stack behind them. "What's got you so skittish?"

"I'm not skittish." She moved to the opposite end of the room and began taking down the papers that hung there. "I didn't know you'd finished whatever it was that had you so distracted." She nodded her head in the direction of the desk. The notes he'd made were missing from the neat desktop.

He patted the pocket of his coat. "I was just writing down a list of things to check on today." He gave a grin that reminded her of a cat who'd just eaten a brave mouse. Did he think she'd snoop behind him, so he'd taken away the evidence of his actions?

"You've no need to guard your notes from me, Jared Ivy. I can assure you that nothing you do outside the paper is of any interest to me." She resisted the urge to huff out a breath as she slapped another paper on the growing stack.

Jared added his paper to the stack simultaneously, causing hers to flutter to the floor. He gave a small chortle. "You do tend to drop a lot of things, Miss Ellison. Your notes, men running by in the street, your composing stick when it's full of type, and now the paper. Are you always so clumsy?" Was he laughing at her?

"I am not. I distinctly remember your involvement in every one of those scenarios."

Now he did laugh. "I'll concede that point on one condition."

She retrieved the paper and added it to the others. Hands on hips, she asked, "What makes you think I'll accept any conditions you have to offer?"

"I think this one will be in both our interests."

"I'm listening."

"I propose that you stop resisting my presence so fiercely. Perhaps that's the reason for your mishaps." He lowered his head and leaned toward her. "Because I'm not going anywhere." Blue eyes sparkled beneath heavy lashes. Gorgeous eyes that could pull an unsuspecting lady into their depths. She knew the truth about men, though. They might be handsome and strong, but none ever stayed when it mattered. Even if they wanted to, death could take them.

His face was open, not hiding anything. Determination oozed from him. Determination that threatened her livelihood.

Mary Lou straightened to her full height and squared her shoulders. She surprised herself when she dared to lean closer to him. There was only room for breath between them. "Nor am I."

Andrew opened the front door and stared at both of them as they jumped apart. Why did she feel guilty? She'd only been making her point to Jared. There was no reason to blush with embarrassment, but she felt the heat in her cheeks just the same.

"Good morning, Andrew." Jared greeted the apprentice with a completely normal tone.

"Mr. Ivy." Andrew looked at her then. "Miss Ellison. Are you okay?" He looked back at Jared. Mary Lou almost laughed at the idea that Andrew thought he might need to protect her from Jared Ivy when she was the one who had advanced on him.

"I'm fine, Andrew."

The young man didn't seem convinced. "Are you sure? I can stay here today instead of working my other jobs, if you need me to." He never took his eyes off Jared, who'd turned to pull down more newspapers.

"Miss Ellison is under no threat from me, Andrew. You merely caught us drawing the battle lines for how we'll be working together until the judge comes to Pine Haven." He turned to Mary Lou. "And when I say 'working together,' I mean working in the same building. I'm not convinced we'll be able to manage to accomplish anything together."

So he felt it, too. There was a constant tension in the air between them. Try as they might, there was no removing the sense of an impending storm. The air was charged like a hot summer day with low, dark clouds rolling in on the horizon. Rumbles of thunder warned of the coming chaos. How would she survive two months in the same office with a man who wanted to take her business?

God, I need Your help. This man has me at my wits' end. Two months on tenterhooks is more than I can manage on my own.

Jared put the last paper on the stack. He'd been watching Mary Lou's reactions since she'd come into the office. Sure, she thought he was disinterested, but he wanted to see her true actions without his influence. Stepping up to him and daring him to take the *Pine Haven Record* from her showed spunk. No wonder Grump had liked her. Under different circumstances he'd like her, too.

Mary Lou was open. Honest. Spoke her mind.

His mother had shown none of those characteristics. How he hated that with her deathbed confessions she'd rubbed out all the memories he'd cherished. Times when she'd comforted him as a boy and told him she'd always protect him. Never once had she told him how Grump wanted to be in his life, too. She'd kept him away from his only connection to his father. He'd tried to forgive her before she died. Had promised her he had. But the bile in his throat over the lost opportunities evidenced his need to keep praying until the forgiveness he knew in his mind must be given, took root in his heart.

"If you're sure, Miss Ellison?" At her nod, Andrew pulled a stack of newspapers from the table and headed for the door. "Then I'll be back for the rest in an hour." The wind caught the door and it slammed shut behind him.

Mary Lou put on her coat and picked up another, somewhat smaller, stack of papers. "There won't be anything else to do until after lunch." She headed for the door.

Jared grabbed his coat from the tree by the door and shrugged into it as he followed her into the brisk morning air. "Wait."

She shook her head and said over her shoulder, "Don't have time to wait."

He trotted a couple of paces and caught up to her. "Where are you going with these?" He reached for the papers in her arms, but she pulled back. He put a hand on her arm, giving her no choice but to stop.

"Really, Mr. Ivy, I must insist you not hinder me in my work."

"Our work." At her sigh he added, "Until the judge decides, it is indeed *our* work." He reached for the papers again. "At least allow me to be a gentleman and carry them for you. You can show me where you sell them. I need to learn as much as I can as quickly as possible."

Mary Lou's shoulders sagged just a bit and she handed over her bundle. "I guess it won't hurt to let you meet the people who allow us to sell the newspaper in their establishments." She took off at a brisk pace. "But you mustn't slow me down."

He chuckled and followed her. Yes, she was someone he'd like to know. If only they weren't at odds over the only thing either of them wanted. The *Pine Haven Record*.

Chapter Four

Mary Lou drew on all her patience and pushed open the door to the general store. With Mr. Croft having been in the middle of the shooting scene on Saturday, Mrs. Liza Croft was bound to be inquisitive today. There was no way to explain Jared Ivy. Mary Lou would just have to make the best of the situation.

She relaxed when Mr. Croft greeted her. "Mary Lou, how are you today?"

"Well, Mr. Croft. Thank you for asking."

Jared pulled off his hat and put it into the hand under the stack of papers he carried. "Nice to meet you, Mr. Croft. I'm Jared Ivy."

The two shook hands. "I heard you'd come to town. Sorry about your grandfather. He'd have loved to see you again."

Jared dropped his gaze to the floor for a quick moment before he responded. "Thank you. I'd have loved an opportunity to spend time with him, too."

"So—" Mr. Croft scratched the crown of his balding head "—what's in the paper this week?" He took a copy from the stack Jared held.

"There's a fine piece about the—"

Mary Lou interrupted Jared's attempt to answer. She wouldn't be pushed aside as if she wasn't the owner of the paper. "I've written about the contested ownership of my paper and about the harvest celebration."

Liza Croft came through the doors that led to the stock room. "I hope you wrote about the lost business the shop owners suffer when the town closes down for a celebration like that." Her tone was snooty, as usual. Mary Lou chose to ignore her, but Jared didn't.

"I would imagine an event that drew everyone from the surrounding area into town would bring extra business to your store." Mary Lou caught sight of the muscle in his jaw as it worked to contain a smile.

"You'll never convince my wife that money is made when the hours of the store are shortened." Mr. Croft stepped behind the counter.

Jared was apparently not a man to be put off easily. "But if more people patronize your establishment before the celebration starts, the volume of sales in a shorter time frame is bound to increase profits. Even if the store closes early."

Mrs. Croft shifted from one foot to another and spoke to Mary Lou. "Well, I see your new business partner has a good head on his shoulders." Mary Lou tried to ignore her ire when Mrs. Croft looked down her nose at her. "You could use someone like that at the paper. Things have gone a bit soft in recent years."

"Mrs. Croft, I—"

This time Jared interrupted her. "I'm certain you didn't mean to imply that my grandfather didn't run a serious newspaper."

"Of course not. But Mary Lou here doesn't have the strong sense for real news that Mr. Ivy did."

Mary Lou's blood began to boil. How dare the woman speak to her like that?

"From what I've seen since I arrived in Pine Haven, Miss Ellison knows a good story when she sees it. She's also very careful to only print the truth."

Mr. Croft chuckled. "I'd say from what she wrote here—" he punched a line on the paper he'd placed on the counter "—she didn't hold back on this story about you coming to town."

Jared laughed along with the man's joke. Mary Lou had been surprised when he'd jumped to her defense. And more than a bit pleased. She shook her head. He was only defending the paper's reputation. She wouldn't let him win her over with kind words meant to protect his own interests.

Not for the first time, she decided to ignore Mrs. Croft. "Mr. Croft, will you please put the money for the papers on my account? We're in a bit of a hurry today. I've got to introduce Mr. Ivy to several people."

"Sure thing." Mr. Croft lifted a hand in dismissal. "Good to meet you, Mr. Ivy."

When they were on the sidewalk outside the store again, Mary Lou headed for the hotel.

"Wait just a minute." Jared stopped walking.

She turned. "What is it? Can't we talk as we go? There's a lot to do today."

He shook his head. "I need to ask you something."

"What?" Still smarting from Mrs. Croft's accusations, she didn't want to waste any more time on trivialities. She could ignore the insults and bite her tongue at the time, but the accusations always stung. She had to get to work on the next edition. She'd make certain there was something so newsworthy that not even Liza Croft could refute it.

"You asked Mr. Croft to credit your account with the proceeds from the sale of the papers."

"Instead of paying me for all of the papers when I drop them off, he credits my account for the ones he sells. It's an arrangement he prefers." Why did he stop her for this? "It makes no difference in the end. The money comes by week's end."

He'd put his hat back on when they'd stepped outside, yet his blue eyes didn't dim in the shade of the brim. "But all the money isn't yours."

"Oh. Is that what has your back up? You think I'm going to control the money and you won't have any?"

"I'm not accusing you of anything."

She pivoted on one foot to angle away from him a bit. "Really?"

"I'm saying that things have to change now. You can't just carry on as if I'm not here."

"Believe me, Mr. Ivy, this is nothing like the way my day would be going if you weren't here."

He didn't flinch at her biting attitude. In fact, he lowered his tone and spoke with more deliberation. "You get my point."

She sighed. "I do." She turned back toward the general store, but he reached out a hand and caught her by the elbow.

"Don't do it now. Mrs. Croft will never let it rest if she thinks I sent you back in to change things."

He was right. The woman would never let go of a tidbit like that. Mary Lou nodded. "Okay. Let's go to the hotel next. They pay in cash. We'll accept it and divide the profits when we get back to the office, taking the amount that usually comes in from the general store into account."

Jared smiled at her. "That wasn't so hard, was it?"

"What?" This man had her flummoxed. He'd defended her when he didn't have to and protected her when she hadn't considered the consequences of a quick reaction. Why would he do that?

"It wasn't so difficult to discuss an aspect of the business and come to a mutual agreement."

"Hmm…no. It wasn't."

"Do you think we can handle the other areas of the paper like that?"

So the motive for his actions came out. Much quicker than she'd expected.

"That's why you defended my reputation to Mrs. Croft. And the reputation of the paper. And now you're offering an olive branch, but with a goal of increasing your foothold in the business. You're a slick one, Mr. Ivy." She stood straight. "I'll have my eye on you."

Why did Mary Lou think he was trying to manipulate her? Had no one ever taken up for her? Surely,

Grump wouldn't let someone accuse his staff of shoddy work or speak ill of someone he cared for.

Jared took a few quick steps to catch her as she crossed the street and headed for the Pine Haven Hotel on the corner. "Slow down, Mary Lou."

She stopped abruptly in front of him and spoke over her shoulder. "You'll have to keep up, Mr. Ivy. The newspaper business doesn't wait for anyone." She set off again at the same pace.

He didn't move. She'd accused him of manipulating her. He wouldn't let that accusation stand. She would realize soon enough that he wasn't following her. After all, he had the newspapers.

Mary Lou mounted the steps to the hotel entrance and reached for the door. He watched as she turned toward him and dropped her hand. She clasped both hands together and waited.

Jared approached at a measured gait.

"Join me for a moment?" He indicated the rockers on the porch in front of the hotel.

"We really don't have time." When she moved toward the door again, he dropped into one of the chairs and set it into motion.

"I have all the time in the world." He knew time was important, but moving forward in agreement was more important. "We'll waste more time in the long run if we don't clear the air about some things now."

Reluctance and resolve warred on her face until she sat on the edge of the chair beside him. "What?"

"I am not a manipulator."

"No?"

"No. I am straightforward." At her raised eyebrows he added, "And diplomatic."

"Ah…diplomacy. So that is what you call it when you try to coerce me into doing things your way."

"I didn't try to coerce you. I merely pointed out that you would have to make some changes to accommodate our joint venture."

"Joint venture? This venture, or whatever you choose to call it, isn't joint."

"We are in the midst of a circumstance beyond our control. We can do our best to make it work or argue and struggle until the judge comes to town. I am not a man given to conflict. I'd prefer to come to an arrangement that is beneficial to both of us. The time will be unbearable if we don't."

"Then why didn't you just say that in the beginning." He could see her resistance fading.

"I think I did." He took a risk and said, "You may have overreacted."

She hung her head. Every ounce of her was full of conviction and strength. He didn't like that his words had caused that to ebb. Then, just as quickly, she raised her head and met his gaze. "I can see how you might think that. Let's finish distributing the papers this morning. When we get back to the office, we can lay out some ground rules while we have our lunch. Then there will be no time lost." She stood. "Shall we?"

He nodded. "After you." With his free hand, he opened the hotel door for her to precede him.

She went to the registration desk. "Mr. Warren. How are you this morning?"

"Well, Miss Ellison. Very well, indeed." The man caught sight of Jared behind Mary Lou. "And you, Mr. Ivy?"

"I'm fine, sir. Thank you."

"Learning to work with our Miss Ellison, are you?" Mr. Warren spoke to him but he smiled at Mary Lou. Why had she suddenly become Mary Lou and not Miss Ellison in Jared's mind? Was the stubborn way she defended her stance at every turn endearing her to him?

"We are sorting through the details as we go along." He cut a glance at Mary Lou.

She reached for some of the newspapers he carried. "He's learning the business." She didn't smirk but he thought she wanted to. She placed the papers on the corner of the desk. "I'd love to interview Jasmine about the wedding."

Mr. Warren's chest puffed out a bit. "Two weeks from Saturday I'll have all my girls settled. Then me and Mrs. Beverly will be happy while we wait for some more grands. Maybe someone will want to take over the hotel for me in the future."

Mary Lou smiled. "You haven't even had time to spoil your newest grandson yet." She looked at Jared. "Mr. Warren has three daughters. Two married and one betrothed." She turned back to Mr. Warren. "I met Tuck after church last Sunday. Daisy and Tucker are so proud. And I think baby Rose is still a bit jealous."

Mr. Warren laughed. "That little girl hasn't slowed down since she learned to walk a few weeks ago. I think she thought the new babe would be a playmate, not someone who took her momma's time and attention."

If Jared was going to fit into the community of Pine Haven, he needed to build relationships with the people he was meeting. "Congratulations on your new family member, sir."

"Thank you, Mr. Ivy."

"Jared, please. I trust the *Record* posted a nice birth announcement on his arrival."

He felt Mary Lou stiffen beside him. "We certainly did. Just like we do for all the new babies in Pine Haven. The *Record* plays a big role in celebrating the good things that happen in our town."

A door opened from the side of the lobby and a woman dressed like a ranch hand came into the room. She was striking in her beauty and wore the clothes like she was made for them. In the years he'd worked on a ranch, Jared had never encountered a lady rancher.

She joined Mr. Warren behind the desk and kissed his cheek. "Hello, Papa." She was tall and graceful. "Good morning, Mary Lou."

"Jasmine, I'd like you to meet Jared Ivy. Mr. Ivy will be working with me at the paper for the next month or so." He wanted to smile at the way Mary Lou had insinuated their time working together would end with his departure, without actually saying he would be leaving. Their time at the paper together would end. But he wouldn't be the one going anywhere. "This is Jasmine Warren. She's Mr. Warren's daughter and will soon be married to Doc Willis."

"It's a pleasure to make your acquaintance, ma'am." He dipped his head in deference to the lady.

Mary Lou continued. "Jasmine, I'd love to interview you for the paper. Your wedding is big news."

Jasmine Warren smiled. "If you really think there's something to write about, I'll be glad to share with you. Maybe we could have lunch one day soon before the wedding."

Jared answered for both of them. "We'd be most agreeable with that. You just name the day."

Miss Warren's face creased. "Will you be joining us, Mr. Ivy?"

"No, he won't." Mary Lou answered on top of his "Yes."

Mary Lou tilted her head to one side and spoke to Miss Warren. "Mr. Ivy has brought a claim of ownership against me for the newspaper."

Mr. Warren didn't seem to like the sound of that. "Is that so?"

"Jacob Ivy was my grandfather. He left me the paper in his will."

Mr. Warren's expression widened as he took in the announcement. "I see."

Miss Warren said, "Then I'll be happy to meet you both on Wednesday at noon. Naomi will be serving her famous chicken and dumplings in the restaurant that day." She lifted the papers Mary Lou had placed on the desk.

"Papa, have you seen my cameo? It was right here." She began picking up the items on the desk one at a time and looking under them. She opened the drawer on her side of the desk.

"No. Are you sure you left it here?"

"Yes. I was showing it to Momma Beverly on Saturday afternoon. You must remember. It was just after lunch."

"I haven't seen it." Mr. Warren opened another drawer on the desk.

A thought he didn't like entered Jared's mind. "Saturday afternoon?"

Mr. Warren stopped his search. "Yes. You were here that afternoon. Did you see it?"

"No, but if you'll think about anyone who may have come through the lobby that afternoon, maybe you can remember someone who could have seen it." Jared knew one person who'd been here that afternoon. Someone who was desperate for money.

"Well, you were here." Mr. Warren began naming everyone he could think of, but his memory wasn't as sharp as a younger man's would be.

"What about anyone local who came in to do business with you? Or perhaps someone who ate in the restaurant?" Jared wanted to stir the man's memory but he didn't want to be the one to say Andrew's name out loud. Mary Lou wouldn't thank him for it. Her fondness for the youth had been made clear.

"There were the usual guests on Saturday. Evan was here."

Miss Warren headed for the door. "I'll go ask if he saw it. He may have picked it up for safekeeping if he did."

Mary Lou explained. "Evan is Doc Willis."

Jared gave a nod of acknowledgment. "Mr. Warren,

was there anyone else? Someone who came but didn't go into the restaurant."

"Well, I hired Andrew that day as the new errand boy, but he was only here a few minutes."

Mary Lou gave a slight gasp and spun to pin Jared with her gaze. "Are you suggesting that dear, sweet Andrew took Jasmine's cameo?"

He held up a hand. "I'm saying that the only way to find it will be to remember who was here. If Andrew was here, he may have seen it."

Mary Lou's words were barely more than a whisper. "Andrew is not a thief."

Mr. Warren cleared his throat. They both started. The hotel owner handed Mary Lou money for the newspapers. "If you two will excuse me, I'm going to help Jasmine search for the cameo. I bought it for her mother because it had a rose corsage on the shoulder of the lady's dress. Her mother's name was Rose."

"I'm sure you'll find it soon." Mary Lou thanked him for the money and they left the hotel.

Jared couldn't understand why she wasn't more curious. "Mary Lou, if you're as good at the newspaper business as you say you are, why aren't you the least bit interested in what happened to a valuable family heirloom?" They turned at the center of town and headed back toward their office.

Their office. It sounded odd in his mind. It was his office. He must keep his focus on the ownership of the newspaper and all the responsibility that went along with that. If someone in town was stealing things, he was determined to get to the bottom of it. Solving a crime would show the people of Pine Haven that he was serious about the paper and about bettering the community.

"People misplace things all the time. Especially small things. I daresay Doc Willis picked it up, just as Jasmine suspected."

He shook his head. "But you don't know that. Aren't you making a lot of assumptions?"

She opened the door to the office and went inside.

He followed her, waiting for an answer.

"I am not. It is not an assumption to refuse to believe that a trusted friend is a petty thief. It *is* an assumption to suspect someone you don't know when you aren't even sure there's been a theft."

"I've only been here a few days, but I've seen you rely on your opinion of situations more than once."

"My opinions, as you call them, are based on years of experience in the newspaper business and a personal knowledge of the parties in question."

Her shoulders stiffened. Even though she stood on the opposite side of his desk, the friction between them filled the room.

"You did not know the newsagent from the train, yet you dismissed him as innocent without interviewing him."

"There was no crime there, either."

"True, Elmer Finch didn't shoot the man in the saloon, but he is harboring a secret. One I think needs to be investigated."

"Really, Mr. Ivy, you do go on." She picked up her pad and pencil from the desk. "If I were to run the paper by following your imaginations, we could become the biggest work of fiction in Texas before the judge arrives."

His mother had ignored him. Even hidden truths from him. But she had never dismissed him out of hand.

Jared mustered all the strength of character he possessed to answer her charges. "Objectivity is the cornerstone of good journalism. I suggest that your years of association with the people in Pine Haven may have dulled your sense of neutrality. Once you become allied with anyone, you lose your ability to consider them in any light other than the one you've cast upon them."

"Your grandfather trusted my instincts. I have yet to err in my assessments of the good people of Pine Haven. I stand confidently on that record."

He crossed his arms over his chest. "Then, as the Good Book says, take heed, lest ye fall."

Chapter Five

Mary Lou looked out her front window on Tuesday morning. Her heart still stung from the rebuke Jared had laid at her feet on Monday.

She'd come across as arrogant. Confidence had united with stubborn defensiveness and she'd allowed them to rob her of her objectivity.

Lord, please help me not to be lifted up in myself. I know You give grace to the humble. And I feel like I'm going to need a lot of grace to get through working with Jared Ivy until the judge comes to town.

After checking her hair one last time in the mirror by the front door, she added another earnest plea to her prayer.

Please let me keep the paper. It's all I have.

When she entered the back of the office, she found Jared at her desk.

"Good morning, Mr. Ivy." She wasn't surprised when he followed the pattern of his grandfather and ignored her. He filled another page with the words that flowed from his pen before she cleared her throat with deliberation.

The pen stilled and he looked up at her. "Oh, good morning."

"You've taken great liberty with the use of my desk."

"I consider it to be my desk, Mary Lou."

"And that's another thing. I am uncomfortable with your use of my given name. We are business partners, not friends of long standing."

"So you admit that I am an equal partner in the newspaper?"

He was quick with a turn of phrase. "I do not. I point out that you have taken liberties without so much as a by-your-leave."

Jared stood and offered her the chair he'd just vacated. "Please do have a seat and let us work out the details of these liberties."

She twisted her hands together behind her back and said, "I'll sit here," as she lowered herself into the chair facing the desk.

The corners of his mouth tweaked for a brief moment but he turned the threatening smile into a neutral expression and sat. "Let's talk of the office and desk first." He put his palms flat on the desk. "I think we can share the desk. In the mornings, I like to make notes on what I'd like to accomplish during the day. If that works for you, fine. If not, I can come in earlier and use the desk before you arrive."

"I use the desk to write articles for the paper. I have no idea from one day to the next what time I will need it."

"What if I'm willing to relinquish my time to you in the event you need to write a story?"

He was being reasonable. Rational and reasonable. If she didn't accept, he could tell the judge she'd refused to cooperate. If she did accept, she'd have to watch him work at the desk every morning. Watching the confident way he put pen to paper without pause reminded her of the elder Mr. Ivy. He always knew what he was about. Never did he stop and question his course.

She wished she could be that bold. The boldness she exuded was manufactured nightly in earnest prayer that she wouldn't falter with each new day. Could she keep up the facade of successful business owner, ready to face the world on her own, in the presence of his natural confidence?

He must have taken her silence for disagreement. He offered another solution. "What if we decide to treat everything as belonging to the *Record*? The furnishings and everything. Then it won't be as if either of us is using the other's personal property. It will be both of us sharing the duties and responsibilities of the paper."

"That seems reasonable." She had taken ownership of all the contents of both buildings when Mr. Ivy died. Save her clothing, there really wasn't anything here that belonged exclusively to her.

The front door swung open and a gust of October wind came in with Andrew.

Jared stood again. "Andrew, just the person I need to see."

Andrew closed the door and cast a leery glance at Mary Lou before turning to Jared.

Jared came from behind the desk. "I need to buy a horse. Mary Lou tells me you reside at the livery."

"Mr. Robbins always has a couple of horses for sale. He's got two fine animals right now."

Jared snagged his hat from the coat tree near the door and thanked Andrew.

Mary Lou asked, "Aren't you going to work today? I intended to show you how to take last week's plates and prepare for a new paper."

"I've got some things to take care of first. You and Andrew go ahead without me."

She put her hands on her hips. "You need to know all the aspects of publishing the newspaper." He couldn't just waltz in and out of the office—and the work—like he didn't have any responsibility.

"I'm sure that can't be the most difficult part to learn. I've got an idea I'm following up on. If I'm right, I'll have a contribution of my own to add to the next edition." He gave her a smile that she knew meant he expected her to grant him permission.

"I won't do your work for you. And nothing will go into the paper without my approval. Perhaps you'd like to share this idea before you waste your time on something we won't print."

"Oh, we'll print it. I'll try to be back before supper." He snagged his saddle from its place near the front door and left.

"Wonder what he's working on." Andrew shrugged out of his jacket.

"I don't know." Mary Lou pushed her sleeves up and reached for her garters to hold them safely away from the ink while she worked. "But if it's anything like what I've heard since he got here, it will never see print."

She and Andrew set to work removing the type from the articles that wouldn't run again and sorting the letters into trays. The next edition would be easier to prepare if they kept the work area organized and clean.

The two of them worked the remainder of the morning, but Mary Lou's mind was on Jared. Where was he? What idea was he pursuing? If he proved to be a better journalist than she was, would Mr. Ivy have wanted her to turn the paper over to him? The thoughts became a jumbled mess in her mind, but she pushed them away after lunch when she set off in search of the next article worthy of the front page.

If Jared was going to compete with her for ownership of the *Pine Haven Record*, he'd have to prove himself a strong challenger. She might need to pray for strength every night, but she set about her job with determination every day. If anything, Jared only made her more determined than ever to succeed.

Jared went straight from the newspaper office to the livery. He entered through the open doors and stopped as his eyes adjusted to the shadows of the interior. "Mr. Robbins? Are you here?"

A man in his forties came from one of the stalls. "That'd be me." He wiped his hands on a rag and stuffed it into his hip pocket.

"I'm Jared—"

"Jared Ivy. Jacob's grandson. You're Ben and Agnes's boy."

He hadn't thought about what it would be like to meet people who'd known his parents. Jared put out his hand. "I am. It's good to meet you, Mr. Robbins."

"I'd have known you anywhere. You're the spitting image of your pa and your grandpa."

Jared chuckled, mostly to clear the awkward feeling that filled his throat. He'd been so long without either man that he hadn't known he looked like them. Only when Mary Lou had pointed it out had he realized it. The picture on the wall in the news office floated to the front of his memory. He'd missed so much. "So I've been told just recently."

"I'm guessing Mary Lou Ellison was surprised when you showed up in town. That's a fiery girl if ever I saw one. She's been committed to the success of the *Record* since your grandpa took her in. Never seen a girl more focused. You'd think she'd want to get married like all the other young ones."

Jared's curiosity pushed to the front again. "Surely she had offers."

"One or two, but no one could get her attention. She's always off in search of the next story. Can't tie a woman like that down. Not many men would be willing to try. They want a woman to be at the house taking care of the little ones while the man runs the business."

Jared shook his head. "From what I've seen of Miss Ellison, she wouldn't be content without a challenge." He dare not push for more information on the woman he hoped to have removed from his business. If word of his snooping into her personality got back to her, he'd have more trouble than he wanted.

"Mr. Robbins, Andrew told me you keep a few horses for sale. I'm in need of a new mount." He cast his eye around the livery and noticed two exceptional animals. "Something like this fellow would do nicely." He stepped up to a stall and put a hand on the nose of a black stallion. "He's a beaut."

"That one's not for sale."

"Are you sure? I've brought cash. And I'll need to board him here with you, too. I think we could come to a fair agreement."

"That's Midnight. You're right. He's a fine horse. But he belongs to Andrew."

Surprise kicked off another line of questioning in his mind. "How can a boy like that afford such a horse?"

"He brought me a little money every week. Sometimes twice a week. He's worked here doing a man's chores for about three years now. Set his eye on Midnight the day I got him. Wouldn't let me sell him to another soul."

"It's unusual for someone his age to be so determined."

"Andrew's no stranger to hard work. He's so busy, you'll see him coming and going all over town. Never know where he'll pop up wanting to lend a hand and make a few coins."

That agreed with everything Mary Lou had said about Andrew. But it didn't sit right with Jared that the boy had been able to raise that kind of money by mucking out stalls and working as an apprentice.

Mr. Robbins pointed to the next stall. "This is Noel.

She's a bit headstrong, but a good horse. I daresay she's only bested by Midnight in the livery."

Jared took the horse for a brief ride. When he returned, he haggled with Mr. Robbins and made the deal for Noel, a chestnut mare with good lines.

He left the livery on Noel and turned toward the Circle W Ranch. The hotel owner had told him that Mr. Willis ran the largest ranch in the county. Jared wanted to meet the man and put forth some of his ideas for expanding the topics covered by the paper. He caught sight of Mary Lou as he passed the office and lifted a hand in greeting. Her expression let him know he'd be bombarded with questions from her as soon as he returned.

His meeting with Mr. Willis took longer than he anticipated, but the man confirmed his instincts about a new direction for the paper. More articles on changing cattle markets and any news in the business world that related to ranching could help the ranchers not only stay in business but make more profit in the long run.

On his way back into town, Jared decided to go to the church. He hadn't been to Grump's grave. It was time.

There was no sign of Mary Lou at the paper when he rode by. The noise from the saloon still confounded him. How did so many men have time in the middle of the day to carouse? When he turned right in the middle of town, he noticed the preacher going into the Pine Haven Hotel. That was a good thing. He'd rather find the cemetery empty than have Reverend Dismuke see him and seek him out for conversation. He preferred to pay his respects in private.

The church was at the edge of town at the end of

Main Street. The river ran alongside the church property. It was a peaceful setting. The cemetery stood on a hill behind the church and its parsonage. Stone markers rose from the ground to honor the dead. A large water oak stood like a sentry at the back of the graves.

Jared slid from Noel's back and ground-tied her near the church. He took off his hat and let the early afternoon sun warm his head. His stomach rumbled to remind him that he'd missed lunch. At first, he walked with his head down, reading the stones. After making his way through several disorganized rows he looked up to search the landscape for a fresh grave.

Then he saw her.

Mary Lou knelt at a grave with a new marker. She put a gloved hand on the stone and traced the letters. Jared felt like an intruder as he walked closer and heard her talking.

"Lord, if I only knew what to do. You gave me Mr. Ivy when I needed him most, and now that You've seen fit to take him back, I'm not sure who to ask for advice. The grandson he wanted so desperately to know has shown up, and I don't know what Mr. Ivy would want me to do."

Her prayer was sincere and without malice. Jared wasn't sure he could pray with that kind of openness if he were in her situation: threatened with the loss of her home and livelihood. Yet, no bitterness rang in her tone.

Guilt at overhearing made him clear his throat. Mary Lou stumbled to her feet and wiped at her cheeks. "Mr. Ivy, I didn't know you were here." She kept her focus on the grave.

"I'm sorry you didn't hear me approach." He pointed over his shoulder, not that she would see, and said, "I left my horse closer to the church. I didn't know exactly where to look for Grump's grave." He stood beside her now. "Please forgive my intrusion on such a private moment."

She sniffed and shook her head. "You've just as much right to be here as I do."

"The stone is nice." He read the verse below Grump's name aloud, "'Also now, behold, my witness is in heaven, and my record is on high.'" He nodded his approval. "Very fitting."

"It seemed the best way to honor his work on the paper and his commitment to the Lord." She turned to Jared. "He loved God. Lived every day hoping to please his Maker. God's got the record of that."

Her eyes glistened in the sun. Her jaw twitched as if Grump were her kin and she felt the need to convince Jared of his character.

"Mary Lou, you've honored him well."

Her face softened a bit at his tone. "Thank you. It's nothing compared to how he cared for me."

She took a step back and indicated the next grave. The stone was weathered but stood straight. Twenty years had faded the color but not the words: Benjamin Ivy. Beloved Husband, Father and Son.

Tears stung his eyes. He didn't expect to react physically to seeing his father's grave. The tears coursed down his cheeks and he dropped to his knees. He didn't hear Mary Lou walk away. His mind was filled with the flashes of events that made up his memory of his father.

A man who stood on the riverbank and taught him to cast a line. A man who laughed when Jared teetered and fell from a hitching post as he tried to walk the straight board while holding his father's hand. A vague voice that sang in church. A smile for his mother as his father looked over his head at her during the service. His father and Grump laughing at something. Being tossed in the air and the wind swooshing from his lungs as he landed in his father's strong grasp.

These snatches in time were the only things he had left of a loving father, but Jared hadn't really known the man at all.

Jared mourned at the graves without realizing the passing of time. The legacy these two men had left him had cost them all they'd had. His father had given his life constructing the building. His grandfather had used his life to build the paper. In that moment, at their graves, Jared vowed he would dedicate his life to carrying it on. It was all he could do to honor them.

Nothing and no one—not even a sweet, determined young woman—would stop him.

Mary Lou didn't know what was the most sad, Jared's grief for the loss of his father and grandfather or the fact that he could have known one of them but didn't. In any case, he suffered from the loss.

She walked away from him toward the parsonage. Perhaps the preacher's wife would know if anything of interest was going on in the community. She needed a good story. A trip to see Liza Croft might be a quicker route if Mary Lou was just in search of gossip, but she wanted to spend a few minutes with Peggy Dismuke. The woman's calm nature always soothed her soul.

"I'm so glad you stopped by today, Mary Lou." Peggy invited her into the kitchen of the parsonage. "David isn't home, and I've just pulled a cake from the oven. I've always believed pound cake should be eaten while it's still warm. At least the first few slices." A trill of laughter punctuated her confession.

"It smells delicious." Mary Lou pulled off her gloves and reached for the plates Peggy always used for dessert. The parsonage was a place where anyone in the community could come for advice, comfort or just a visit. Most of the ladies in town knew where everything in the kitchen was stored. "I've come to ask if you know of any upcoming events or situations that I should include in the next edition of the *Record*."

Peggy put teacups on a tray with the cake slices and led the way to the front parlor. "What about the wedding of Jasmine and my brother?"

"I'm interviewing Jasmine tomorrow at lunch." Mary Lou tried to sound neutral but a bit of anxiety crept into her voice. "Jared Ivy will be joining us."

"That shouldn't be too awkward for you. You've been working together for several days now."

"We've been working in the same space, but I don't think we've managed to work together on anything yet. Certainly not a story. It won't surprise me if he's got ideas for making a lot of changes to the paper. My goal is to maintain the tone and character his grandfather established. But let's not talk about Jared. I need a good story. Unless I want him to bring in something better than I do. If that happens, he could take over the spirit of the paper before the judge comes to town and decides who will keep it."

"So you don't want to talk about Jared, do you?" Peggy was gracious and didn't point out how much of Mary Lou's conversation centered on the newest resident of Pine Haven. "Let me see." She poured tea, and the two of them soon were deep in conversation about the upcoming social planned for Christmas Eve.

Mary Lou took the last bite of cake and set her plate on the tray. "Has Reverend Dismuke arranged for the use of the barn at the Circle W?"

Peggy nodded. "He's spoken to Evan. With Jasmine running the ranch now, David knew Evan could arrange the details with her."

"It still seems a bit odd for Mr. Willis to have turned over the reins of the ranch to Jasmine before the wedding." Mary Lou knew what it was like to work in a man's job. Jasmine was in a more difficult position as a lady rancher.

"Jasmine played such an important role in the healing of our family before she and Evan became engaged. Pa loves her as much as he loves me and Evan and Milly."

"Do you think your father's somewhat obstinate personality will keep him from letting go of the decisions?" Mary Lou knew Peggy's family had recently reconciled after years of tension. Jasmine Warren's friendship and ultimate betrothal to Peggy's brother, the town doctor, had been the turning point.

Peggy laughed. "I don't think Pa will cease to be ornery, but I think he does it now to tease us."

"I'm so happy for your family. Not everyone gets that kind of happiness restored." Mary Lou knew there was no one to restore for her. No one alive claimed her as their family. Her father and mother had passed, then her aunt. Now with Mr. Ivy's death, everyone she'd ever truly loved was gone.

Movement outside the front window caught her attention. Jared walked across the churchyard, leading his new horse by the reins. His pace was steady but not fast.

Peggy went to stand by the front window. "So you don't want to talk about Jared Ivy, but you still do. And you're watching him out the window, too." She turned to Mary Lou. "Is there something besides a news article you'd like to talk about with me? You know I'm more than happy to lend an ear."

Embarrassment at having been caught staring jolted Mary Lou back to the moment. She put her teacup on the tray and stood. "I need to be going. There's a lot of work to be done for the paper." She pulled her gloves on and smiled at Peggy. "Thank you for the information about the Christmas social. I think I'll try to find a way to make the preparations into a series of articles. I'll start by speaking to your husband."

Peggy followed her to the front door and put a hand on her arm. "You're more than welcome, Mary Lou. Please be cautious. I don't know what I think about this new man coming into town and trying to take the paper from you. I don't want you to be hurt."

"I'm trying to be wise. One minute I'm concerned about losing everything Mr. Ivy gave to me, and the next I'm wondering if Jared really does deserve it. He is an Ivy, after all."

"The only reason your name isn't Ivy is because you insisted you were too old to be adopted when Mr. Ivy offered."

Only a few people knew that. "Please don't mention that to anyone. His grandson already questioned whether I tried to plant myself into Mr. Ivy's good graces in order to inherit the paper."

"Oh, Mary Lou, no one would ever believe that."

"No one who truly knows me." She stepped onto the front steps. "But Jared Ivy doesn't. All he knows is that he wants the *Pine Haven Record*. And he's determined to have it."

"I'll pray for you. God always has the right answer."

"I thought God had answered my prayers for a home when I came to stay with Mr. Ivy. Then he passed away. I thought the paper was his way of providing for me even though he's no longer here." She watched Jared mount the horse and head toward the middle of town. "I wonder where God will lead me if the judge takes it all away."

"Don't you borrow trouble. It's only a couple of months. The answer will be there when you need it."

They said their goodbyes and Mary Lou followed the same path Jared had traveled moments before.

Would God give it all to him? Would she have to start over and build a new life for herself? Again.

Her mind screamed for her to worry, but she refused. Instead she started considering possible articles she could write about the Christmas social. With just under ten weeks to go, she could write nine stories. She'd start with one about Reverend Dismuke and the true meaning of Christmas. She could do one about the children and their practices for the reenactment of the journey to Bethlehem. Maybe one about families and how they celebrated...

She was so successful in thinking about her work that she didn't see Jared until he reached out to catch her when she almost stumbled off the edge of the sidewalk.

"Whoa!" He wrapped his arm around her waist and set her to rights. "You are deep in thought."

The strength of his arm was a surprise. She was never touched by any man unless it was inadvertent. She'd jostled into someone leaving church before, or when she handed Andrew a stack of papers. But nothing like the strength of Jared Ivy as he protected her.

She remembered to breathe at that moment and gulped in too much air. A fit of coughing ensued. That was something she didn't need to repeat because his hand as he clapped her on the back was large and firm but gentle at the same time.

Mary Lou held up a hand and caught her breath. "Thank you, Mr. Ivy. You can stop now."

"What were you thinking about that nearly had you toppling into the street?" He released her and took a step back. She was close enough to see the beginnings of tiny lines in his forehead. Days in the sun on a ranch would be the cause. His eyes were flawless. No imperfections or hints of other colors to obscure the crisp blue.

"Not you." Her hand flew up to cover her mouth when she heard the words.

His heavy brows lifted. "Really?"

She was completely flustered now. "If you must know, I'm planning a series of articles for the paper. There's going to be a Christmas social for the community on Christmas Eve. I was thinking about that."

"To keep yourself from thinking about the fact that the judge may well have come to town and decided our fate by then?"

He thought she was fearful of losing the paper. That was true. But she was more afraid of letting herself think about Jared, the man. He was the kind of man she'd have dreamed of, if she'd allowed herself to dream.

Why was her mind playing the cruel trick of telling her this while she was standing so close to him?

"I won't deny that has occupied my mind." She looked up and squared her shoulders. She couldn't let him think she was afraid. "But that is not what I was thinking of just now. The quality of the paper is important to me. Planning ahead is one of the ways I maintain it."

Jared smiled. A brief smile that tilted his thin lips upward on the ends but didn't reveal his teeth. "You should be pleased to know that's what I've been working on today, too." He held an arm out toward the hotel. "Let me buy you lunch. We can compare ideas over a meal."

"We can compare notes, but we'll have to eat at my house. Lunch is prepared and waiting on the stove. It will spoil if it's not eaten today."

He offered her his arm. "That's even better. I haven't had a good meal since the stew you shared with me the other night."

Without realizing how it happened, Mary Lou found

herself dipping up bowls of soup and serving lunch to the man who could very well take away her home and job.

The most disturbing thing was that she was enjoying his company.

Jared dropped his spoon into his empty bowl. "That was delicious."

"Thank you." She took the bowl away and replaced it with a plate of fresh oatmeal cookies. "I enjoy cooking." She sat opposite him at her small kitchen table and picked up a cookie. "Tell me what you mean when you say we should plan ahead."

He took a bite of a cookie and nodded his approval. After taking a sip of tea he said, "I want to include articles about ranching and the cattle markets around the country."

"The people here are excellent ranchers. I'm not sure they need that."

"I'm not talking about how to raise cattle as much as I'm talking about the business side of things." He picked up another cookie. "I just left a job on a ranch that had to be sold because the owner didn't keep up with the ways things were changing. The railroad and barbed wire could eliminate long cattle drives entirely. Cattle prices are affected by any change like that. It's important for the ranchers to have this kind of knowledge before the changes occur."

"We do a good job of covering the local news. I'm not sure the *Record* is capable of predicting the future, Mr. Ivy."

He ate the rest of his cookie. "If we were able to do

that, Miss Ellison, we'd have the best-selling publication in all of Texas."

She laughed. He had taken her sarcasm and turned it back on her. "Let me think about it. Pine Haven isn't a large town yet. I want to consider the good of any such changes and weigh it against the space we have in the paper for what absolutely must be covered."

"That's reasonable. I want what's best for the paper. And helping the community will help the paper in the long term."

"On that one point, Mr. Ivy, we can agree."

Once again she'd let her guard down. Mr. Ivy would warn her to be observant and not be drawn into the story.

Could she resist the charm and intelligence of the man who sat across from her and had even offered to say grace before they'd eaten? Her fear of no man ever staying could be replaced by a fear that the one man she might want to stay would want her to leave.

Chapter Six

Jared finished his notes for the day and vacated the desk chair. The back door to the office opened and Mary Lou entered. She looked lovely in a dark green skirt and vest. The lacy collar of her white blouse brushed against her jawline with every move. She didn't know how beautiful she was. Never had he met a woman as pretty as her who could, but didn't, use her appearance to her advantage.

"What time should we arrive for our meeting with Miss Warren today?" He went to look out the front window. He wouldn't be distracted by the way her hair curled around her ears if he wasn't looking at her.

"We should arrive at the hotel at a quarter till noon. I never like to keep anyone waiting."

Having lunch with Mary Lou for the second day in a row might not be the smartest thing he'd ever done. Listening to her yesterday as she'd shared her ideas about a series of articles for Christmas, he'd kept wondering what she'd have thought of him if he'd come to town before Grump passed. Would she have welcomed him as he knew Grump would have?

Not unless he'd been able to convince her that he hadn't stayed away on purpose.

"I'll meet you at the hotel then." He opened the door.

"Where are you going?" Mary Lou stood at the corner of the desk like a captain at the wheel of a ship. She was poised to direct the paper at her will. And he needed to learn more about the town of Pine Haven so he could focus on having a plan in place before the judge arrived.

"I'm going to check on some ideas I have for a story for the paper."

"Which ideas?"

"About the thefts. I'll let you know if the clues develop." He wanted to find out if Jasmine had located the missing cameo. To mention that would stir up Mary Lou's ire.

"You may just be wasting your time. Let me see what you've written when you finish it."

"Mary Lou, I haven't decided if there's enough to write yet."

"And that's something else, Mr. Ivy. You've insisted on the informality of using my Christian name."

"We work together every day. All day. You should call me Jared. Don't you think it would be best if we approach some semblance of friendship?" He hadn't meant to start calling her Mary Lou. It had been spontaneous. Her name floated in his mind like it belonged there. He didn't think of her in a formal way.

"Will that offer of friendship remain in the event the

judge decides in my favor?" Her question wasn't unkind or abrupt. But the truth of it rang in the air. They
weren't friends. The easy lunch and going about town to
meet people was a front to keep the name of the paper
in good standing with the community. He would be
wise to remember that.

"I would hope to be your friend after the judge vali-
dates Grump's will."

"If this is your attempt to wear me down and hope
there will be no battle in court, you are mistaken. I
worked hard for your grandfather. Nothing he faced in
those last years was faced alone."

Andrew came through the front door. "Good morning, Miss Ellison." He took his hat off as he spoke. "I'm
sorry to be late. I took Midnight out for some exercise
and lost track of the time. Is there anything you need
me to do for you this morning?" He stood with his coat
on, his hair rumpled from the hat, and breathing as if
he'd run from the livery.

"Not this morning, thank you, Andrew." Mary Lou
sat behind the desk. "I'll be writing up an article. If
you'd like to come by later to start pulling the tiles and
compositing it, you may."

Andrew agreed. As he turned to leave he said, "Mr.
Ivy, you bought yourself a fine horse yesterday."

"I quite agree, Andrew." He watched for any sign
of reaction from the young man as he made his next
statement. "I was interested in Midnight, but Mr. Robbins informed me that you are the proud owner of that
fine animal."

Andrew's face lit up. He spun his hat in his hands.

"I am. Took me a lot of hard work to get him, but he's the best horse in town. I aim to be a rancher. He's the kind of animal I'll need."

"How did you afford a horse like that?"

Mary Lou shot him a sideways glare. "Andrew worked hard for that horse. Every odd job he could find."

Andrew showed no annoyance at the question. "When a man sees a horse like Midnight, he'll do whatever it takes to get him." He shoved his hat on and headed for the door. "Which means I better get on to my next job. I'll be back after lunch, Miss Ellison."

Jared nodded at Mary Lou as Andrew left. "He didn't exactly answer my question."

"He doesn't know your question was an attack on his character."

"It wasn't an attack. Do you believe everyone you interview thinks you're attacking them?"

"Of course not. But I know you think Andrew is a thief. You don't even know if the cameo was stolen, yet you seem determined to find a motive for Andrew to be a thief. I warn you, it won't sit well with me for you to keep following this train of thought."

"I'm on my way now to see if the cameo has been found." Jared pulled on his jacket.

Mary Lou stood and followed him. "I'm coming with you. We'll put an end to this once and for all." She took her coat from the tree by the front door. "Then we can get back to working on a real story."

It took only a matter of minutes to reach the hotel and speak to Mr. Warren.

"No, we didn't find it. As a matter of fact—" Mr.

Warren pointed to a table between two chairs near the front window "—we're missing a porcelain dish, too."

"What?" Mary Lou's face fell and she wrung her hands. Jared watched all the starch go out of her. He hated it, but it was not a surprise to him that something else had disappeared. "Do you know if it went missing at the same time?"

"We think it did. Josephine dusted the lobby that morning, and it was there. We noticed it missing when we were looking for the cameo."

Jared's suspicions that someone in town was a thief were validated. If it wasn't Andrew, it could easily be someone who comes and goes on a regular basis. "Josephine is the maid, right?"

Mr. Warren answered. "Yes. I believe you met her when you were our guest."

Mary Lou walked to the table by the window. "How large was the dish?" She ran a hand across the surface of the table.

"About the size of a lady's hand," Mr. Warren answered. "What are you thinking, Miss Ellison?"

She looked up and her gaze met Jared's. "Whoever took these items had to have done it quickly. I've almost never seen this room unoccupied."

Mr. Warren scratched his chin. "We try not to be too far from our guests. If we ever leave the desk unattended, we prop the door to the residence open. It's easier to keep an eye out for arriving guests. Except at night, of course."

Jared's curiosity wouldn't be stopped. "Have you had anything go missing from any of the rooms? Or from your residence?"

"No. I'd have the sheriff involved if that happened. I am hoping these things have merely been misplaced." Mr. Warren shook his head. "You think we have a thief here in the hotel, Mr. Ivy? As much as I'd hate to believe it possible, I'd have to contact Sheriff Collins if that was true."

"Not necessarily. Although, it would be wise to keep an eye out for anything else that might go missing. Those things could still turn up." If it was Andrew, Jared didn't want the man to involve the sheriff. He'd like to give the boy a chance to make things right and earn Mary Lou's faith in him.

Mary Lou asked, "Has anything else like this happened since you purchased the hotel?"

"No. We haven't had the first problem. I can't imagine we'd have a thief on our staff. Why, I couldn't even imagine a thief in Pine Haven." Mr. Warren's apparent disbelief was as sincere as Mary Lou's.

Jared pushed forward with his thoughts. "It happens more than people realize. Someone you trust finds themselves in need and, before you know it, they've done something they'd never done before. Trusting folks is well and good, until someone gets hurt." He'd trusted his mother. Her efforts to conceal a grandfather who'd loved him had robbed him of family he would never know. "Sometimes people very close to you do things that hurt you, and they do it for reasons they justify in their own minds."

Mr. Warren and Mary Lou stared at him. Did they suspect he was no longer talking about a missing cameo and a porcelain dish?

"Well, I've got somewhere I need to be. If you'll both excuse me." He turned and left in an instant.

Mistrust was new for him. It had consumed him when his mother died. Without warning it swarmed over his every thought.

Mary Lou might not think people capable of robbing or hurting others, but he knew it could happen. And he wore the pain of it in his heart. No matter how he tried to bury it.

At fifteen minutes before noon, Mary Lou stood on the porch of the hotel. Jared was nowhere in sight. She searched the street in both directions. A check of the pendant watch she wore pinned on her vest told her she couldn't wait for him any longer. Mr. Ivy had given her the watch on her twenty-first birthday. He'd told her that punctuality would open doors for a journalist that would never be open to someone who was late. She smiled at the engraved words—*A broken heart is an open heart*—knowing he'd meant it to encourage her but that it would probably never be true for her. Her heart had been broken by loss in her life. Never had she felt open after it happened.

She turned on her heel and entered the lobby. Mr. Warren was still at the desk where she'd left him after Jared had walked out earlier that morning, with both of them staring after him.

She couldn't put her finger on why, but there was pain in Jared Ivy. Pain that she'd witnessed at the cemetery. Was that what made him so suspicious?

She stopped in the middle of the lobby. Jared accused

her of being too trusting, of not looking at the possibility that things weren't what they seemed. She didn't have any problem doing that when it came to him. She'd questioned everything about him since he'd arrived. Every action and motive was dissected in her mind.

"Miss Ellison?" Mr. Warren stepped from behind the desk. "Are you feeling ill?"

"No. I'm quite all right." Was she?

"You just look a mite pale." Mr. Warren nodded toward the restaurant. "Evan will be joining Jasmine and Mr. Ivy in a few minutes. You're welcome to wait for him with them."

"Mr. Ivy is in the restaurant?"

"Yes. He's been in there about a quarter of an hour with Jasmine. Said he wanted to ask her a few questions. Didn't you agree to the meeting the other day?"

"I did. It was scheduled for noon." She rose up to her full height and took a deep breath. "If you'll excuse me, I need to get to work."

In the restaurant, Jared sat facing the entrance. He was speaking to Jasmine, and though Mary Lou couldn't hear the words, she knew the instant he saw her. His eyes widened a bit and he leaned in closer to the table as he made a note.

Mary Lou approached them. "Hello, Jasmine." She smiled a greeting to her friend. "Mr. Ivy." The look she shot at him was for his eyes only. He smiled away what she'd intended as a scorching rebuke.

"Mary Lou. So glad you could join us."

"I was waiting for you on the porch." She had been clear that they should arrive together.

"You were so right to warn me to be early." He took his seat again. "I arrived just as Miss Warren was returning from the Circle W. It seemed a good opportunity to ask her some questions about the ranch." Their interview was supposed to be about the wedding. Jared meeting Jasmine early and asking questions about ranching made Mary Lou appear unprofessional. And she didn't like it.

Jasmine signaled to Naomi, the cook.

The older lady came to the table with a happy greeting. "Good day to you, folks. What can I get for you?"

Jared answered for all of them. "We've been invited here today on the promise of tasting the absolute best chicken and dumplings."

Mary Lou's respect for Naomi Grant increased when she gave him a suspicious look. "Sir, if you mean to flatter me into an extra helping, you'll have to know Miss Warren here won't cotton to special favors to the menfolk." Then she winked at Evan Willis as he joined them, and Mary Lou realized the look had been for Doc Willis's benefit. "Unless it's her intended."

Doc Willis put a hand on Naomi's shoulder. "Please tell me you've saved a large portion of dumplings for me."

"You know I did." The cozy cook confirmed their orders and headed through the swinging door that led to the kitchen.

"Hello, love." Doc Willis dropped a kiss on Jasmine's proffered cheek.

"Hi, Evan." She gestured toward Jared. "Have you met Jared Ivy?"

Doc Willis took the chair beside Jasmine. "Not formally, but I've heard a bit about the uproar you started by coming to town and trying to take the newspaper from our dear Miss Ellison." A light tone kept the words from being mean-spirited, but they stung of truth to Mary Lou.

"Have I started a commotion? Really?" Jared turned to her.

"You'll soon learn that the town doctor is known for his direct manner." To the doctor, Mary Lou said, "He came to see his grandfather, but sadly he arrived too late." After seeing him grieve at the grave, she couldn't doubt his true sorrow over not coming sooner.

"My condolences to you." Doc Willis put an arm across the back of Jasmine's chair. Mary Lou watched how Jasmine, in full rancher attire, leaned into the gesture. Two more opposite people she couldn't imagine. The town doctor and a lady rancher. She hoped for a good story about their upcoming wedding.

"Thank you. I hope to learn about Grump from the people who shared his life." Jared spoke to Doc Willis but his eyes were on Mary Lou.

"We're working together at the paper until the judge comes through town. It seems that Mr. Ivy left the *Record* to his grandson in an old will that has surfaced." It took great effort to keep her tone from giving away the anxiety the words caused her.

Naomi returned with several plates of food. "Here we are, ladies." She set a generous portion of dumplings in front of each lady and put a plate piled high with her fresh biscuits in the center of the table. "I'll be right back with something for the gentlemen." Her wide skirts swooshed as she returned to the kitchen.

Jared leaned back in his chair and crossed his arms over the leather vest he always wore. Mary Lou thought it odd that he dressed like Jasmine yet wanted to run her paper. "I'm hoping to carry on the vision Grump and my father had for the *Record*."

Doc Willis looked at Jasmine and smiled. "Seems to me they're at a crossroads in life."

Jasmine chuckled. "Don't you start trying to solve their problems, Evan."

"What? I was merely going to say that a sensible solution would be to run the paper together. Why divide it, if it's what you both want to do?"

"Doc, you know how hard I've worked at the *Record*. Mr. Ivy taught me everything I know." Mary Lou couldn't let his words go unchallenged. What if everyone started to assume they should run it together? What if the judge ruled they should share it? No. That would never do. The *Record* was hers. She would fight for it.

"Seems to me two adults with similar goals might be well suited to one another." Jasmine pressed her elbow into Doc Willis's side as he spoke.

Jared put up both hands. "Hold on there, Doc. If you're suggesting we join forces for the paper, I'll have to agree with Miss Ellison. And believe me, we don't agree on much."

"Not just the paper. I'm saying why not consider joining your lives? Miss Ellison is as fine a woman as you'll meet in Pine Haven. You came here alone. Why not think of the possibilities if you aren't against one another?"

"Evan, you're starting to sound like Papa when he tried to convince you and me to court." Jasmine was clearly uncomfortable with the turn of the conversation.

"Look how well that turned out, my dear."

Mary Lou couldn't have been happier to hear what Jared said next.

"Thank you for your observations, Doc, but Mary Lou and I aren't searching for life partners. We're here for a story about you and Miss Warren."

Mary Lou seized the opportunity to change the subject. "Jasmine, I want to do a story about the wedding. Not just the facts of the event, but I want to include a personal touch about how it felt for you to move to Pine Haven and find your true love."

Naomi came back with the other plates and served the men. "Can I get you anything else?"

Jasmine thanked her. "Naomi, it smells delicious. You've outdone yourself again."

"Thank you, ma'am. You folks enjoy your lunch." She took a step away from the table. "But save some room for the chocolate cake Mrs. Beverly baked this morning." Then she left them to the meal.

Jared took a bite of the dumplings and hummed his approval.

Jasmine laughed. "I told you they were famous." The crowded room bore witness to Naomi's cooking skills.

"This might be the story for the paper." Jared took a biscuit from the platter. "I'd love to do an article on how Naomi came to be in Pine Haven."

"I wrote that story six months ago." The arch of his brow was minute, but she saw it. He knew she was challenging him. Jared silently signaled his acceptance before he bit into the biscuit.

Mary Lou asked Jasmine, "Will your house be finished before the wedding?"

"We think so. The men are working feverishly."

"So the men on the ranch are building your home?" Jared seemed surprised.

"Some of the workers are ranch hands. We hired a few men who help Mr. Thomas at the lumber mill, too." Doc Willis grinned at his betrothed. "We needed to hire the extra men to get the work done." He asked Jared, "Why would that matter to the story?"

"Your families are two of the most influential in Pine Haven. I'm looking at how your union will affect the business opportunities in town. A lot of people rely on your families for their livelihood."

Mary Lou thought her heart might stop beating. Was Jared suggesting their marriage was a business arrangement?

Doc Willis put his fork down. "What exactly are you asking?"

The serious tone caused Mary Lou to interject, hoping to calm what she saw as a brewing storm. "Let's talk about the ceremony. Have you decided to hold the reception at the ranch or the hotel?"

Jared wasn't deterred. "I'm thinking the two families working together could have a great impact on the local economy. It could be a good thing for Pine Haven. And as owner of the *Record*, I feel it's my duty to keep the community informed of anything that could make their lives better—or worse. That's the kind of story readers want in a local paper."

Doc Willis leaned back in his chair. "You think our marriage will impact the economy?"

"I do. With the resources and business experience of Mr. Warren and Mr. Willis pooled, there would be no end to what they could accomplish. If any member of your family were to run for public office, you'd most likely succeed. You could influence the direction of the future development of Pine Haven."

Mary Lou almost dropped her jaw. Where had this line of questioning come from? She wanted a piece about a lovely couple. Jared was turning it into a political and economic article. His grandfather had never done stories like that, nor had she. If she could get him out of this meeting without making enemies of two of her dear friends, she'd be relieved.

She directed her comments to Jasmine. "The readers care about the people of Pine Haven. They loved the reception your father hosted to honor your sister, Lily, and her marriage to Edward." To Jared she added, "The entire community was invited. It was the finest event we'd seen in a long time. There was delicious food and dancing. The hotel was decorated beautifully, too."

Doc Willis smiled at Jasmine. Again. "That's where we met."

Relieved that the couple followed her to a less controversial topic, Mary Lou asked several questions about the upcoming wedding.

Jared ate his lunch and listened with every indication of attention.

When the meal was over, and the cake was eaten, the four parted ways in the hotel lobby. Jared held the door open for Mary Lou to precede him onto the porch. As soon as Jasmine rode off in the direction of the Circle W and Evan closed the door of his doctor's office in the building next to the hotel, Mary Lou poked a finger into the center of Jared's chest.

"What were you thinking? You could have ruined the very good friendship that I enjoy with the two of them. Why did you want to pry into their personal business? And to suggest they run for office! That is making a story where there is none."

He narrowed his eyes and tilted his chin down to meet her gaze. "It's not about sparing personal relationships. The *Record* is a newspaper. And your small-town approach will not help it succeed in the fast-changing world we live in. It's not 1855. We are approaching a new century. The world won't stand still while we tell cute stories about pretty dresses and fancy cakes. The only chance you have of making an impact on the community should not be wasted on frivolity."

He hadn't raised his voice but he'd threatened her very way of life with every word.

She had to stand her ground. "Your grandfather would have approved the story I intend to write."

"Then you better do a bang-up job. It may be among the last stories you write for the *Record*." Jared jammed his hat on his head and left her standing there.

Chapter Seven

Jared rode out to the Double Star Ranch and met with Tucker and Daisy Barlow after breakfast on Thursday morning. The visit proved to be informative. As he suspected, most of the farmers and ranchers who called Pine Haven home would appreciate more news on the markets in the Record. The railroad had only come to town the year before. Things were changing rapidly. He hoped Mary Lou would see the need to stay ahead of the times.

He rode back into town in the afternoon and stopped in front of the general store. He tied Noel and, as he went up the steps, Doc Willis came out of the store.

"Afternoon, Doc."

"Hello, Mr. Ivy."

"Call me Jared. I'm starting to feel like an old man. Everyone in town calls me Mr. Ivy."

Doc Willis chuckled. "It's a close-knit community. They'll warm up to you. Unless they feel like you're trying to come in and put Miss Ellison in the street. That poor woman had a rough life before your grandfather took her in. He was good to her." He paused. "And she was good to him. Loved him like her own."

"I didn't come to put her out. I came to be with Grump. I had no idea he had passed."

"Would you have come if you'd known?"

Jared hadn't considered that. Would he have moved this far west? There had been other ranching jobs in Maryland. Just because the ranch he'd worked on had gone under didn't mean he couldn't find work closer to home.

But it wasn't really home. This was his home.

"Pine Haven is my home, Doc. My father and mother lived here before I was born. Pa and Grump built this paper for me when I was a small boy. I came to carry on the legacy they created."

Doc nodded. "Then God will work it all out for you. He has a way of bringing folks to the things—and the people—they need in their lives."

Jared wasn't sure. "God didn't show much interest in me in Maryland."

Doc Willis shook his head. "Sometimes things happen that God didn't have anything to do with. It doesn't mean He isn't interested. It can mean He wasn't consulted. Or even that it wasn't time for a particular thing to happen. Either way, I've learned something about God. He's always good." The doctor gave a quick nod for emphasis. "And He's always right."

"I've got no argument with that."

"Don't close yourself off from things—or people—

too quickly. There just may be an answer waiting for you if you're willing to hear it."

"Doc! Come quick!" An older gentleman waved at the doctor from the center of town. "There's a fight at the saloon! Looks like they're gonna need you again."

"I wish the town council had never let Winston Ledford build that saloon." He stepped onto the street.

"Would they have approved it if men like you or your father-in-law had been one of their number?"

Doc Willis paused to ponder his question. "They wouldn't have had my vote. Mr. Warren didn't move here until after the saloon opened."

"That's just the sort of thing a man can influence when he involves himself in political matters."

"That's a thought worth thinking on, Jared." The doctor nodded as if it were something he'd think about immediately. "You have a good afternoon. I'm sure we'll meet again soon."

As the doctor made his way toward the waving man, Jared thought about what Doc had said about God working things out for people. Grump had read him Bible stories when he was a boy. Every story had ended with something good that God had done. His mother had read to him, too, until he'd learned to read for himself. But not with the enthusiasm of Grump. When Grump read, the characters all took on different voices. He'd even made the lions roar before Daniel had been thrown into the den. The memory warmed his heart.

Doc was right. God was always good.

And in his heart, Jared knew God was always right.

If only he could see God's plan for the future. He'd known coming to Pine Haven was the right thing to do.

Why hadn't God told him to come sooner?

For the first time he acknowledged that he couldn't blame that on his mother or God. Jared was twenty-four years old. He'd been working on the ranch for years before his mother passed. He could have come to visit Grump any time after he'd started working. No, it wouldn't have been an easy trip, and his mother wouldn't have approved. But the fault was his alone.

I'm sorry, Lord. Please forgive me for the hurt I've bottled up inside and the blame I've held against my mother. Help me to forgive her. And myself.

Elmer Finch came out of the general store. He was looking down and bumped into Jared.

"Hey, be careful." Jared put out a hand and caught the man by the arm to keep him from tripping off the porch.

Mr. Finch snatched his arm from Jared's grasp. "What are you doing standing in the middle of the sidewalk like a stumbling block?" Jared saw the moment the man recognized him. "Oh, it's you. Every time I see you, you're hindering me."

"Every time I see you, you're in a big hurry." He nodded toward the store. "Is there someone in there with a gunshot wound?"

"You know I didn't do that." Mr. Finch stepped by him and down to the street.

"Have a nice day, Mr. Finch." Jared couldn't resist taunting him. Something about the man made him suspicious.

Jared went into the store and Mr. Croft greeted him.

"Mr. Ivy, good to see you again so soon. What can I do for you today?"

"I've come on a hunch." Jared cast an eye to the street outside. "Have you had anything go missing of late? Small things maybe. Things that might fit into a pocket and be taken without your notice."

The store owner frowned. "Can't say I've noticed anything missing." He bellowed to his wife in the back storeroom. "Liza, have you noticed anything missing?"

Liza Croft sashayed through the swinging doors. "What are you looking for?"

"Nothing. Mr. Ivy here wants to know if we're missing anything."

Her tinny voice rose. "Has someone been taking things?" She pivoted first one way then another. "We'll do a complete inventory after we close tonight."

"No, we won't. It was just a question." Mr. Croft addressed Jared. "Why did you ask?"

He hoped a smile and a sincere tone would help him calm the situation he hadn't meant to instigate. "No reason. It's the newspaper instincts. Always looking for a story."

"Has the sheriff been told?" Mrs. Croft would not be silenced as readily as Mr. Croft. "Is there a thief among us?"

"No, ma'am. There's no need to talk to the sheriff. I have no reason to believe you've been robbed."

The bell rang as the door opened and Mary Lou entered. "Mary Lou, I'm glad you're here. I was just about to see if the Crofts have any of the supplies we need for the paper, but I didn't think to make a list before I left the office." Perhaps a possible sale would divert them from their conversation.

"You are a master of lists, Mr. Ivy. I find it hard to believe you would forget such a thing." Mary Lou studied him with her ever-present suspicion. "I am unaware that we are low on anything at the moment."

Liza Croft put a hand to the base of her neck. "Miss Ellison, Mr. Ivy has been telling us there's a thief in town." She darted her eyes along the rows of shelves. "I'm going to look around right this minute. I won't rest until I know no one has taken anything from us." She scurried toward the front of the store. "Donald, these small things you insisted on putting near the front door are a temptation no crafty-minded crook would pass up." She arranged and rearranged the trinkets on a low table.

"Liza, no one wants those trinkets. They're ugly. I put them there hoping people would see them and buy them. You paid too much for them. We'll never get our money back." Mr. Croft went to help pick up the things his wife had knocked onto the floor in her hurry to inspect them.

Jared watched the scene unfold and saw Mary Lou's face tighten. She whispered to him, "You told them there's a thief?"

"No." He kept his voice low. "I asked Mr. Croft if he'd noticed anything missing."

"Mrs. Croft is excitable. You may as well have told her there was a gang of renegades coming to town for supper." A smile pulled at the corners of her mouth. This close to her, he caught the scent of the soap she'd used on her hair. The light fragrance teased his senses. "I doubt you and Mr. Croft, with the help of the sheriff, will be able to calm her down now." She laughed. "It's no more than you deserve. I warned you not to try to make a story where there wasn't one."

Mrs. Croft cried out like a woman in great pain. "It's gone!" She had moved to the front window display in her frantic search to find something missing.

Mr. Croft followed her. "What's gone, Liza?"

"The music box I set there this morning. It played the sweetest tune and fit in your hand. The lid lifted and a tiny bird tweeted a melody."

"You put that in the front window? It should have been in the case on the back counter." Mr. Croft wasn't happy.

Jared stood with Mary Lou and watched from across the store. "It seems I was right to question whether they were missing anything."

Mr. Croft lifted several items in the window in search of the missing music box.

"I put it right there." Mrs. Croft pointed to an empty spot in the window display.

The doors to the storeroom swooshed open and Andrew entered the shop. "Mr. Croft, I couldn't find what I need. Thanks for letting me look around." He was heading for the front door when he saw Mary Lou and Jared.

"Miss Ellison, do you need me at the paper this afternoon?"

Mary Lou darted a glance at Jared. He saw the look of surprise in her eyes. "No, Andrew. I'm working on a story this afternoon. You can check with me in the morning after you do your work at the livery."

Mr. Croft called out, "Here it is." He held up the music box for them to see. "It was under that length of fabric Mrs. Ledford was looking at earlier." He handed it to his wife. "Go put it in the case."

"I'm sorry for the confusion, Mr. Croft." Jared hadn't intended to upset the couple.

"Don't worry about it. If anything, we learned a lesson in preventing such a theft from happening." He clapped a hand on Jared's shoulder. "You've done us a service today, Mr. Ivy. I'm grateful to you."

Andrew cleared his throat. "What happened?"

Jared watched Andrew's reaction as Mary Lou answered him. "A music box was misplaced. They were concerned it might have been stolen."

The lad cocked his head to one side and drew his brows together. "Who in Pine Haven would steal something?"

"Exactly what I was saying," Mary Lou agreed. "Thank you, Andrew."

Andrew said his goodbyes and left. Jared watched through the front window as Andrew cast a glance over his shoulder and looked into the store before he headed in the direction of the hotel. Mary Lou might not want to consider it, but there was still the matter of the missing cameo and the porcelain dish. It wouldn't hurt to keep an eye on the young man. Though part of Jared hoped, for Mary Lou's sake, that he wasn't a thief.

One thing was certain: Jared was not going to ask

himself why it mattered to him if Mary Lou's trust was misplaced.

She had stepped to the back of the store to speak to Mrs. Croft. The two ladies were admiring the tiny golden box. Her hair hung loosed from the side of the bun at the nape of her neck and hid her face from him. She reached up and tucked the loose strand behind her ear, upsetting the pencil that was always at the ready for taking notes should she run across some interesting detail during the day.

Jared went to stand near Mr. Croft as he straightened the window display. Mrs. Croft had turned it on its heel in her frantic search.

Mr. Croft stood back to inspect his work. "I'm glad there wasn't a thief."

"I'm not sure we'll be able to convince the two of them that I had a right to speak up to you. Mary Lou doesn't care for my habit of asking too many questions."

"You're supposed to ask questions. You're a newspaper man."

"Getting her to see that will take a bit of doing."

"You're already calling her by her Christian name. I'd say, if she's letting you do that, she'll be open to most anything you put to her." Mr. Croft laughed and headed to the back of the store.

Jared took the opportunity to slip away unnoticed.

He took Noel back to the livery and brushed her down, all the while wondering if Mary Lou was right. Was this town so small no thief would dare to violate the trust of his neighbors? It was doubtful. Even as he considered it, he heard shouts coming from the direction of the saloon.

There were definitely people in this town who wouldn't consider the good of others. They might not be part of the community, but they were in Pine Haven. Even if they were only passing through.

Mary Lou sat at the desk, writing up her notes from her interview with Jasmine. The details were coming together for a lovely wedding. She'd just finished polishing the story she intended to include in the next edition when Jared came into the office. The fall air that ushered him in and caused the flame of her lantern to flicker filled the room before he could shut the door.

Jared hung his hat and jacket on the coat tree. "You're working late."

"It's best to stay ahead of schedule. Every article I have ready will be something I don't have to fret about on Saturday." She blew the ink dry then set the story on the edge of the desk, placing the magnifying glass on top of it to keep it from flying away.

Jared took the pages up as soon as she moved her hand.

"That's not a story I need your help with." She sounded like a protesting child even to her own ears.

"I will want to read everything before the next edition is printed." He spoke as though he wasn't hearing her. He was focusing his attention on the document in his hand.

What choice did she have? The right to input was his. The sheriff had given it to him.

"This is a good start."

"It's not a start. That is the story."

He shook his head and put the paper under the magnifying glass. "That is your perspective on the story. I propose that, while we are sharing the duties of the paper, we will offer alternate views of the stories on which we disagree." When she opened her mouth to protest, he held up a hand. "Hear me out. I'm only suggesting that for the stories on which we do not agree. For stories such as this—" he pointed at the paper on the desk "—we may both write an article and compare content. I suspect we will be able to combine the two efforts into one article on most occasions. But I reserve the right to print an opposing viewpoint on any subject."

She took her time before answering. "What if we each write different articles on different subjects? We could sign the articles so the people of Pine Haven will know who the author is."

"How would we choose who would write which story?" That he didn't reject her idea out of hand was a surprise. She'd expected him to resist any thoughts from her.

"I can write the stories I bring in, and you can write the ones you bring." She resisted the urge to give a sharp nod as punctuation to her words.

"Then you may print this article and I will print one about the power and influence of the two families combining."

Mary Lou didn't like it, but it was better than letting him ruin her article by trying to combine it with his. "Very well."

She reached for another piece of paper and pulled some notes toward her. The next article should be finished before she retired for the evening. She read through her notes again without really seeing them. Jared standing over her from the opposite side of the desk was disconcerting. She put the notes in order before stopping to ask, "Is there something else?"

"I told you I want to read everything before it goes into the paper. What are you working on now?"

"If you must know, it's the first in the series on the Christmas Eve social."

Jared sat on the corner of the desk. "What approach are you taking for the series?"

"Nothing as fanciful as suggesting the wise men gave the Christ child stolen gifts." She didn't mean to snap, but he'd accused Andrew of being a thief and stirred the idea of theft to others.

Jared chuckled. "Well, I'm glad to see you're basing the story in fact." He went to the table that held the font tiles and pulled out his notebook. "If you don't mind, I'll work a bit longer tonight. I've got this story ready and don't want to wait. Who knows what may come up tomorrow? Perhaps another shooting or a stagecoach robbery. A mysterious passenger from the train could come into town and turn the peace that is Pine Haven on its ear." He plopped onto a stool and began putting tiles onto a composing stick.

They worked in silence for several minutes. Mary Lou didn't make a lot of progress. She'd crossed out more information than she'd kept. She wanted to know what he was writing.

She put her pen down and asked, "What story is that?" She wouldn't let him read her work without demanding to see his.

He picked up another tile and added it to the stick, carefully pushing the letter close to the others. He reached for another. Mr. Ivy had often been so engrossed in his work that he'd ignored her. She'd soon learned it was his deep concentration and not an attempt at rudeness. Jared had no way of knowing how like the man he was. If he wasn't a threat to her independence, she might even like him. Or at least not be so upset at his presence.

"Jared, what story are you working on?"

He started and dropped the tile onto the table. His "What?" was absentminded as he retrieved the letter.

Mary Lou came to look over his shoulder. "What story are you working on?"

"One about the ranches in the area and how the railroad has changed their business." He didn't look up but kept working.

"What made you choose that subject?" She leaned in to try to see the words he'd chosen, but he angled his hand so she couldn't. "It's not something that's come up much in the last year."

"That's why I want to write it. The train came through Pine Haven almost a year ago. I want to show the ways it has helped the town progress."

"The people know that. They don't need an article about it." She put a hand on his arm. "Let me see."

He stopped working and looked down on her from

his place on the stool. "You will get a better picture if you wait and read the entire article."

"Who did you interview? The sources you spoke to will determine whether people will accept the merit of the story."

"I didn't stop people in the street and ask their opinion. I went to the Circle W and the Double Star. Mr. Willis and Mr. Barlow were both eager to share their experiences. Mr. Barlow had the benefit of having worked on a ranch in East River before he moved to Pine Haven. It's a good story, Mary Lou."

"Let me see what you have so far." She tugged on his sleeve. "You haven't worked with the tiles before. You'll be wasting your time if you aren't doing it right."

"All right." He turned toward her and held out his hand for her to see. The first few words were lined up evenly.

She tried to keep from laughing, but it bubbled up in her throat and spilled out.

"What?" He looked at the composing stick and then at her. "You know this is a good story."

"I'm sure it is." She reached for the stick but he pulled it out of her reach.

"If you're only going to laugh, why should I show it to you?"

"Well, if you want the readers to understand the content—" she stifled another chuckle "—we're going to have to print it so they can read it."

He looked at the letters. "It's perfectly legible."

"Yes." She pointed to the printing press. "Come look at these."

He followed her to the press and groaned. All the starch went out of him. "For all my telling you I can manage without your help, I've just proved myself wrong." He smiled at her. "You don't think me foolish, do you? I couldn't bear it."

Heat filled her face. "Why does my opinion matter to you?" She knew he wanted her gone. But something about him pulled her to him. He was kind and intelligent. A smile threatened to cover her face again. Even if he had a lot to learn about the newspaper business.

"Because you're the one Grump chose to work with him. If I'd been here, he might not have needed anyone, but he chose you. I'd have been family, an obvious candidate. You were a choice. I'd like to earn your respect, even if we can't both win in this situation." He held out his hands to indicate the office.

"Hmm. Well, if you keep using your words with that kind of charm, you'll have the whole town eating out of your hand." She reached for the composing stick and he relinquished it to her. "But first, you're going to have to learn to read backward." She started to remove the tiles and drop them into their slots.

"I don't know why I didn't notice that all the type is set backward." He fumbled to put his hands in his pockets, face downcast.

"Don't let it upset you. Anyone could have made the same mistake." She finished sorting the letters with the speed of experience. "Thankfully, we caught it before you had too much time invested." She handed back the composing stick and returned to the desk.

She picked up the dictionary Mr. Ivy had kept there

and handed it to him. "You might want to keep this close at hand."

He frowned. "Why do you say that?"

"Because in the few lines I sorted and put away, I found three misspelled words. If you find it hard to spell them forward, wait until you've done a few backward." She sat back down and picked up her notes.

"Don't you want to read the story?"

"I do. But not on the composing stick." She didn't look up. Let him see how it felt to hold a conversation with someone who wasn't paying attention. Not that she was ignoring him. Even with her eyes lowered, she could see the hem of his vest and the watch chain that hung between the pocket and the button. She didn't want him to notice that she was taking in every detail of who he was. She pointed to the corner of the desk. "Just leave it here. I'll read it when I've finished sorting these notes."

He turned back to the composing table and leafed through his papers.

Lord, everything he puts in this paper will reflect on me. I've got to maintain Mr. Ivy's high standards. Help me to be kind but firm, if needed. And please help me get my emotions under control. This is no time for me to become interested in a man. Especially not one who wants to take away everything I have.

Jared slid the paper across the desk in front of her. "I'm going to eat supper at the hotel. You can tell me what you think when I return." He reached for his hat and coat.

"I'll leave a note with my recommendations on the desk. I'm sure to be gone by the time you return."

The door closed behind him and Mary Lou watched his silhouette as he walked by the front window.

Jared was more of a distraction and threat to her than anyone she'd ever known. How was she to maintain ownership of the *Record* if she lost her heart to the man who wanted to take it from her?

"That will never do, Mary Lou." She scolded herself out loud. "Mr. Ivy trained you. Jared Ivy is his grandson, but you were his choice to run this paper."

Jared's words to that effect echoed in her mind as she read his story. It was good. Well written, if poorly spelled.

As much as she was loath to admit it, he was right. The ranchers and farmers would be helped by the information he'd included in the article.

Was it time to change the direction of the *Record*? Could Jared Ivy make it better with his business articles and political opinions? Only time—and the judge—would tell.

Chapter Eight

Two weeks of learning how to set type, lay out the paper in a logical order, balance social news and business news—and honing his spelling skills—had Jared feeling better about the future of the *Pine Haven Record*. He'd also learned what a good newspaper woman Mary Lou was. For all her protestations that the paper should be personal and relevant to the everyday lives of the people of Pine Haven, she had a good head for the difficult subjects. She'd written an article about the increase in violence since the saloon had opened and another about the railroad increasing the number of trains stopping in Pine Haven.

He finished compositing the last of his story for the top of the paper and set it in place. The only thing left to add would be Mary Lou's article on the Warren and Willis wedding scheduled to take place later that morning.

The front door opened and Andrew came in. "Morning, Mr. Ivy." Andrew removed his hat. "Is everything set for the printing this afternoon?"

Andrew had proven himself a hard worker in the few weeks that Jared had been in Pine Haven. Jared appreciated his determination but still didn't know if Andrew was trustworthy.

Jared eyed the young man's clothes and knew everything he wore was something Jared had seen before. He never appeared to spend money, but the horse he owned still had Jared confounded.

"Everything is ready except Miss Ellison's article on the wedding."

Mary Lou entered through the back door. "Good morning, gentlemen." She was lovely in a dark green skirt with a matching cape. The lace collar of her blouse nestled against her neck. She carried delicate gloves in one hand and a notebook in the other.

Andrew greeted her first. "Hi, Miss Ellison. If you don't need me, I'd like to go ahead to the church. I want to see Tucker Barlow before the wedding. Someone said he might have a ranching job coming open." Excitement filled the youth's words.

Jared wondered if Andrew was strong enough to work on a ranch. "That's mighty hard work for one so young."

Andrew bristled. "I'm sixteen. Been working since I was twelve. I don't claim to know all there is to know about ranching, but I'm a hard worker. Mr. Barlow is a fair man. I think his foreman, Paco Morales, would make the final decision, but Mr. Barlow could give me permission to show the foreman what I know."

Mary Lou came forward like a protective sister. "That's a good opportunity for you, Andrew. I'd be proud to see you settled in a good job that would pay a man's wages in time."

The look she gave Jared seemed a silent plea for him to encourage Andrew. He couldn't acquiesce to everything Mary Lou wanted, but this request gave no cause for disagreement.

"I met Paco when I went out to the Double Star Ranch with Mr. Barlow. He seems a fine boss. You've got a good horse, too. That will help you."

Andrew stood a bit taller at the praise of Midnight. "I got a new saddle yesterday. Not near as fine as yours, Mr. Ivy, but it's the best I could get here in town. Not so fancy as I would have liked, but it's a fine leather."

"That must have set you back a pretty penny." Caution ran through Jared's mind. He could see Mary Lou tense at the turn in conversation.

"Took every bit of the money I've been able to scrape together since I bought Midnight. It ain't right to have a fine horse and a poor saddle."

"Andrew, what did I tell you about 'ain't'?" Mary Lou scolded in her best schoolmarm voice.

"Yes, ma'am." In a slow, steady tone he corrected himself. "It isn't right to have a fine horse and a poor saddle." Andrew put his hat back on. "I'll see you both at the wedding. It's sure to be the best meal I've had in ages." He scooted out the door and down the steps in front of the office.

Jared watched him from the window.

Mary Lou's voice came from behind him. "I know what you're thinking."

"It doesn't make sense, Mary Lou. A boy that age, no matter how hard he's been working, shouldn't have enough money to pay for things like that. I'm just surprised no one else in town has been suspicious of him."

"Only two items have gone missing in the two weeks since Jasmine's cameo and the porcelain dish disappeared from the hotel."

He turned to face her. "Two very expensive items."

"Where would a boy like Andrew be able to sell things like that?"

"I admire your loyalty, but someone is taking small things from unsuspecting people in Pine Haven. And Andrew is the only person flaunting new treasures."

"He's not flaunting anything. He told me about the saddle because he knows I respect how hard he works. We share a bond of trust."

Jared shook his head. "I hope you're right."

"I know I am. And you didn't answer my question. Where would he sell those things?"

"The last items could have been sold to any drunk in the saloon after he won a good hand at cards."

"Why would a drunken card player want a fancy ink pen? Most of the people who come and go from the saloon don't appear to be literate."

"An inebriated man would be easily convinced to purchase a shiny object as a way to show off his money."

"But a brush and comb set?"

"What better way to pacify an angry wife after having spent the night in town gambling away all his money? And after the way Donald and Liza Croft started watching their merchandise more closely, it would have to be someone they trusted to take the items right out from under their noses."

Mary Lou seemed to ponder his arguments. "I'll grant you that those things may have been sold at the saloon. May even have been sold by someone from here in Pine Haven, but I know in my heart it wasn't Andrew." She straightened her cape, picked up her gloves and headed for the door. "I want to get to the church early, so I can get a good seat and sketch the details of the church and Jasmine's dress." She opened the door. "I'm sure I'll see you there, as well."

He caught the door and pulled it wider. "I'm coming with you."

She paused and turned to him, her face mere inches below his. "It isn't necessary. You can come at your leisure and sit where you choose."

"Are you saying you don't want me to accompany you?" If she told him that was her reason, he'd be disappointed. The thought of sitting with her in all her finery was inviting. The more he learned about her, the more he appreciated Grump's decision to take her in. If she could get past the notion of trying to keep his grandfather's paper, they might grow to be good friends. Or even more.

Her answer was quiet, so he had to lean closer to hear her. "No. I'm not saying that. I'm offering it. I don't want you to feel obligated to escort me."

He couldn't resist the urge to smile. "I consider it an honor, not an obligation."

"Well then." She cleared her throat and pulled on her gloves. "Shall we?"

When she took his offered arm, he was relieved. He wasn't sure she'd think his politeness was professional. On more than one occasion, she'd reminded him that their business arrangement did not necessitate friendship. As they stepped off the porch and into the street, he was glad to realize she hadn't repeated the mantra in the last several days.

The closeness of working together on different stories, using the press and sharing a desk had forced them to be civil. The civility had grown into an easy camaraderie.

Having a true friend in Mary Lou Ellison would be a wonderful thing. She was like no one else he'd ever known. Her loyalty was in complete contrast to his mother's mistrust and secretiveness.

Even when Jared disagreed with her, she was kind and professional. She'd even laughed with him at some mistake he'd made in a story he'd written, and the spelling errors he was working to overcome.

If she noticed people looking their way as they walked through the middle of town, she gave no indication. When they entered the church, she stopped just inside the door to study the decorations. He offered to take her cape while she stared at the greenery draped from every possible surface. She refused and he followed her to sit near the front of the church. Several people must have had similar wishes to arrive early and see everything. A low hum of chatter filled the building as everyone gathered for what promised to be the social event of the season.

And though he should have been focused on who was entering and who they were speaking with, all Jared could do was watch the beauty of the woman beside him as she reveled in her work as a journalist. He had no doubt she was memorizing the details.

She turned at that moment. Her green eyes were so close he marveled at the black line that circled the green. Their breaths mingled together as she whispered to him, "It's so lovely. Any woman would be honored to marry in such a setting."

Without taking his eyes from hers, he agreed. "It is lovely. The green is perfect. It's difficult to have flowers in a cold season, but the beauty of evergreens is incomparable in the right setting." He hoped she didn't realize he spoke of her eyes.

What was he thinking? This was the woman who would stand and tell a judge that he wasn't worthy of his grandfather's inheritance. Why, after a lifetime of avoiding women, would he be drawn to the one woman in the world who wanted nothing more than for him to walk out of her life?

Mary Lou stretched up on her toes to see over the shoulders of the crowd, trying to glimpse the full length of the bride's dress as she came down the aisle on her father's arm. Leaning forward a little too far to peer around the sheriff, Mary Lou would have stumbled, but Jared put out his arm and she fell against its steadying force.

Her breath caught. He was too close. Too familiar. Too tall. Too handsome.

She planted her feet and turned as Jasmine passed the end of their bench. The bride was lovely. Lace and ruffles adorned her dress. It was unusual to see Pine Haven's resident lady rancher dressed in such finery, but it was lovely all the same.

When Reverend Dismuke instructed the congregation to be seated, Mary Lou felt Jared's hand cup her elbow. *He's just being kind. He's a gentleman.*

The words did nothing to calm the distraction his presence had become.

The ceremony was everything a wedding should be. Solemn vows were exchanged between Doc Willis and Jasmine. A chuckle went up from those gathered when the preacher gave permission for their first wedding kiss and the doctor pushed up on his toes to kiss his new wife.

After the couple went back up the aisle and out the front doors, Reverend Dismuke extended the family's invitation for everyone to join them at the Pine Haven Hotel for a wedding celebration.

Jared spoke close to her ear. "Did you get all the notes and sketches you need?"

Mary Lou rubbed a hand against the side of her neck where his breath had stirred her hair. "I still need to get a better look at the front of the dress, but I made good notes about the decorations beforehand."

He stood behind her as they waited their turn to exit the church. She felt him pull at the shoulders of her cape to straighten it. Did his hands rest there a moment longer than necessary?

She took a step away from him. "I'd like to try to get to the hotel before everyone else, if possible."

He chuckled. "I don't think we'll make it before everyone, but we may be able to arrive before most of the guests."

The brisk November air helped to calm her. She'd worked for weeks with Jared and he hadn't affected her like he did today. It must be the nostalgia that is common at a wedding.

The bride and groom had stopped in the churchyard and were being congratulated by well-wishers.

Mary Lou skirted the gathering crowd and walked up the street, dodging in and out of the groups of people making their way to the celebration.

"Whoa, Mary Lou." Jared touched her arm. "You're making it very difficult to keep up with you. I'd rather not trip over some unfortunate person who happens to not anticipate your approach. I don't think it would be good for me to pummel a little old lady before everyone learns what a good person I am."

"If we slow down, we won't get a good look at the room before it fills with people. Then the details of the story will be vague."

"Okay, but be prepared to take the credit if I bowl someone over."

"Come along, and it won't happen." They arrived at the hotel and followed Naomi Grant into the lobby.

Jared stepped around Mary Lou and she would have protested until she heard him offer to take Naomi's coat.

As he helped the cook, he asked, "Mrs. Naomi, would you be willing to give Mary Lou and me a peek at the restaurant before anyone else arrives?"

Naomi smiled at him in her kind way. "Oh, Mr. Ivy, I don't know if Mr. Warren wants any of the guests inside before he arrives."

Jared persisted. "We'd like to be able to cover today's events to the best of our abilities. I think we could give a better account if we can see what a wonderful job the family and hotel staff have done with the decorations before the others crowd into the hotel." He swept his arm wide to indicate the lobby area. "If the lobby is any hint, the restaurant must be beautiful."

Mary Lou watched Naomi pause, as if having second thoughts. "The church was lovely. May we please just take a peek?"

Jared added, "We'll only stay a moment. We'll be back in the lobby before anyone else comes."

"I just want to take a few notes before anything is disturbed." Mary Lou held up her notebook. "Please."

Naomi shook her head. "You two are a powerful force for persuasion when you work together." She waved them on. "Follow me." She stopped still. "But if Mr. Warren comes in, I want both of you out the back door without a peep."

They all laughed. Jared and Mary Lou answered in unison, "Yes, ma'am."

A half hour later the celebration was in full swing. The thin strains of music from a phonograph filled the room, and the tables and chairs had been arranged to allow for dancing.

Mary Lou watched as Jared spoke to Mr. Warren across the restaurant. Jasmine and Doc Willis were dancing in the center of the room. Jared looked up and caught her eye. She felt her face grow warm when he smiled at her.

The room was full of happy friends and relatives milling around and visiting with one another. One song ended on the phonograph and another began.

The sheriff blocked her view of Jared. He had shaved, like most of the men today, only he'd kept his heavy moustache. It never ceased to amaze Mary Lou how much stock people put in a special occasion. Why didn't they keep themselves looking their best all the time? She cast a glance at the sheriff's boots and almost laughed. His attention to detail had stopped before he'd polished the well-worn leather.

He rubbed his chin as if uncomfortable without the rough whiskers. "Miss Ellison, have you come up with any ideas on who our thief might be?"

"I am not convinced the thief is ours, Sheriff. It could have been someone who was here and is now gone. Or it could have been a coincidence of more than one thief. Perhaps a series of strangers who rode through town and took a memento with them. A keepsake of their time in Pine Haven."

Jared's voice came from her right. "You can't really think that is the explanation." She'd been so focused on the sheriff that she hadn't noticed Jared come to stand beside her. He carried two cups of punch and held one out for her to take.

"I don't." Sheriff Collins looked at Jared. "Do you have any thoughts on who it might be?"

Jared looked at Mary Lou. "I have given the matter some thought."

"Who do you think it is?" The sheriff's persistence was in keeping with his reputation. Many people felt he was comfortable letting others bring answers to him. More comfortable than finding those answers on his own.

Mary Lou spoke up. "We have no right to say a name based solely on suspicion and not on fact." She twisted the cup of punch she held with both hands.

"So you do have a name." The sheriff pressed again for Jared to answer.

"He doesn't have any proof." Mary Lou tried to steer the conversation.

Sheriff Collins turned to her. "Why are you trying to protect a thief, Miss Ellison?"

Jared said, "I'm not willing to share my observations."

"What have you observed, Mr. Ivy? You may be the publisher of the newspaper, but I'm the law in this town."

"I am the publisher of the *Record*, Sheriff Collins," Mary Lou insisted.

"I'm asking Mr. Ivy the questions now."

"He doesn't know the people of Pine Haven like I do. He can't give you a valid opinion on this matter."

"Not give a valid opinion?" Jared's eyes grew wide and one brow arched upward. "I believe my opinion to be plausible."

She wouldn't listen to him. "No. You have no evidence. All you have are your suspicions."

The sheriff continued to address Jared. "What suspicions?"

She wouldn't stand by and let Jared cast Andrew in a poor light. "Just because someone was in the vicinity of the missing items on the day they were taken doesn't make them guilty."

"Mr. Ivy, I've been fair to you since you came to Pine Haven. Matter of fact, you wouldn't be working at the paper right now if it weren't for my good graces." The sheriff narrowed his eyes at Jared.

"Hard work can give a boy the money he needs for things. He doesn't have to steal." Mary Lou wanted to tear down Jared's case before the sheriff bought into it.

"What boy?" Sheriff Collins turned to her and she realized she'd said more than she meant.

"Any boy."

The sheriff raised his voice a notch. "Miss Ellison, you were speaking of a particular person. I know you were." People who were standing nearby stopped talking and turned toward them.

Jared put a protective arm around Mary Lou's shoulders. "Sheriff, if you'll allow me to suggest that we not interrupt the festivities, I'll be glad to drop by your office on my way back to the paper this afternoon."

Sheriff Collins hooked his thumbs in his belt. He looked around as people stared and nodded. In a quieter tone he agreed, "I think that's a good idea." Those around them turned their attention back to other things. The sheriff leaned in close to Mary Lou and Jared.

"Mind you don't forget or I'll be looking for you before dark." He walked toward the table of refreshments set up against the back wall of the restaurant.

Mary Lou thanked Jared. "I'm sorry he almost caused a scene." Jared dropped his arm from her shoulders and she missed the warmth of it.

"So am I."

"What will you tell him?"

Jared took a drink of his punch. "I wasn't going to tell him anything." His gaze followed the sheriff as he spoke to her. "It will surprise me if he doesn't figure out who you were talking about before I get to his office."

Mary Lou's heart sank. She played the conversation over in her mind. "I'm the one who gave him the clues." She sighed and hung her head. "You didn't tell him anything."

"Don't fret. If I'm right, the sheriff would eventually figure it out, anyway. If I'm wrong, the truth will come out in time."

"What have I done? You warned me about making assumptions. I assumed you would tell the sheriff, and in trying to protect Andrew, I gave him away."

Jared spoke to the sheriff and headed back to the office. Andrew was preparing the papers and ink for the printing and Mary Lou was at the desk. She looked up when he came in.

"How did it go with the sheriff?" She cut her eyes toward Andrew.

The sheriff had been called away to the saloon just after Jared arrived. They hadn't had time to talk about the thefts. Jared shook his head. "Nothing new for the paper tonight." He hoped she understood his meaning.

Her shoulders slumped in obvious relief. "Oh, good."

Andrew turned from the press. "What's happening with the sheriff?" He fumbled and dropped the stack of paper he held. Sheets floated across the room. He was retrieving them almost before they hit the floor.

Jared picked up the sheets that landed near his feet and handed them to Andrew. "Are you all right?"

"I'm fine. A little clumsy is all. Sorry."

Mary Lou retrieved the papers that had slid under the desk. "No harm done." She handed the pages to Andrew, who sorted them back into an orderly stack.

Was the boy nervous? He'd never been clumsy before today. The comment about the sheriff could have set him on edge. It was a consideration.

"As soon as I finish compositing this story, we'll be ready to print." Mary Lou brushed her hands together and took her notes to the composing table.

The three of them worked together until the next edition was hanging to dry and the press was clean. Andrew's awkwardness continued throughout the evening. He dropped freshly printed papers and got ink on his trousers. By the time they finished, he seemed eager to be gone.

"How did your talk with Mr. Barlow go, Andrew?" Mary Lou took off her sleeve garters and put them away.

Andrew slid his arms into his coat. "He said I can go see Paco Morales on Monday afternoon." A smile broke across his face. "If I get this job, I'll be set. No more sleeping in a loft. I'll have a bunk in a real bunkhouse."

"I hope you get the job. Though I will miss you here." Mary Lou patted Andrew on the shoulder as he went out the front door. "You're a hard worker. They'll be glad to have you on the Double Star."

She closed the door behind him. "He's excited."

"He sure was jittery." Jared rolled his sleeves down and reached for his coat.

"It's his first real job opportunity. Don't you remember how it was to be his age? He's ready to take on the world, but he's had so many obstacles to overcome. This is a way he can build a future without being at the mercy of the good graces of others."

Jared took a step toward the door. And her. "You seem to have done well for yourself. Are you hoping the same for Andrew?"

She clasped her hands together in front of her and lowered her gaze. "I know what it's like to be alone. I want Andrew to be settled. To have all the things in life he deserves."

"Do you think anyone ever gets all they deserve in life?" He looked down on her upturned face. The glow of the lantern lit her soft features.

Sadness crossed her eyes. "No. I'm not sure anyone does. And it's sad. We should, you know? We should be able to get the things we work hard for. We should all be able to have happiness and true joy."

"What is the source of your joy, Mary Lou?" He wanted to reach up and brush his knuckles across the line of her jaw, to take the sadness out of her expression.

"I find joy in the Lord."

He wasn't surprised. Her faith had showed itself

in her character in the weeks he'd known her. But he wanted to know more. She had layers of mystery yet was open at the same time. She made no pretense, but she was complicated. Jared asked, "And what makes you happy?"

She tilted her head to one side and thought before she answered. "I'd say it's the little things. A beautiful morning." She pointed at the papers that hung around the perimeter of the office. "The smell of the ink drying on a freshly printed edition. A smile on the face of a young man who's worked hard and may now be branching out into what could very well be his lifework."

Jared saw the hope for Andrew in her eyes. "I hope you aren't disappointed."

Chapter Nine

A gunshot woke Jared. Would he ever adjust to the sounds of living across the street from the saloon? He climbed out of bed to go look out the window, thinking he'd see a drunken cowboy hanging on to his horse as he rode into the night, firing his gun in the air. A scream drew his attention to the stairs. Another gunshot sounded. Both had come from the newspaper office. He grabbed his trousers and hopped on one leg as he pulled them on and made his way to the door.

"Mary Lou!" He stumbled in the darkness as he flew down the steps.

God help her! Don't let anyone harm her!

He caught his balance and burst into the office. Mary Lou stood trembling, her coat tied snug around her middle and a pistol in her hand. A lamp on the desk cast a circle of light on the floor and one of the biggest snakes he'd ever seen. Its tail writhed in the last throes of death.

"What in the world is going on here?" Jared didn't mean to shout but he couldn't believe his eyes.

"I came to get my notebook. I forgot it. This fellow—" she indicated the now-still snake with the barrel of her gun "—decided he'd come in from the cold and take up residence under my desk."

Jared leaned against the doorway and put a hand over his chest, rubbing the soft fabric of his union suit. "So you decided to shoot off a gun underneath my rooms without so much as calling up the stairs to warn me?"

"I didn't have a lot of notice myself."

"Why on earth did you have to scream? You scared several days off the end of my life. I know you did."

"I missed him with the first shot. He was coming my way fast."

"And you just happened to have a gun?"

"I carry a gun whenever I go out in the middle of the night. In case you haven't noticed, it's not always safe for a lady to be out on her own."

"Well, not counting the screaming part, I can see you're well able to protect yourself in an emergency." He pushed away from the jamb. "I'll get a broom and handle the cleanup here."

Mary Lou took a step back. "You might want to put a shirt on over your…" She pointed at his union suit. In his haste to get down the stairs he hadn't bothered with a shirt.

She picked up her notebook and headed for the back door. "And throw him in the alley, not out the front."

The door closed behind her.

How did she wake him from a dead sleep, scream like she was being murdered and then scold him for not being properly attired?

Exasperating. That's what she was.

Then he smiled. He didn't know another woman who wouldn't have screamed first and climbed onto the furniture to watch the poisonous snake slither off to hide. He went upstairs for a shirt and then got the broom. He was relieved he wouldn't be hunting a live snake in the morning.

It was a long time before he went back to sleep. He lay awake wondering what conversations between Mary Lou and Grump had been like. He rolled onto his side and punched his pillow into a better shape. He'd have to ask her to share some of her stories about Grump.

Mary Lou picked up her notebook and headed to the office on Monday morning. Approaching the back door, she noticed a place near the edge of the alley where the dirt had been disturbed. Jared had not only removed the snake, he'd buried it.

He kept surprising her. First when he came to town, then with his innate curiosity and knack for finding a story. His determination was impressive.

Mr. Ivy would have liked him. She knew Mr. Ivy loved him, but the man who buried a snake and dug for truth where she didn't even see a story was someone Mr. Ivy would respect and admire. She was glad to know Jared wouldn't have disappointed his grandfather.

The office was empty when she entered. Jared hadn't attended the church services the day before, nor had she seen him in the afternoon. It was unlike him not to be at the desk before she arrived.

Andrew knocked on the front door and she let him in.

He rubbed his hands together. "It's almost cold out there today."

"I'm sure it won't last. These cold snaps come for a day or so and leave. We won't get much real cold weather before Thanksgiving Day. Maybe even December." She started to take the papers down and stack them. "What time do you have to be at the Double Star Ranch?"

Andrew pulled the papers from the opposite side of the office. "I'll leave right after I get the papers delivered."

Mary Lou brought her papers and added them to his stack. "You'll have to let me know when they want you to start."

"They may not hire me. Mr. Barlow said Paco Morales is a good foreman, but he's picky about his hands, too."

She put a hand on his shoulder. "Andrew, you're a fine young man. There's not a reason in the world for them to hesitate."

"I hope you're right." He went to pull down another row of hanging papers.

"You come by this evening and let me know. If I've already left the office, come to my house." The front door opened and Jared entered. "I'm not sure I could rest for wondering if you don't."

Jared reached for the papers nearest the front of the office. "What could keep you from resting, Mary Lou? I wasn't aware you slept at night. I thought you were more of a prowler."

"Only when the need arises." She felt the heat spill into her cheeks as she remembered standing in this very room with him in the middle of the night. "Andrew was telling me he has to leave for his interview at the Double Star as soon as he finishes helping us."

"Why don't you go ahead now, Andrew? I can deliver to the places you usually go." Jared pulled his pocket watch from his vest pocket and checked the time. "It might make a better impression on the foreman if you go in the morning instead of the afternoon. A lot of work gets done on a ranch before lunch."

Andrew dropped the last of his papers onto the stack. "You mean it? I can go now?"

Mary Lou wanted to laugh at his childlike excitement, but she knew it could hurt Andrew's feelings. "That's a fine idea, Mr. Ivy."

Andrew was pulling his coat on and opening the front door in one motion. "Thank you, sir! Thank you, Miss Ellison!" They watched him jump from the porch to land on both feet in the dirt and launch into a full run in the direction of the livery.

"Mr. Ivy, you made that young man very happy. Thank you for offering to do his work today."

"Jared. You must remember to call me Jared." He put the last of the papers on the stack. "And don't thank me. I may not have done him any favors. They may send him back without a job. I don't know how he'll take it if they do."

Mary Lou pushed a pencil over her ear and tucked her notebook into her belt. "There's no reason for them to refuse him. He's a fine young man." She straightened the stack of papers. "I just reminded him of that." She stopped and asked, "Where were you?"

"When?" He didn't look at her but went to sit at the desk and make his usual morning list.

"Let's see. When?" She curled a hand at her chin and tapped her cheek with one finger. "Yesterday? Why weren't you in services at church? You have been there every Sunday since you arrived in Pine Haven."

He didn't look up or answer. The list grew longer under his steady hand. One day she would get a look at the notes he made in that journal.

"Well?" She stepped directly opposite him and put her palms on the desk. She leaned in and cast a shadow over his work.

He put the pen down. "Well what?" He stood, and she was forced to stand straight to look at him.

"Where were you Sunday?"

"Oh, I had to speak to someone about a story I'm working on." He put on his coat and slid the journal into the inside pocket.

"And this morning?"

He took a large stack of papers. "The same. It's like the saying about the early bird. Only, I was digging for worms. We can't wait on someone to bring them to us."

"What story?" Mary Lou picked up some papers and followed him out the door.

"The sheriff wanted to talk to me about the thefts. It seems he figured out who you were talking about and was trying to see if it was possible for Andrew to be the thief."

Mary Lou looked quickly around them. "Please don't say that where anyone could hear you. I don't want poor Andrew to be maligned in any way."

"I'm sorry, but the sheriff has already spoken to several people about it. More things have gone missing. Miscellaneous items small enough to be pocketed without notice. Seems Andrew was in the general store the day the things were taken from the Crofts. And we already knew he'd been at the hotel."

"But you were so kind to him just now. Do you honestly think he could have stolen those things?"

"I don't like to think that. But I'm determined to take an unbiased stand on this and all matters that may have to be written about in the paper. I can't afford to make up my mind one way or another until I have the facts."

Disappointment weighed her down. "If only I hadn't said anything. No one would be considering him."

"That's not true, Mary Lou. I was. And it wouldn't have taken the sheriff long to discover who had been seen when the things were stolen. It was bound to come out soon enough."

"But what about the things? He couldn't sell them. No one here would buy them. I know Andrew hasn't been seen at the saloon, either, so don't even suggest it." The harshness of her words was aimed at herself more than him. She hated that her conversation with the sheriff had led him to pursue investigating Andrew.

"You've no cause to be upset with me." He tugged on the brim of his hat in dismissal. "I'll be back this afternoon to help you pull the stories we won't reprint from the plates on the press."

He turned away from her and left. She'd have to let him know she wasn't upset with him. But, right now, she had to go see the sheriff. As soon as she dropped off the papers at the hotel and general store.

"Mr. Croft, I'm in a bit of a hurry today. Will you please divide the credit for these papers between Mr. Ivy and me? Just put them on our accounts." She placed the papers on the counter.

"Will do." He opened the store ledger.

"Mary Lou Ellison!" Liza Croft's voice rang out through the general store. Several ladies who were shopping turned to see what the commotion was about as the owner made her way through the barrels and displays to stand beside her husband.

"Good morning, Mrs. Croft." Mary Lou didn't know what was coming, but it didn't bode well for anyone in her way when Liza Croft got something in her craw.

"It is not!" She pointed to the ledger her husband was writing in. "Why we've lost more than anyone else in town to this petty thief. And I hold you personally responsible."

"Now, Liza." Mr. Croft raised a hand in caution.

"Don't you 'now Liza' me, Donald Croft. We've taken these newspapers—" she thumped the stack of freshly printed copies of the *Record* "—and spent our time and energy to sell them for the benefit of Miss Ellison, and she repays us by harboring a criminal in our midst."

A small gasp came from near the fabric tables. It seemed Mrs. Croft had decided Andrew was guilty without the benefit of evidence or a trial.

Mary Lou kept her voice low. "Mrs. Croft, there

is no proof that anyone associated with me has stolen anything."

"You've no need to whisper. Everyone will know to be on pins and needles around Andrew Nobleson if I have anything to do with it." Mrs. Croft sniffed the air as if that were the end of the subject.

"We all know you will." Mr. Croft finished his notations and put his pencil down. "You always do."

"Humph! You think what you will, Donald, but it's the good people of Pine Haven that I'm thinking of when I tell them to be on guard when that young man is around. No one will say I didn't warn them." The bell on the front door rang and she twirled in a flurry of skirts and poor temper. She marched from behind the counter to help the arriving customer.

Mary Lou left the store and dropped onto a bench on the front walk.

How did her one slip to the sheriff have the town buzzing with ugly rumors about Andrew? All she'd ever done was try to help him. The same way Mr. Ivy had helped her.

If Jared hadn't put the thoughts out into the air, this never would have happened. It was a good thing Andrew was getting a job on the Double Star. It would keep him away from the gossip until the rumors died down.

She jerked her head up. "Or until the real thief is caught." The pencil she kept tucked over one ear flew across the paper of her notebook. She would solve the crime and clear Andrew's name. She tapped her lip with the end of the pencil, trying to think of any other suspect or victim that wasn't on her growing list.

"Trying to come up with a story for the next edition so soon?" Jared stood on the street in front of her.

"What?" She closed the notebook and tucked it back into her belt. She wasn't prepared to share her growing list of suspects with him until she had time to carefully consider each one. She didn't want to cast suspicions on an innocent person by speaking too quickly. "Never you mind. What happened in there is all your fault." The fact that Mrs. Croft had accused her of harboring a thief could destroy her. Not only could she lose the paper, she could lose her good name in Pine Haven.

He leaned back. "What is my fault?"

The door of the general store opened and two of the ladies who'd overheard Mrs. Croft's accusations came out. They looked from Mary Lou to Jared and turned to go in the opposite direction.

Jared took the two steps onto the porch in one motion. "Ladies, would you have a moment to answer a question or two?"

The younger of the two ladies sent a coy look to the older one and put a hand out to stop her. She gave Jared a slight nod.

"Do either of you know why Miss Ellison is accusing me of causing something that went on in the general store just now?"

His smile and familiar manner irritated Mary Lou. The ease with which he captured the attention of anyone who would listen, all the while deflecting any scrutiny from himself, was maddening. In less than two minutes the ladies had assured him that he could in no way have had a part in anything that Mrs. Croft was saying about Mary Lou.

He tipped his hat to them. "Thank you for your time. You ladies have a nice day." The women walked away with their heads close together, sharing words that Mary Lou had no doubt would spread everywhere they shopped.

"May I?" He indicated the empty place beside her and sat when she didn't respond. "There seems to be a misunderstanding."

She still didn't speak. He had branded Andrew as guilty from the moment Jasmine's cameo went missing. She wouldn't waste her time trying to convince him.

"You may be able to charm a silly girl who is enjoying your attention, Mr. Ivy, but your charm has no effect on me." She stood and brushed her skirt smooth. "If you'll excuse me, I have business for the paper."

Jared followed Mary Lou to the office. "I'll take the papers to the train depot. You can do whatever it is you're doing. I need to speak to the station master, anyway."

"Whose reputation will you be out to destroy today? Someone new, or will you just be finishing the job of ruining mine? Is this all part of your plan to get the paper when the judge comes to town? Turn all of Pine Haven against me, so you can insist that the paper will collapse if you don't gain control?"

"I don't know what you're talking about. What happened in the last hour?"

"What happened is that you've sullied the name of a fine young man, and in the process you've sullied mine."

"You're going to have to explain."

Andrew slung the front door wide and stomped into the office. He stopped in front of Jared and pointed up at him. "You and your gossip cost me the best job I could have hoped to have in Pine Haven. I know you've been talking to the sheriff. Then all of the sudden he's asking people all over town if I was near their place when things got stolen. I don't know what gave you the idea that I'm a thief. But I'll be happy to meet you in the street and settle this like men."

Jared held up both hands. "Whoa, boy."

Andrew took a step closer. "I ain't a boy."

Mary Lou came from behind the desk. "What's wrong, Andrew? This isn't like you."

"On account o' him—" Andrew punched the air with his finger and didn't look away from Jared. Anger and pain filled his young face. "Señor Morales said he's gonna have to wait about offering me a job. Said the sheriff needs to finish investigating the thefts in town before they could bring me on as a hand. Said the rest of the men need to know they can trust the people who work with them."

The thunderclouds in Mary Lou's eyes darkened. "Oh, no! This has gone too far."

Jared could see the tide turning against him. The two of them had been skeptical of his motives since he'd first come to town. His goal had never been to destroy anything or anyone.

He took a step back. "First, I think we should all calm down." The tension in Andrew didn't lessen, but he lowered both hands to his sides and clenched his fists. "Violence is not the answer."

Mary Lou spoke to Andrew. "He's right about that. The answer is to find out who did steal those things and clear your good name."

She spun to face Jared. This time it was her finger pointed at him. "And you are going to help us do it."

He shook his head. "I never set out to prove Andrew was guilty—only to find the truth."

"Well, if that's the case, you haven't been successful."

"All I can do is search for the truth. What would the two of you do if I wasn't here?" He spread his arms wide. "The thefts would still have taken place. You'd still have a paper to publish. What would you do?"

"We wouldn't be accusin' one another of stealing the things." Andrew's anger still boiled at the surface.

"No, we wouldn't." Mary Lou twisted her mouth into a tight pucker. If she wasn't so angry with him, Jared would consider it adorable. "We might, however, ask you where you were when the things were stolen. It occurs to me that we had no theft in Pine Haven until you arrived."

"What? Are you honestly accusing me?"

Andrew nodded. "That's right. How does it feel to be the one people are looking at?"

"But I didn't take anything. And no one has a reason to suspect I did."

"You was at the hotel the same day as me. The day the cameo and dish were stolen!" Andrew seemed to latch on to this possible theory of Mary Lou's.

"Mary Lou, you know I didn't steal anything." He couldn't believe they'd turned on him like this.

Mary Lou raised her eyebrows. "How would I know that, Mr. Ivy? You've only given me your word. I have no basis for knowing the value of that word."

"You've worked with me all these weeks. I've given you no cause to question my integrity."

She turned to Andrew and chuckled. "I think we're getting somewhere now."

Jared was incredulous. "What?"

Andrew didn't seem to understand her, either. "What do you mean?"

She brushed her hands together and went to sit behind the desk. "Mr. Ivy, you have just used the very arguments I presented to you about young Andrew." To her assistant she said, "Now Mr. Ivy understands how you felt when you were falsely accused."

"You mean, you didn't actually think I stole the things, but you were making a point?"

"I sometimes have to remind myself to be objective. Your grandfather taught me to look at every situation without bias." She picked up a pencil and opened her notebook. "I'll admit it's something I struggle to remember."

Jared protested. "It's one thing to be unbiased and another thing to discount the facts you have. You know me."

She shook her head. "Not for as long as I've known Andrew."

"I see." Jared dropped into a chair near the front door.

"I don't." Andrew leaned against the press. "And I'm the one who doesn't have a job now."

"You still have a job here." Mary Lou asked Jared, "What do you think your grandfather would have done in this situation?"

He sat on the edge of the chair. "You tell me. You knew him a lot better than I did." The sadness of the statement jarred his chest. He was trying to carry on the legacy of a man he barely remembered. She was carrying it on with full knowledge of Grump's likes and dislikes, his habits and opinions.

Andrew said, "He wouldn't think I did it. I've been working here too long. He trusted me."

Jared met Mary Lou's confirming stare. "You're right, Andrew. I shouldn't have suspected you. I should have considered the respect you had from Grump and Mary Lou. Please forgive me."

"I can forgive you—" Andrew slapped the side of his leg "—but that don't get me a job on the Double Star."

Mary Lou leaned back in her chair. "I'd say we're making real progress in this investigation today. What if we all share what we know about the thefts and see if we can figure out who the guilty party is? Then Andrew can get his job and Mrs. Croft and the sheriff will focus on someone other than the two of us."

They spent the next few minutes talking about what they knew. Mary Lou gave her opinions about who it wasn't, but she never gave a guess at who it could be. Was she hiding something? Some clue?

She closed her notebook and stood. "I'm glad we've cleared the air among the three of us. We're all going to have to keep an eye out for anything, or anyone, suspicious. At the same time remember, the townsfolk are thinking they know who did it. Andrew, don't do anything or go anywhere that might lend weight to their arguments.

"Jared, you said you would speak to the station master. Ask if he's seen anyone who might have been to Pine Haven on more than one occasion. Perhaps there's someone who came to town before the first theft and left after the others."

"What can I do?" Andrew had calmed down and shared his thoughts about the thefts. Like Mary Lou, he had ideas about who was innocent but no clue about who could have committed the crimes.

"Bring the newspapers and come with me to the train depot. You can make the other deliveries like any Monday morning. I've already been to the saloon. I don't want you to go there."

Mary Lou stopped. "You took papers to the saloon?"

"I did."

"We don't sell our papers in the saloon."

"We do now. Mr. Ledford was most helpful." Jared put on his coat. "If a bit surprised."

"You didn't discuss this with me." The tension of their earlier conversations returned to her voice.

"We are in the business of selling newspapers. The fact that many of the men who go to the saloon want a paper made it a good business decision. I thought you'd want more sales."

"I want to keep the reputation of the paper immaculate. Seeing it in the saloon could damage that."

"The paper is for everyone in the community. Not

just the churchgoers. The same people who frequent the saloon shop in the general store."

"And that's where they can buy their paper."

"Must we argue about this now? We've just come to agreement again about finding the thief. Let's not get distracted from that." He put on his hat and opened the door.

"This isn't the end of our discussion."

"A fact of which I have no doubt." He closed the door and walked with Andrew toward the train depot.

"You should ask her stuff like that." Andrew didn't look at him.

"Why do you say that? The paper is mine. I have as much, or more, right to make decisions as she does."

"It ain't the same." Andrew shook his head. "She's worked hard. If you're gonna change things, you oughta at least talk to her first. She ain't hard to get along with."

"That's not true of my experience with Miss Ellison."

"Hadn't seen her argue with no one but you. Seems like that makes you the problem."

They walked in silence to the depot. Was Andrew right? Mary Lou did have a good rapport with just about everyone else.

Lord, if Doc Willis was right about needing to ask You for things, I'm asking for You to help us sort this out. It's not fair for Andrew to be falsely accused while a thief goes free. And I'd like to keep Mary Lou's reputation secure.

Grump had invested so much in her. For Jared to destroy it because he didn't think through his first attempt at uncovering a good story for the *Record* would be wrong.

He wanted ownership of the paper, but he didn't want to cause her pain. Somehow she'd burrowed her way into his conscience. What happened to her mattered to him.

In a few weeks everything he'd thought he wanted out of life had changed.

And Mary Lou had played a large—and unexpected—role in the changes.

Chapter Ten

Mary Lou interviewed the sheriff and Mr. Warren again. Neither man gave a hint of anything that she or Jared hadn't already discussed. By the time she finished writing up her notes in the hotel lobby, it was well past the noon hour. Lunch in the hotel might warm her insides and cheer her mood.

"Here you go." Naomi put a bowl of vegetable soup on the table in front of Mary Lou.

"Thank you." Mary Lou put her napkin in her lap. "Would you care to join me? It looks like the lunch rush is over."

"Don't mind if I do. I'll be right back." The cook made her way through the empty restaurant and the swinging door that led to the kitchen. She reappeared in moments.

"I thought I'd get us some corn bread, too." She set a plate of the golden-brown bread in the center of the table and took a seat.

Mary Lou offered a prayer of thanks and then dipped her spoon into the thick soup. "This is always delicious."

"It's one of my favorites. Any time you see it on the menu, you can know one of two things has happened. Either I've had a chill to the bone or I'm thinking about my Elijah. It was one of his favorites, too." Naomi often spoke of her deceased husband. "Today was his birthday."

"I'm glad to share your meal on such an important day." Mary Lou, like most everyone in Pine Haven, respected Naomi Grant. Her good food and sound wisdom had brought comfort to many people on more than one occasion. Sharing a meal with Naomi was like dinner with a wise grandmother or aunt.

"How are things going with you and the young Mr. Ivy?" Naomi took a piece of the corn bread and crumbled it into her soup.

"Not very well, I'm afraid."

"Would you like to share? Sometimes saying things out loud takes the tension out of them."

Mary Lou took a sip of her coffee. The fact that she'd forgotten to put sugar in it reminded her of how distracted she was today. "He's gone about the newspaper business with an approach that is opposite anything his grandfather did."

"Opposite?"

"That might not be fair." She added sugar to her cup and stirred the coffee until it dissolved. "He accused me of being biased because I didn't suspect someone I knew of theft."

"Ah… Andrew."

Her heart sank. "If you've already heard of this, too, then it's more widespread than I thought."

"People do love to talk."

"Especially Mrs. Croft." Mary Lou still rankled from her attack this morning.

"She probably found it easy to talk to Mr. Ivy. Just like most of the men in town."

"What are you saying?"

"Don't tell me you haven't noticed. If the two of you are talking about a story for the paper, folks just tend to answer him more than you."

"I didn't know anyone else noticed."

"Might be because he seems to ask in such a way that the person wants to give him the answer. More like he's charming it out of them than interrogating them."

"A woman should have just as much respect as a man."

"She should. But you and I both know it isn't often true. A man would rather tell a man a thing, and a woman will tell almost anyone."

"I just wish he hadn't started people to thinking of Andrew as a possible thief."

"Do you think Jacob Ivy would have suspected Andrew?"

"I don't. He would have eliminated him because he trusted Andrew."

"So the real issue for you is the trust." Naomi dipped her spoon into the bowl again.

"You have to trust your instincts in this business." She couldn't remember how many times Mr. Ivy had told her that. *Follow your instincts. Train yourself to look for clues. Be observant. And follow the trail of clues to the truth.*

"I thought the newspaper business was all about asking questions. It seems young Mr. Ivy was seeking answers without the advantages you had. You already knew Andrew. He didn't."

Mary Lou put her spoon down with a sigh. "I was unfair."

"That's not like you. Do you feel threatened by Mr. Ivy?"

"I could lose everything. The judge could come at any time. If he decides to honor the old will, the *Pine Haven Record* will no longer be mine."

"So are you worried about Andrew or are you worried about losing the paper?"

"Both."

"Would you say being worried about losing the paper intensified your anger about Andrew?"

Mary Lou looked up from her soup. "Naomi Grant, you have a way of digging out the core of a problem. I could have helped Jared see the truth about Andrew if I hadn't been so determined to best him at every turn."

"While we're searching for the truth, have you thought that Mr. Ivy may be just the kind of man God would send your way? Sometimes we put up a powerful defense against something we didn't expect, when it may be just what God has in mind for us."

Mary Lou choked and sputtered on her coffee. "Mrs. Naomi!"

"This soup sure is good." Naomi's dark eyes twinkled. The smooth, brown skin of her face and the beauty of her spirit defied her years. The joy that resonated from her was a reminder that God could do anything. She winked at Mary Lou.

"It sure is." Mary Lou spent another hour with the wise cook. By the time she left, she knew that Jared Ivy wasn't just a man after her paper. He was a man she could lose her heart to if she wasn't careful.

Friday morning dawned and they were no closer to solving the mystery of the stolen items than they had been on Monday when they'd shared their ideas.

Well, most of their ideas.

Mr. Robbins had told the sheriff on Wednesday that one of his finest crops was missing from the livery, and then Mr. Ledford had reported some cigars stolen from the saloon. Both places had insisted that Andrew had been seen nearby before the items went missing. The poor youth couldn't go anywhere in town without being suspect.

Mary Lou decided she'd been right to withhold a few of her ideas from her conversation with Jared outside the general store on Monday. She had followed up on several of her possible suspects to no avail, but she wouldn't give up hope.

Jared was at the desk when she went to the office. It was a good opportunity to speak to him without Andrew present.

"Good morning."

A grunt was his only reply.

"What are you working on?"

He kept writing. "Just making some notes."

"I think I owe you an apology."

The pencil dropped to the desk and he closed his notebook. He leaned back in the chair and took a deep breath. "I'm ready."

"You don't have to make such a big deal of it."

"It's more that I'm savoring the moment." He put his elbows on the arms of the chair and waited.

"I was unfair to be upset with you about Andrew."

"I see."

"And I think if I'd have told you more about him, you might have seen him like I do." She drew an imaginary circle on the top of the desk with her fingertip. "Like your grandfather did."

"Hmm." He stared at her. Not an accusing stare. Not a forgiving one, either. "Then I think it only fair for me to apologize to you, too. If I'd asked for your insight, I might have spared the poor boy a lot of grief."

"If he hears you calling him a boy again, I'm not going to stand up for you. You'll be on your own."

They both laughed.

"Well, I just wanted you to know that I'm sorry." She tucked a pencil over her ear.

He stood and joined her in front of the desk. "Where are you off to today?"

"I want to follow the steps of the thief, map it out in my mind. Someone had to see something. No one could be so unobtrusive as to never be seen."

"May I join you?" He took her coat from the coat tree and held it for her.

Having him along could be distracting. She couldn't

recall a single instance since he'd come to town where she'd done her best work with him present.

Naomi's words came back to her. Her defensiveness against Jared's presence could be the reason for that. If only she could convince herself that he wasn't indeed a threat to her. For the paper—or as a man God may, or may not, have sent to her.

"Why not? Neither of us has succeeded alone. Perhaps together we can arrive at the truth."

Jared held the door open for Mary Lou to enter the train depot that afternoon. All morning they'd retraced the thefts. No new information surfaced. No one seemed to be looking for anyone except Andrew.

They approached the ticket window side by side. Chester Meadows looked up through the metal grate that separated his office from the lobby area.

"What can I do for you folks today?"

Mary Lou offered Mr. Meadows one of her friendliest smiles. "Good afternoon. How is Mrs. Meadows these days? I don't think I've seen her for at least two weeks."

"She's quite well, thank you."

Jared got straight to the point. "Have you remembered anything you didn't tell us before that might help find the thief?"

Mary Lou shot a frown his way. The speed with which her expression changed was comical. She whispered at him, "I was getting to that."

He spoke low to her. "Yes, but I'm already there."

To Mr. Meadows he said, "Were you able to think of something else?"

"Nope. Sorry I can't help. Even asked the missus. It's a mad rush in here when the trains are coming and going. The in-between times, there's only people from town buying a ticket or a straggler who missed his train—"

Mary Lou interrupted. "What about while the train is in the station? The people who get off to walk around. Did you notice anyone in particular?"

"No, Miss Ellison. The only people I recognize are the ones who come all the time. I know the conductors, the engineers, the newsagent and such. You see the same people I do. They might go to the hotel for a meal or to the saloon for a drink, but most of the time they aren't here long enough to leave the station for more than a few minutes."

Jared listened to every word. There must be a clue in something they'd heard today. "Have any of the regular train workers said or done anything that stuck in your craw?"

Mr. Meadows scratched behind one ear and thought. "Not as I can think of."

The door opened and two men entered the depot.

"If you folks don't mind, I need to see to the paying customers." Mr. Meadows gave a friendly wave of dismissal.

Jared and Mary Lou were almost at the door when he called them back. "I just thought of something. If you can wait a minute, while I take care of these tickets, I'll be glad to tell you all about it. Not sure it will help, though."

Mary Lou sat on a bench by the door. She pulled out her notebook and made several notes. The pencil she wore over her ear was tucked back in place when the two men left and Mr. Meadows signaled for their attention.

"The engineer came in a couple of weeks ago. He was asking for a copy of the paper. I got it for him, but asked why he didn't just buy one of the ones the newsagent sells. He gave a snort and said he didn't like the fellow. Said he was new to the line but carried himself like he owned the whole company."

"Thank you so much, Mr. Meadows." Mary Lou's face lit up a bit too brightly at his words.

"I don't know if that matters, but it's the only thing I know that was out of the ordinary."

Jared tapped his hand on the ticket shelf. "Thank you, just the same."

When they stepped outside, the whistle for the afternoon train sounded in the distance and Mary Lou put a hand on his arm.

"If we hang around the depot while the train is here, we may notice something untoward for ourselves."

"I'm not sure there's anything to notice."

"If it hadn't been odd to him, Mr. Meadows wouldn't have called us back to tell us about it."

He didn't think there was much point, but they'd tried everything they could think of in town. "I'll stay for a few minutes, but I don't know if it will matter. I'm of a mind to agree with Mr. Meadows. A highfalutin' attitude doesn't make a man a thief."

She spun on him. "Neither does a fancy horse and saddle."

"All right. You win. I'll stay with you. We'll see if we can catch the thief among us." He dipped his head near her ear. The sweet floral scent she favored filled his senses. "I meant it when I said I was sorry for misjudging Andrew. I really do want to help find the thief."

The train chugged into the station and squealed to a stop. In no time at all, passengers streamed from the cars.

The conductor paced on the platform and called out in a loud voice, "Departing at four o'clock sharp. Departing at four o'clock sharp."

Mary Lou opened her pendant watch. "It's only three now. We have a full hour." She looked first one way and then another. "Do you think our presence would cause a thief to change his pattern?"

He pivoted and leaned in close again. "How do you know we are looking for a man?" Mary Lou would have backed away from him but he held her elbow. "Don't move away. Look over my left shoulder."

Her eyes grew wide. "What do you think is happening?"

"I'm not certain, but it seems as though the sheriff is questioning the personnel from the train."

"Why does that mean you have to stay so close to me?"

"If the workers think we are on the same mission as the sheriff, they'll never talk to us." He nodded in the direction of the conductor. "But if they think we're a young couple asking questions about the best place to go on a trip together, they may cooperate."

She stiffened. "But we aren't a young couple. That would be lying. I will not use a lie to learn the truth."

"I didn't say we were going to lie."

He guided her toward the conductor. "Excuse me, sir."

The man stopped on the platform. He was of average height and weight, probably going on for forty years old. Nothing noticeable in his demeanor that Jared could see.

"Yes. How may I help you?"

"We..." Jared paused and chose his words carefully. "That is, I was wondering where might be a nice place for a young man to take his sweetheart—if he had one—on a trip. I reckon you've seen almost everything there is to see for miles in every direction. Seems to me like you'd be the man to ask."

Mary Lou might not realize it but her blush only lent a note of sincerity to his request. In truth, the conductor would know the answers to the question Jared asked. All Jared needed now was a sweetheart. A smile pulled at one corner of his mouth. He decided it would add to the effect so he gave Mary Lou a full smile complete with dimples. She might be angry later, but not if he found out who the real thief was.

"Well, son, you two might enjoy a trip to Dallas if you've never been far from Pine Haven."

"I'm from Maryland, and I would like to see some of the sights farther west." He cut his eyes at Mary Lou. Her stare seemed to warn him again to be honest. He looked back at the conductor. "But I haven't been able to secure a sweetheart for myself since I moved here. We're from the *Pine Haven Record*. We're working on an idea for a story for the paper." He wouldn't lie. Not just because Mary Lou didn't want him to. He wasn't a liar. Not for any reason. She was right. He could find the truth with the truth.

"Then I'd say a trip to San Antonio might be just the thing. There's good food, and the land is pretty between here and there. Some folks just enjoy the train ride."

"That does sound like a good suggestion. Can you tell me, though, what kinds of things are available on the trip? Would a couple have to get off the train to eat or shop? Just in case they wanted to get a memento of their trip. Nothing fancy, mind you. Money can be a real issue."

"It depends on the trip. Most of the trains stop in places where you can get a meal. But if you're watching your coins, you could bring a basket of food with you. Or buy something from the newsagent. Some of them only carry candy and cigars, but the one on our route has a small business going."

"Really? What kind of things does he sell?"

"Sandwiches, sweets, sometimes baked goods. He's even started selling an assortment of souvenirs. Little things. Trinkets mostly. But he offers a good price for them. He even has a little piece of jewelry from time to time. To be honest, it's more than I've come to expect from a newsagent."

Jared nodded his head and offered his thanks. "You've been a great help to us, sir. Thank you for your time."

He moved his hand to Mary Lou's back and guided

her toward the street. She stood a bit straighter and he dropped his hand as soon as they were out of sight of the conductor.

Mary Lou became animated. "We've got to tell Sheriff Collins." She turned to walk toward the sheriff but he put out a hand to stop her.

Jared was relieved to have a possible suspect for the crimes, but he knew jumping to conclusions about the newsagent would be no different than falsely accusing Andrew.

"Tell him what? That someone on the train sells things? We can't go to him without more than that. He won't believe us in the future if we take him every possible thought without evidence."

Her shoulders slumped. "You're right. I just want it to be over. For Andrew and for us."

"I know. We just have to be patient and discern a way to find out if it is Elmer Finch."

Mary Lou watched Jared go into the bank before she went to the general store. He might be willing to be patient, but she wasn't.

She stepped inside the dim interior and noticed several passengers from the train milling around. She made her way to the back of the store, picking up first one item then another as she went. When she got to the back counter she saw Andrew on the opposite end. He was looking at a small mirror with a decorative pink handle.

"Hello, Andrew." She waved at him and he acknowledged her with a nod.

"May I help you, Miss Ellison?" Liza Croft came to

stand at the counter midway between her and Andrew. She spoke to Mary Lou but kept her eyes trained on Andrew. He turned his back to them and eventually left without purchasing anything.

"No, thank you. I just want to look around for a few minutes."

A short time later she stepped out onto the sidewalk again. Perusing the streets for anything suspicious, she spotted Mr. Finch in the distance. Had he been inside the general store? She hadn't seen him but there had been several people inside.

As Mr. Finch turned in the direction of the hotel, she saw Jared move off the sidewalk and fall into step behind the newsagent.

Did Jared leave her and go into the bank so he could follow the agent alone?

She couldn't be upset. That had been her plan, as well.

Mary Lou trailed along at a distance, hoping not to be noticed by either man. Even in the Friday-afternoon crowd of townsfolk and passengers from the train, she could follow Jared easily. Not because he was taller than those around him, but because she'd grown accustomed to keeping an eye out for him.

He had an annoying habit of showing up everywhere she went. She would be interviewing someone for a story and he would come up behind her with a question that stole the attention of the person she was talking to—and ultimately the story.

But it was more than that. She watched the top of his head as he bobbed in and out of sight. She'd memorized the shape of his head and the untamed texture of his hair. His gait was more familiar to her than any she'd ever known.

Without her knowledge or permission, Jared Ivy had become the object of her attention.

And at this very moment he was following Elmer Finch into the hotel lobby.

Chapter Eleven

"Mary Lou, how nice to see you." Jasmine Willis greeted her when she entered the lobby.

"Hello." Mary Lou scanned the room for Mr. Finch and Jared, seeing only Jared seated on a sofa near the front window. "Did you have a lovely honeymoon?" It was unusual to see Jasmine in a dress when she wasn't at church.

"Yes, we've only just arrived on the afternoon train. I wanted to come say hello to Papa and Momma Beverly before we go home."

Mary Lou tried not to be jealous of the glow of Jasmine's joy. Would she ever know the fulfillment of a happy marriage?

Jared spoke from behind her. "Mrs. Willis, it's nice to see you back in Pine Haven."

"It's good to be home, Mr. Ivy." Doc Willis came through the front door and Jasmine excused herself.

"Why are you here, Mary Lou?" A sparkle of teasing lit Jared's eyes.

"I might ask you the same thing, Mr. Ivy." She didn't look away. Couldn't look away. The side of his jaw twitched with a suppressed smile.

"I wonder if perhaps you followed me here." He darted his eyes in the direction of the restaurant.

"I'm sure I don't know why you'd think that." She looked over her shoulder and could see Mr. Finch seated in the restaurant.

"If you're going to require complete honesty from me, I must insist on the same from you. I saw you trailing after me as I followed Mr. Finch."

Rather than admit guilt, she asked, "Since we're both here, would you care to join me for a piece of pie?"

With a hand on her elbow, he escorted her into the dining room. She resisted the urge to look up at him. Knowing he wore a grin was enough. She didn't have to see it. Working *with* Jared was more pleasant than competing with him. If only they could come to some sort of agreement.

Naomi brought apple pie and coffee for both of them and returned to the kitchen.

Jared took a bite. "She is a wonderful cook."

"She is, but many of the desserts are made by Mrs. Warren." She stirred the sugar into her coffee and cast a glance at Mr. Finch. "What have you observed?"

"Nothing. He went into the general store just before I entered the bank. He was walking up the sidewalk when I returned to the crossroads in the center of town, so I followed him here."

Naomi stopped by their table. "Is everything good here? That pie is scrumptious."

Jared agreed with her and added in a casual tone, "Does the newsagent eat here often?"

Naomi looked over her shoulder at Mr. Finch. "He comes in most days when he's in town. He fancies my biscuits."

Mary Lou smiled. "Everyone fancies your cooking."

Naomi thanked her and left them to their pie.

"When I saw the two of you in the street, I had been in the general store. There were so many passengers from the train shopping that I didn't see him." She hated to add the next part. "Andrew was there, too. Mrs. Croft was watching him like a hawk."

Jared kept Mr. Finch in sight while they talked. "I'm sorry for that. He's probably being treated like that everywhere he goes."

Mary Lou looked through the restaurant doors into the lobby and saw Andrew again. "Now he's here."

"Wouldn't that be common when the train arrives? He helps with the passengers' luggage."

"Yes, I guess so. I just hate that he's been everywhere we've seen Mr. Finch. If we are going to show that the newsagent is a possible suspect, it won't help if Andrew is there at every turn."

They finished their pie as the train whistle blew a warning for the upcoming departure. Mr. Finch paid his bill and made his way out of the restaurant. Mary Lou and Jared waited a couple of minutes before they followed at a modest distance. Andrew was carrying a valise up the stairs when they went through the hotel lobby.

Jared strolled beside her toward the depot. "If we

discover that anything was stolen today, we'll be able to suggest that the sheriff investigate the railroad personnel."

"Mr. Finch in particular?" She'd give almost anything to have the suspicion off her trusted assistant.

"I haven't seen anything that would make that reasonable. I don't want to make the same mistake about him that I made about Andrew."

They watched from the shadows as the passengers filed onto the train and it left minutes later. Nothing they saw stood out as questionable.

"The entire day feels wasted." She wondered out loud, "I don't know what will go on the top of the paper when we print it tomorrow."

"Something will come up. It always does."

"That thought almost scares me while we're trying to solve this crime."

"Don't worry. We'll figure it out." He gave her a reassuring look but she knew he was just as stumped as she was. "I'll stop by the sheriff's office again and ask if he has any news. About this or anything else we could use for a good story."

"Then I'll go back to the paper and finish compositing the next installation of the Christmas Eve stories. Maybe I can add a bit more detail and it will take up more of the page. This is the piece about the children's involvement. Parents will love to buy the paper just to see their child's name in print."

When they would have gone in different directions at the center of town, Mary Lou heard Andrew call her name. She turned as the sheriff led Andrew, holding one arm pushed behind his back, into the jailhouse.

"Oh, no!" She hurried down the street with Jared right behind her.

"Wait, Mary Lou." His voice faded in the background as she wondered why Sheriff Collins had taken Andrew into custody.

She burst into the sheriff's office. "What is going on here?"

Andrew was seated on a bunk against the back wall of a cell. He wore a brave face but she could see the terror in his eyes.

"There's been another theft, Miss Ellison. If you'd like to write a story for the paper, you'll have to give me time to talk to the prisoner first."

Jared came in behind her. "Why is he in a cell?"

The sheriff pulled a small mirror from his pocket and put it on his desk. "Found this in his pocket after Mrs. Croft sent for me. She said he'd been looking at it earlier this afternoon and it was missing after he left."

Mary Lou lost her breath. It was the mirror she'd seen Andrew holding in the general store. "Oh, Andrew." The words were more moan than diction. "How did this happen?"

"I didn't do it, Miss Ellison." Andrew looked at Jared. "You've got to believe me!"

Jared wanted to believe him. In his heart he almost did. With no evidence until this moment on anyone, it was difficult to dismiss the mirror.

Mary Lou walked closer and stood in front of the cell bars. "Andrew tell us what—"

Sheriff Collins interrupted. "You're all going to have to let me talk to the boy first. As far as I'm concerned, you're journalists, and I've got a string of crimes to solve."

"Sheriff, I am the closest thing to family Andrew has. I won't be pushed aside while he's sitting in…" She sniffed and pointed at the cell. "In there."

Jared understood her concern. "Is that absolutely necessary? It's not like Andrew is going to run off. Can't he sit out here like a man and talk to you at your desk?"

"It's customary to keep prisoners in a cell." The sheriff's voice wasn't as gruff as it had been when he'd put Mr. Finch in the same cell the first day Jared had come to town. His personal knowledge of Andrew was the likely reason.

Mary Lou took advantage of the silence. "But this isn't a normal circumstance, Sheriff. If Andrew was going to run away, he'd have left when…" She cleared her throat. "When people started accusing him of being a thief. With a horse like his, he could have been anywhere by now."

Jared closed his eyes. If only she'd stopped and not mentioned that horse.

"That horse is one of the things that's got folks wonderin'." The sheriff sat behind his desk and leaned back in the chair. His dirty boots clunked onto the desktop and his hands crossed behind his head. "You two can stay—as long as you don't interfere with my questions."

"Thank you." Jared pulled a chair from against the wall for Mary Lou to sit close to the cell. He stood near Mary Lou, but turned to have a good vantage point of everyone in the office.

"How did you come to have this mirror in your pocket, boy?"

Mary Lou jerked around. "His name is Andrew." She looked at Andrew. "And he's not a boy."

Jared watched Andrew draw strength from her support, but he also saw the sheriff bristle.

"I won't warn you again, Miss Ellison. You're here as a courtesy."

She didn't answer, only nodded.

"Now tell me how you got that mirror."

"I don't know, Sheriff Collins. I was in the general store about an hour ago." He shot Mary Lou a look that begged for her help. "But I didn't steal anything."

"Mrs. Croft said she saw you looking at it. Saw it in your hands."

Mary Lou leaned forward. "Tell the whole truth, Andrew. It's always best."

Andrew hung his head. "I did hold it." He bolted from the bunk and came to stand at the bars. "But I didn't steal it!"

The sheriff lowered his hands to the arms of his chair. "How do you explain me finding it in your pocket?"

"I can't." Andrew walked to stand in front of Mary Lou. "You have to believe me. You know me."

"I do believe you, Andrew." Her voice was calm and sweet, like a mother soothing a restless child. She put her hand over his where it wrapped around the iron bar.

"We're going to find out what happened. I promise you I won't rest until we do."

Jared wanted all the facts so he could help Mary Lou. He knew her well enough to know she wouldn't stop searching until she had the answers. "Sheriff, you said Mrs. Croft sent for you?"

"Yes. Had the dressmaker's son who lives across the street come for me. Reilly Ledford. He's just a boy, but old enough to run an errand."

"Did Reilly say if he saw anything?" Mary Lou was following Jared's thinking now. That would be good for the investigation, but it was unsettling, too. Their association was supposed to be short-lived. How would it feel to work on important stories after she moved on and the *Record* was his? He forced himself to concentrate on the conversation at hand. If he let her distract him now, they could miss an important clue.

"I didn't ask the boy. He's a kid." The sheriff's annoyance was growing.

"But kids see things others don't. Their perspective is different." Jared moved to the cell. "Andrew, which pocket was the mirror in?"

Andrew pointed to the front pocket of his jacket. It was low and sewn at an angle, perfect for slipping your hands in when the weather necessitated it.

Jared turned to the sheriff. "So we're all agreed that pocket is where you found the mirror?"

Sheriff Collins stood. "I don't know what you're gettin' at, Ivy. Yes, that's where I found it."

"I'm not sure. I want to talk to this boy Reilly." Jared

pointed at Andrew. "Don't you worry. We'll take care of this."

Mary Lou stood to follow him as he headed for the door. "Sheriff, will you please let Andrew come with us? I promise to keep a close eye on him."

The heavy mustache moved to one side as he shook his head no. "'Fraid I can't let him out. There's been too much of a fuss about town these last couple of weeks."

Andrew called out as they went through the doorway. "What about Midnight?"

Jared answered him. "I'll take care of your horse and speak to Mr. Robbins and Mr. Warren about your jobs. Your job at the paper will be there when you get out."

The sheriff returned to his chair and Jared closed the door. "He doesn't seem to think there's anything for us to learn from young Reilly."

"No. I dare say he thinks we're on a fool's errand. How often does he get the evidence and the suspect so neatly handed to him?"

"That's the thing that doesn't sit right with me." Jared held out his arm to assist her down the steps. The motion was done without forethought, and only when she laid her hand on his sleeve did he realize how seamlessly they were working together. It was empowering, yet dangerous to his peace of mind.

She matched his pace as they hurried toward the Ledford Dressmaker Shop. "You think someone put the mirror in Andrew's pocket, don't you?"

He nodded, pleased by the fact that she still kept her hand looped around his arm as they walked. "How else could it have gotten there? And it wasn't Mrs. Croft.

She wants the real thief caught. Her motivation is more about her profit than framing Andrew. She won't care who it is. But she'll be suspicious of everyone, especially Andrew, until someone is caught."

A smile crossed Mary Lou's face and lit up her eyes when she looked at him. "I like the way you think, Jared." Then a stain of pink filled her face.

"I like that you've decided to call me Jared." He put a hand over hers and gave it a light squeeze. "Here we are." He walked up the steps to Milly Ledford's shop and opened the door for Mary Lou to enter.

"Hello, Milly. Is Reilly here?"

Milly Ledford sat behind her sewing machine with yards of pink fabric spilling over the table and onto the braided rug that kept the fabric off the floor. "He's upstairs. Is something wrong?"

Jared greeted her and said, "No, ma'am. We just want to ask him about Andrew Nobleson."

"Such a dreadful business. It makes me sad to see a young man taken off to jail like that. I know how much you and Mr. Ivy invested in that young man after he came to work for you, Mary Lou. I do hope you know my Reilly wasn't involved."

Mary Lou assured her they only want to ask Reilly if he'd seen anything. "Maybe he noticed something no one else saw. You know how children see things that adults look right over."

Mrs. Ledford stood and pushed the pink fabric into a heap on her chair. "I'll get him." She paused on her way to the stairway in the back corner of the room. "But

I'll stay with him while you talk to him. If I feel you should stop, you will stop immediately."

Jared answered for them. "Yes, ma'am. I promise we'll be respectful of his age."

Reilly didn't remember anything special at first, but when Jared asked if he'd noticed anyone hanging around the general store who didn't seem to be buying anything, Reilly perked up.

"I saw that man from the train. The one who comes around every time the train comes."

Mary Lou leaned over to be closer to Reilly's height. She put a hand on his shoulder. "Do you remember what he looks like or what he was wearing?"

"He was just a man. I don't remember nothing special about him."

Mrs. Ledford signaled to them that she wanted them to take what Reilly had given them.

Mary Lou patted his shoulder and stood. "Thank you for all your help, Reilly."

"Nothing special, 'cept he was wearing one of them funny hats. You know, the kind Doc Willis likes to wear. I don't know why any man wouldn't want a Stetson. The Mosley twins got Stetsons when their ma married Mr. Barlow. That's the kind o' hat a man oughta wear. Ma, if you get married again, can I have a hat like that?"

Mrs. Ledford struggled to cover her embarrassment. "Reilly, we will not discuss that now. We have visitors."

Reilly turned to Jared like they were allies and held up a finger to his lips. "Don't tell Doc Willis I don't like his hat. He might wanna give me some of that nasty-tasting medicine next time Ma makes me go see him when I ain't even sick." He grinned a boyish grin and bounded up the stairs.

Jared laughed and Mary Lou and Mrs. Ledford joined in. "I'd say he was very clear about that."

Mary Lou thanked Mrs. Ledford before they left.

"What do you think Sheriff Collins will do with this information?" Jared could hear the concern in her voice.

"I'm not sure there's enough information for him to use. We've got to do more than prove that Mr. Finch was there. We've got to prove he's a thief. If he is a thief."

"I know you're right." She stopped still. "I just realized something that won't help Andrew at all."

"What?" He watched the color drain from her face. "Mary Lou, you have to tell me."

"I saw Andrew in the general store, holding the mirror, but I didn't see Mr. Finch." Her eyes glistened with sorrow. "How will it help Andrew if no one saw Mr. Finch with the mirror?"

Jared finished her thoughts out loud. "You seeing Andrew could be all the proof a judge would need."

"Can you handle the ink or do you want to load the papers?" Mary Lou tied on her apron Saturday afternoon as she and Jared prepared to run the newspaper for the first time without Andrew.

"Why don't I load the papers and you load the ink?" He pushed his sleeves up with Andrew's garters.

She looked at the printing plate and prayed that God would use the paper to help prove Andrew's innocence. She'd memorized the words of the story asking the community to come forward with any clue, no matter how small, to help the sheriff solve the crimes. It had been difficult to pen the story without pleading for everyone to help Andrew. In the end, Jared had written the article. His words emphasized the responsibility of the community's citizens to protect themselves from crime by being aware of their surroundings and reporting anything suspicious.

Separate and apart from the article, they'd offered a twenty-five-dollar reward to the person who revealed the true thief. Jared had insisted that to include it in the story would show a distinct bias in the paper. By having it posted like an advertisement and declaring themselves as the individuals who offered the money, they gave a modicum of protection to the paper. At best.

Mary Lou inked the plate. "I hate the contrast of the Christmas Eve story about the children beside the piece about crime."

"If you think about it, the two stories show how the paper is an integral part of the community." Jared pulled the lever to print the page. "We keep the people of Pine Haven informed about current and future events, but we also involve them in things that matter to them. The Christmas Eve social is a big event from what I've heard since I arrived here."

"But the thief and not being able to catch him isn't good for Pine Haven."

He loaded another sheet of paper as they fell into the rhythm of printing. "But if someone in the community comes forward with the answer then everyone will see the good the paper can do. That reinforces their need for the *Record*."

She inked the plate again. "I hope it works. I can't fail Andrew. He needs me."

"You won't fail him."

"When we took him in, your grandfather told me it was my turn to care for someone else. He had rescued me, and I had to do my part to keep the work of the Lord going forward. He said it wasn't right to receive something and never give anything."

The muscle in Jared's jaw rippled as he pulled the lever again. "I wish I'd known him better. It sounds like he was a wise man."

"He was."

The sound of the press and the ink roller were all that filled the space for several minutes. Mary Lou continued her silent prayers for Andrew as every copy came off the press.

"Would Grump have put the reward in the newspaper?"

"Probably not. He was forever warning me to be objective. I have to remind myself that it's not all about throwing myself into the story but about looking at it from different angles."

Jared turned the handle to move the paper under the press and it came off in his hand. Mary Lou laughed as his jaw dropped open, and he looked up at her.

"This is not funny." He bent to pick up the pin that had worked its way loose from the press.

"It isn't, but your expression is."

Without any evidence that he meant the words, Jared replied, "I'm glad I could entertain you."

Mary Lou walked around the press and reached for the handle. "Let me show you how to fix it."

He pulled it behind his back. "I will fix it."

She raised her eyebrows and fought back a chuckle. "How well acquainted are you with the workings of this press?"

He gave a mock glare. "I know enough to keep from being made a fool of. Now back up and let me work." He extended his hands, effectively pushing her back without touching her. He rolled his shoulders and bent close to the press.

Mary Lou reached over his shoulder and pointed. "That's where the pin goes."

"I can see that." He shrugged her arm away with his shoulder.

"Then why aren't you fixing it?" She couldn't help it. A little rumble of laughter caught in her throat.

He twisted his neck to look up at her. "Perhaps you're blocking the light by trying to watch my every move."

She clasped her hands behind her back and turned her head in a deliberate fashion from one side to the other. "I could fix it with my eyes closed."

"Oh, you could, could you?" He rotated his shoulders again and made another show of trying to put the pin through the handle and into the machine.

She reached over and held the handle for him. He maneuvered the pin in several directions before it slid into place and the handle held firm. When she let go of her end of the handle, he overbalanced and landed on his seat at her feet.

He wiped one hand across his forehead. "That was more involved than I imagined."

Her laughter could be held no more. She couldn't form words, so she pointed at his face.

"What?" He rubbed the other hand across his cheek.

"Stop!" She wrapped her hands around her middle. "You've made quite a mess of yourself."

"I have?" He looked at the grime on his hands and then at her. "It's everywhere, isn't it?"

"Pretty much." She reached for a clean rag while he got to his feet. "Let me help you." He leaned over so she could reach his face. The spot on his forehead came off without much effort with the rag, but it was hard to concentrate when his breath mingled with hers in the small space between them.

"Better?" he asked with a grin.

"One more place." She scrubbed at the smear on his cheek. He angled it toward her, all the while keeping his eyes on hers. "This spot is more stubborn than the other one."

He captured her hand with his. They stood, inches apart. Not speaking. She searched his eyes for a calm she didn't find. He leaned forward, ever so near.

"Thank you." His words a low rumble of a whisper.

Mary Lou could hardly breathe with him so close. "For what?"

"For helping me. Teaching me all of this." He nodded his head toward the press without losing her gaze. "For putting yourself at risk to protect Andrew." He looked over her shoulder but she knew his focus was inward. "For sharing my grandfather's life and this newspaper—first with him, and now with me."

"You're welcome." She rubbed the rag across his cheek again.

He stilled her motion and looked into her face. "You never give up, do you?"

"I can't afford to. If I give up, I won't have anything."

"You'll never be without, Mary Lou." He lifted his other hand and brushed her jawline with one finger, stopping to rest it under her chin. "No one as special as you will ever be without whatever, or whoever, they need." She was beginning to need him in her life, but would he still send her on her way if the judge gave him the paper? He leaned close and pressed his lips to her forehead. A gentle, sweet pressure of kindness and closeness. And something else. Something she was afraid to consider.

Chapter Twelve

Monday afternoon Jared stopped in at the jail to talk to Andrew again. Sheriff Collins was out, so he pulled up a chair and sat close to the cell.

"Are you hungry?"

Andrew sat up on the side of the bunk. "Hungry and angry." He dug his fists into the mattress. "How long will it be before someone comes out with the truth? And what if they don't?"

"Don't lose hope."

"That's easy for you to say from that chair. You're on the other side of these bars." He stood to pace the small floor.

"Mary Lou hasn't given up on you. Don't give up on yourself."

Andrew stopped in front of Jared. "What about you? Do you still think it could be me?"

"No." He twisted the brim of his hat with both hands. "The faith Mary Lou—and Grump—put in you is enough for me." He met Andrew with a level stare. "I'm sorry I didn't see it sooner."

With a scuff of his boot against the floorboards, Andrew forgave him. "I can see how all the things made me look guilty."

"Help me think about everything that was stolen and where you were when it happened."

Andrew sat down, and for the next few minutes they went over every item, one at a time.

Jared looked at the notes he'd made. "The mirror is the biggest hurdle. How are we going to convince a judge you didn't take it when the sheriff found it in your pocket?"

"I don't know how it got there." The defeat in Andrew's voice was real.

"We're going to find out. Mary Lou and I will find out." Jared pushed his chair back against the wall. "I promise you that. You just keep praying and thinking. One way or the other, we'll find out."

"I didn't think you believed so much in praying for stuff." Brown eyes dared him to deny it.

Leave it to a young man, barely more than a boy, to get right to the point. "I believe in God."

"I know that. Why else would you go to church?"

"Going to church is the right thing to do. Christians need to be around one another. It makes our faith stronger."

"But I've heard you say you didn't think God was interested in the details. Like you thought He cared about the big stuff, but not the little things."

It was true. "You're right. I used to think that."

"What changed your mind?"

"You. And Mary Lou." He put his hat on. "And that's all I'm going to say on the matter." He had changed. His heart had softened to believe God would help him and Mary Lou find the answers to get Andrew out of jail. And to think God might help him know how to run Grump's newspaper.

He stepped onto the sidewalk and looked across the street to see Mary Lou coming out of Momma's Bakery.

What he didn't know was if God would show him how to get Mary Lou to stay. He couldn't imagine the *Record* without her there. The stories wouldn't be as personable without her knowledge. The heart of the community beat inside her.

Jared could manage the business and print the information about ranching and trends in the market to help the landowners in Pine Haven, but he would never be able to make stories come alive and give people hope the way she did. That was Mary Lou's gift.

He was beginning to realize that she was causing him to let down the barriers he'd erected against women. She had single-handedly scaled the walls he'd put up between him and any woman. He'd done it to protect himself from the mistrust that had flourished in his heart after years of his mother's falsehoods and silence.

He remembered the kiss he'd given her on Saturday. The sweetness in her face as she'd laughed at his dilemma, yet helped him, had drawn him to her. Her gentleness was like a balm to his wounded heart. The memory of the softness of her skin against his lips warmed his soul.

Jared went to check on Andrew's horse and give Mr. Robbins more money for the animal's care. Then he headed to the hotel and arranged for a hearty meal to be delivered to Andrew.

He made his way back to the newspaper office. Maybe Mary Lou had uncovered some new information. They'd gone in separate directions to deliver the newspapers today, hoping that someone would give them a hint of a clue that could rescue Andrew.

Mary Lou sat at the desk with a cup of coffee and two cookies. Jared hung his hat on the coat tree and sat down across from her.

"Those look good." He reached for a cookie but she swatted his hand away.

"They are. I'm sure Jane Sanford would love to sell you some. All you need to do is stop in at Momma's Bakery."

He leaned back in his chair. "So you're really not going to share?" He pulled his most pitiful face for her.

"Not even when you look like a sad puppy." She broke off a piece of a cookie and smelled it before she put it in her mouth.

"You just smelled the cookie?" He laughed out loud.

"Yes. Smell is a large part of taste." To emphasize her point, she inhaled the steam from her coffee before she sipped the dark brew.

"You do savor the small things, don't you?"

"Some people never get big things to savor. It's best to enjoy what you've got. You never know when it will be taken away." The fun that had filled her eyes when she spoke about the cookies faded in an instant.

He knew she was thinking he could take the *Record* from her. He wanted to restore that fun to her but didn't know how without relinquishing everything Grump had built for him.

"I've been to see Andrew."

"How is he?" She picked up the other cookie and handed it to him.

"He's ready to get out." He made a show of taking in the scent of the cookie before he took a large bite. "Mmm, we'll have to bring him some of these. I sent him lunch from the hotel."

"That's very kind of you. I'll buy him some cookies later."

"We talked about all the different thefts. I'm going to go see the Warrens again. I wonder if they've come up with any ideas about the cameo. What are you working on?"

"I've made some notes about the Christmas Eve social article for the next edition. And I'm going to head to the depot when the train comes today. I want to get the paper from Dallas and whatever other papers the newsagent might have. I'd like to pull some articles from the bigger cities to expand our content more. People are responding well to the news of the markets and such from you. I'm thinking it would be good to add a piece or two about politics every week. We've done occasional things. It's time to print more of these stories on a regular basis."

Jared finished the rest of his cookie. "You mean you're going to follow through with some of my suggestions for changes to the *Record*?"

"I am." She stood and pushed her pencil over her ear. "If you'll excuse me, I'm going to get back to work."

When she walked by him, he reached for her hand. He hadn't meant to. It happened without conscious thought. But she stopped and looked at her hand in his.

"We're going to solve this and get Andrew out of jail before the judge comes. We'll have the real thief ready for trial by then. And the paper is going to grow, just like Pine Haven is growing."

She still stared at their hands. "And when the judge finishes the trial for the thefts and decides our fate, what will we do then?" She looked into his eyes and he saw fear in hers. He'd never seen fear there before, and it was there because of him.

"Maybe we can talk about that and come to some solution before the judge arrives."

She slipped her hand from his. "I know we might both wish that were possible, but I'm not sure it is." She left without looking back.

Jared sat for a long time. The afternoon sun was casting long shadows when he moved from the chair, no closer to a solution than when she'd left.

Mary Lou stood on the platform at the train depot a few minutes before the train was scheduled to arrive. Mr. Meadows had warned her that its stop in town would only last half an hour today. No more. The railroad was making a change in the schedule and this train was going to the next town. Then it would reverse the schedule and come back through Pine Haven in the morning.

She twisted her hands together. Jared was getting to her. Was he trying to win her over so she'd give him the *Record*? Or was he as kind and compassionate as he appeared? The more she learned about him, the more she liked him. He was like Mr. Ivy in so many ways.

Why did the type of man that she had only dreamed of in the past come to Pine Haven wanting to take her world from her? She must remember the only reason Jared stayed in town was to have the judge award the paper to him.

The whistle of the train drew closer and the ground rumbled beneath the platform.

Jasmine Willis came out of the station master's office. "Hello, Mary Lou. Are you expecting someone?" Jasmine wore her ranching clothes. The long black braid hanging over one shoulder was at odds with the clothes of a working man.

"I came to buy the newspapers from out of town. Mr. Ivy and I are expanding the scope of the *Record* to include things from outside of our area that could affect us."

"That's very smart. I know the railroad has made a big difference in ranching. Cattle drives were a lot of hard work. Shipping the cattle by rail lowered our risk tremendously. I was just speaking to Mr. Meadows about any rate changes he might know about."

The train came into view, and Mary Lou grabbed Jasmine's arm.

Jasmine asked, "What is it? You look as though you're about to burst."

"I've just had an idea! Will you help me?"

"What is it? I'm not sure I like your tone."

"Please, I only have a few minutes. You have to help me." Mary Lou pulled Jasmine along in the direction of the hotel and shared her newly hatched plan as they walked. By the time they reached Jasmine's old room in the hotel's private residence, Jasmine was on board and happy to help her.

Twenty minutes later Mary Lou stood at the edge of the platform, away from the other passengers making their way onto the train. At her feet was the carpetbag Jasmine had borrowed from her father. They hadn't told Mr. Warren what Mary Lou was doing. They'd slipped out of the hotel unnoticed and taken the back alley to the station. No one would know her plan until the train left the station.

Jasmine came out of the ticket office and handed Mary Lou a round-trip ticket to Gran Colina, the next stop for the train. "Thanks, Lou. I'll bc hcrc to pick you up when you return from your trip." Jasmine winked at her. "Don't try to be anything you aren't. Just remember you're on a mission. Andrew is worth this."

Mary Lou looked down at herself. Jasmine was several inches taller than her, but she'd packed the extra length of the trousers into the boots Jasmine had loaned her. The shirt was tucked in at the waist, and she'd braided her hair and let it hang down her back before putting on the riding jacket that completed her outfit. No one who knew her would believe the transformation.

Jasmine had laughed when Mary Lou had picked up her reticule after she'd changed clothes. Mary Lou had agreed and left the feminine bag on the bed. She'd tucked some money and her pad and pencil into the inside pocket of the coat. At the last second she'd pinned her watch inside the coat, too.

Jasmine asked one more time, "Are you sure he doesn't know who you are?"

"I don't see how he could. He saw me the first day he came to Pine Haven. He plowed into a post trying to avoid me, and the sheriff took him straight to jail. He was too busy trying to stay out of jail to pay attention to me. And even though we were in your father's restaurant the other day, he was across the room and my back was to him much of the time." She looked down again at the trousers and jacket. "I think the change of clothes will keep him from making the connection to who I really am."

"Be careful." Jasmine lowered her voice. "Are you sure you don't want me to let Mr. Ivy know where you're going?"

"You can tell him after the train leaves. If he comes down to the station now, he'll ruin any chance I have of finding out if Mr. Finch is indeed the thief."

The conductor checked his pocket watch and called out, "All aboard!" He walked a few feet down the platform and called out again.

"I better go." Mary Lou felt a rumble of excitement and nervousness in her middle. "Thank you for your help."

"You're welcome. If you find out it's him, I want to be among the first to know."

"You will be. I promise." She laughed. "Besides all that, I'll have to get these clothes back to you." She hoisted the carpetbag that held the clothes she'd worn earlier. "Say a prayer for me."

"I will."

Mary Lou made her way to the rear of the car and sat on a seat alone. No one sat in the row across the aisle. She slid over by the window and put the carpetbag on the seat beside her, hoping no one would try to join her. Jasmine waved at her from the platform as the train pulled out of the station.

She kept her head lowered and scanned the other passengers from under the rim of the Stetson Jasmine had insisted was the finishing touch. Mary Lou almost laughed when she thought about the differences between Jasmine, the lady rancher, and her sister, Lily Stone, the milliner. Both were beautiful and strong women. Businesswomen, like herself. But they also had husbands. Men who valued their character and embraced their intelligence and their beauty.

Mary Lou could never compete with their beauty. She didn't have the softness they possessed. That was another reason she needed to solve this crime. If she could find evidence that Mr. Finch was the thief who troubled the residents of Pine Haven, it would solidify her ownership of the *Record*. The townspeople wouldn't be looking at her or Andrew with suspicion.

No. Mary Lou didn't have beauty or a husband. She had to protect the only thing she had. The *Pine Haven Record*. She hoped Jared would understand that she didn't have a choice. She had to fight for her future. Even if it put her at odds with him.

The door behind her opened. The noise of the track

and the blustery fall wind swirled into the car. Mary Lou kept her head lowered. She saw black trousers and shoes stop in the aisle.

"Ticket, sir?" The conductor held out his hand.

She offered her ticket, lifting her head enough to watch him punch it yet still keeping her face hidden beneath the wide brim.

"Here you go." He stretched his arm to return the ticket to her, but his elbow hit her hat.

She watched it fall onto the floor when she missed the brim in a desperate attempt to catch it.

"Hey!" He leaned over to look at her face. The sound of the car on the tracks muffled his words in the confined seat. "You're a woman."

"I am."

He straightened to his full height. "What's the point of dressing like that?" The conductor made no attempt to confine their conversation to the two of them.

Mary Lou had just put the hat back on as several people turned in their seats to stare. Speaking with only enough volume for the conductor's hearing she said, "I don't believe my attire is a matter of concern for you." She held her hand out for the ticket.

He shoved it at her. "I'll be watching you."

"There's no need." She sat back in her seat. "I'll be right here."

The conductor huffed his way to the next row of seats, mumbling to himself. Mary Lou was glad when he had punched all the tickets in her car and gone through the door at the front. She looked up as he gave a cursory glance over the occupants. His gaze landed on her as if he were memorizing her face before he closed the door.

Lord, help me not to draw any more attention before I accomplish my purpose. Give me the opportunity to find any evidence there is against Mr. Finch.

She could almost hear Mr. Ivy's voice in her head reminding her to be objective.

Or whoever the guilty person is, Lord. I just know it's not Andrew.

Thirty minutes before the train arrived at the next stop, Mr. Finch entered the car. He came from the front carrying a tray laden with newspapers and small items like candy and cigars. He started at the first seat and worked his way toward her, selling things to whomever wanted something as he passed.

The time had come to know if he recognized her as Miss Ellison of Pine Haven, editor of the *Record*.

Hoping to keep him from seeing her features, when he got to her, she stood with her head down and perused his tray of wares.

"Do you have any cigars?"

"The conductor told me about you. Women don't smoke cigars."

"Women buy cigars for men." She reached a hand into his tray and toyed with the cigar choices he had. She noticed newspapers from Pine Haven, Dallas and two other towns.

"A woman who dresses like you doesn't have a man to buy cigars for." He had no idea that the clothes she wore today weren't the reason she didn't have a man in her life. Maybe that was why it was so important to her to protect Andrew. No one ever stayed to protect her. Even if they wanted to.

"They're for my boss." Jared wasn't her boss yet. But if God didn't intervene, he would be when the judge came to town. The weeks were flying by. The judge could arrive any day. Even then, Jared wouldn't be her boss for long. She could never stay and let him tell her how to run her own paper.

"How many do you want?"

"Three." She pointed at the least expensive ones. "I need to take a gift to a sister, too." Jasmine wasn't *her* sister, but she was a sister. And she could give her whatever trinket she bought today. Unless the sheriff determined it was stolen. She'd show everything she bought to Sheriff Collins as soon as she returned to Pine Haven in the morning.

"What about a brush or comb? Or does your sister dress like you?"

She turned her laugh into a cough. He had no idea that the clothes she wore belonged to the woman for whom she was making her selection.

"She loves beautiful things. If you let me see what you have, I'll choose what I think suits her best."

Mr. Finch moved the papers to one side and revealed a small array of gifts for ladies. Watches, hat pins, brushes and combs, and just beneath the edge of a lace handkerchief Mary Lou caught a glimpse of a cameo. In an effort to keep him from thinking she had a particular interest in the cameo, she lifted the handkerchief and handled the fabric.

"I'd like this handkerchief." She fingered a set of hair combs. "How much are these?"

He gave a price that was well below what she knew would be a true cost.

"I don't know."

"What about something less expensive?" He showed her a porcelain dish. Now she knew he was the thief, but she couldn't let him see that she knew.

"It's not the expense. I just want the gift to be something she would like." She picked up a hat pin and put it back. "What about this?" She reached for the cameo. It was Jasmine's. The distinct rose corsage that Mr. Warren had described was beautiful.

He took it from her. "I'm sorry. I don't know how that got in here."

Mary Lou was grateful for her coat when goose bumps rose on her arms. She couldn't make him suspicious now, but she wanted the cameo back for Jasmine because of its sentimental value.

"Are you sure? It's just the sort of thing she would like." She didn't look at him, but kept her eye on the way he slipped it into the pocket of his trousers.

"No. I got it for my mother. Mustn't disappoint her on her birthday next week." He offered Mary Lou the kind of smile she'd seen over and again on an insincere face trying to pacify someone.

"Well, let me have the combs then." They hadn't been stolen in Pine Haven, but she'd stop into the sheriff's office at the next town and see if there had been any thefts there in recent weeks.

He wrapped her purchases in brown paper but pulled

the package back when she reached for it. He held out his open palm and told her the amount for her purchases.

She dug the money from her pocket and dropped it into his hand. "Thank you." She took the package. "Now I'll get a warmer welcome when I get home."

She sat back down and pretended her focus was on putting the items into the carpetbag. He stood over her for another moment before leaving through the back door and going to the next car.

Mary Lou slumped against the seat. She'd done it. She had found the evidence that Mr. Finch was the thief.

She had to speak to the sheriff in Gran Colina before Mr. Finch hid the cameo or sold it to someone else.

When the train pulled into the station, Mary Lou was on the platform of the passenger car, ready to step down.

She was met by a tall, burly man wearing a vest and a badge. Unlike the sheriff of Pine Haven, this man was clean-shaven and looked well rested. He held out his hand to help her from the train. "Miss Ellison?"

She accepted his hand and stepped onto the platform. "How do you know my name?"

"I'm the sheriff of Gran Colina, Scott Braden."

Mary Lou looked over her shoulder and back at him. "Can we talk over there?" She pointed to the corner of the station where they would be shielded from view but still able to observe the comings and goings on the platform.

He nodded and followed her.

She lowered her voice and asked, "Why are you here?

I was afraid I'd lose valuable time seeking you out when I arrived."

"I received a telegram from your boss. He said you were in danger and asked me to meet you."

"My boss?" Her jaw fell in what she was certain was a most unladylike fashion. "I…am my own boss, Sheriff Braden."

The sheriff pulled a telegram from his vest pocket and handed it to her.

Mary Lou Ellison on next train.
Reporter dressed as rancher.
In peril.
Please assist.

Jared Ivy.
Publisher, Pine Haven Record.

She looked beyond the sheriff and saw Mr. Finch on the steps of the last passenger car. He scanned the platform from his elevated vantage point. She ducked behind the sheriff.

"I am the publisher of the *Pine Haven Record*." She crumpled the telegram in her hand and shoved it in the pocket of her trousers. "But I don't have time to explain all of that this instant."

She dared to peek around the sheriff just as Mr. Finch stepped off the train. "Are you familiar with the newsagent on the train?"

"I have seen him once or twice."

"He's coming this way and mustn't see me talking

to you." The sheriff opened the side door to the station master's office and urged her inside.

"Thank you." She looked out the window as he pulled the shade down to prevent her face from being visible from the platform. "Mr. Finch is in possession of several items that were recently stolen in Pine Haven. I would like you to arrest him before he has time to sell or hide a particular item he slipped into his trouser pocket when I asked to purchase it on the train. I believe he may have realized I've uncovered his scheme."

"Miss Ellison, why would you put yourself in danger by following a suspected thief?"

"I'll be glad to tell you all about it later, but right now—" she ducked to see under the shade "—Mr. Finch is leaving. If you don't follow him, the cameo he stole will be gone, and we may never find it again."

Sheriff Braden scratched his temple. "I'll go talk to him, but I won't arrest him without more than the word of a woman who dresses like a rancher and claims to own a paper that I know belongs to Mr. Ivy." He opened the door. "You stay here."

Mary Lou bolted through the door after him. "I will not. I am the owner of the *Pine Haven Record*. And I dressed like this—" she made a sweeping gesture to indicate the jacket and trousers "—to lessen the probability that Mr. Finch would recognize me."

The sheriff was walking along the length of the platform, headed in the direction Mr. Finch had taken. Mary Lou had to trot to keep up with his pace as they watched Mr. Finch step into the local barber shop.

"There's a young man in jail in Pine Haven who has

been accused of the thefts that I know Mr. Finch committed. An innocent boy's life could be ruined forever if he has time to hide the evidence."

Desperation drove her to stay on the sheriff's heels. Jared might claim to own the *Record*, and Sheriff Braden might think she wasn't sane—dressed as a man and insisting she owned a business—but she would do whatever it took to rescue Andrew.

"Please, sheriff! Let me show you he's guilty."

Sheriff Braden opened the door of the barber shop. "You stay out here." He pointed to the sidewalk. "If you come inside, I may have to arrest you for interfering with my work."

She wanted to stomp her foot in protest but knew that wouldn't help her cause. She could see Mr. Finch in the barber's chair. He was leaned back and the barber was wrapping his face in a towel.

An idea popped into her mind and she stepped away from the window with her back against the wall.

"Has anything been stolen in recent weeks in Gran Colina?"

The sheriff closed the door. "What kinds of things?"

Mary Lou dug into the carpetbag and pulled out the package of items she'd purchased on the train. She untied the string and unfolded the brown paper. The sheriff watched without much interest until she lifted the handkerchief.

He picked up the combs. Anger edged his voice and he narrowed his gaze on her. "Where did you get these?"

"I just bought them from the man in that chair." She

pointed at the barber's window. "Who did he steal them from?"

The sheriff clenched his jaw. "My sister. She has a shop on Colina Street." He held the combs in his hand. "Do you mind if I keep these?"

"No. But I'd appreciate if you'd make Mr. Finch give me back the money I paid for them." She was actually able to smile. "Before you escort him to jail and then on to Pine Haven to face justice there. I'll even pay the train fare, if I need to. I made a promise to a young man, and I am thrilled to be able to keep it." The man who'd stolen her peace of mind was about to face judgment.

She stayed on the sidewalk while the sheriff went inside to confront Mr. Finch. The relief gave way to another thought.

When had she decided that Mr. Finch, and not Jared Ivy, was the man who'd stolen her peace?

It didn't matter. She couldn't let it matter. The telegram Jared had sent to Sheriff Braden was proof he still believed he was the rightful heir of the *Record*. Mr. Finch might be on his way to jail, but the matter of who owned the *Pine Haven Record* was still unsettled. Like her heart.

Chapter Thirteen

Jared shifted his weight from one foot to the other. The train was late. It was after eleven o'clock. Chester Meadows had assured him the train would arrive at ten thirty this morning.

Sheriff Collins walked out of the ticket master's office. "You're gonna wear the soles off your boots if you don't sit down." The sheriff folded himself onto the bench by the door. "Meadows said he just got a message that the train left Gran Colina late. Should be here any time."

As if on cue, a whistle sounded in the distance.

"Did they say what caused the delay? Was it Elmer Finch? Do you think he put up a fight to keep from coming back here to face the judge? If anything has happened to Mary Lou…" He hadn't meant to say that last sentence aloud.

"I know Sheriff Braden. You don't have to worry about Finch giving him a problem." He laughed. "Seems

I remember Miss Ellison knocking Finch on his head in the middle of the street the first time she saw him."

Jared paced to the end of the platform. He wouldn't relax until he saw Mary Lou with his own eyes. Maybe then he would find the humor in the sheriff's words. "She put herself in the middle of that situation, too. And the man ran into a post. He knocked himself into the street."

The train came around the last bend of track before it would reach the station. Jared wrung his hands. That woman had found her way into his mind. He couldn't rest or eat if he thought she was in danger. Her stubbornness was maddening, but he couldn't imagine her without it. The sweetness she showed to the people of Pine Haven was endearing. Her loyalty to Andrew was honorable.

But it had put her in danger. He needed to see her. To know for himself that she hadn't been hurt.

Why hadn't she sent him a telegram to let him know she was okay? Sheriff Collins had received one from the sheriff in Gran Colina. She must have known Jared would be worried.

Another long blast of the whistle alerted the town to the arrival of the train. The wheels squealed against the rails as the massive machine came to a stop. Jared looked from one end of the train to the other and didn't see her. The novelty of reversing the routes must have drawn a larger number of passengers. The platform became of sea of people.

Mary Lou came from behind a group of strangers. "Jared! We did it!" She wore the dress she'd had on when she'd left the office the day before. There was no sign of the rancher outfit Jasmine had told him about.

He put his hands on her shoulders and slid them gently to her elbows. "Are you hurt?" His voice shook with the thought of someone bringing harm to her.

"Of course not." She tilted her head to one side and met his eyes. "Why would you think that?"

"You went after a thief! Alone! One who carries a gun!" His voice had risen with each phrase, but he didn't care. "You knew he carried a gun."

Mary Lou backed away from his reach. "I'm capable of taking care of myself, Jared." Her countenance lost the joy it had held when she'd first approached him. "The Good Lord looks after me every day. All day. I don't have to be afraid."

"It's not a matter of being afraid. It's a matter of being cautious."

"Is everything all right here, Miss Ellison?" A large man with a badge on his chest came up behind Mary Lou. He dropped a hand on her shoulder.

She cut her eyes up at the man. "Everything is fine, Sheriff Braden." She extended her hand in Jared's direction. "This is Jared Ivy."

"Your boss?"

Jared cringed at the words. He didn't consider himself to be Mary Lou's boss, and he knew without a doubt she would resent the statement. He offered his hand to the man. "I work with Miss Ellison. We are sharing the publisher's duties at the *Record*."

The visiting sheriff shook Jared's hand but didn't move his other hand from Mary Lou's shoulder. A lot must have transpired in Gran Colina for Mary Lou to be allowing such a familiar gesture from someone she'd just met.

She smirked at Jared. "We are sharing the duties until the judge comes to town and sends one of us on our way." She sidestepped away from Sheriff Braden's hand. "The same judge who will see that Mr. Finch is punished for his crimes." She looked around. "Where is Mr. Finch?"

"Sheriff Collins took him to the jail." Sheriff Braden tipped his hat at her. "I best be getting along, too. I promised a full report on the thefts in Gran Colina to your sheriff."

"Thank you so much for all your help." She smiled and added, "I'll stop in at the hotel and make sure they have a room for you before I go back to my office."

"I'll be looking forward to our supper." He gave Jared a curt nod and walked away.

Jared was so relieved she wasn't hurt, but he was also disgruntled that another man was pressing in on Mary Lou's time and attention. "It appears that you and the sheriff have made good use of the short time you've known one another." The words came out with a bitter tone he hadn't meant to reveal.

"He met me at the train yesterday. It seems he was sent as a kind of protector by someone who thought I couldn't take care of myself."

"I was worried about you." There was no need to deny the truth.

"There was never any danger." She looked away as she said the last word.

"Never? You were never concerned that Mr. Finch might recognize you and harm you in any way?"

"You sent a telegram that I was a reporter and you were the publisher. Sheriff Braden thought you were my boss."

"I sent a telegram worded so that a sheriff I'd never met would see the urgency of ensuring your safety. If I'd told him how strong you are, he might not have bothered to go." He leaned closer. "And I think you were a bit afraid. But you're more worried that relying on me for help might make you vulnerable. You're afraid that trusting me would weaken your position in regard to the ownership of the *Record.*"

Her face blanched at his words.

"Mary Lou, I sent the telegram to protect you. Not to lessen you." He put his hand on her cheek. "You are the bravest lady I've ever met." The softness of her cheek against his palm nearly undid him. The thought of losing her for any reason caused an ache in his chest. A deep heaviness that threatened his breath. "But you didn't have to do it alone. I would have helped."

"Mary Lou, there you are!" Jasmine Willis stepped onto the platform. "I'm sorry I'm late. There were a few details yet to be done on our house. The workers couldn't come until this morning." She stopped a few feet from them.

Jared dropped his hand and slid it into his pocket.

Jasmine spoke to Mary Lou. "I can come back later."

"There's no need. I was just about to go to the hotel and return these things." Mary Lou held up a carpetbag.

"Did he recognize you?" Jasmine turned to Jared. "I

thought her idea to dress as a lady rancher to keep him from suspecting her true identity was good."

So Mary Lou had wondered if Elmer Finch would recognize her and become suspicious of her motives.

He waited for her response. He knew she wouldn't lie.

She answered Jasmine but the glance she sent his way assured him he'd been right to be concerned. "There was a moment where I felt I needed to use extra caution. I didn't want him to think I was searching for specific items. When he slid your mother's cameo into his pocket and refused to sell it to me, I feared it might be lost forever."

"You found my cameo?" Jasmine hugged Mary Lou. "Papa will be so thrilled."

"If you'll excuse us, Jared, I need to go to the hotel. I can take care of the details with Jasmine and Sheriff Braden." There was a distance in her eyes that hadn't been there before she'd gone to Gran Colina. "Will you meet me at the office after lunch? We can talk then."

He pulled his watch from the pocket of his vest. After checking the time, he said, "I'll be at the sheriff's office when you get there. We can arrange our afternoon once we've finished the business at hand."

Jared watched her walk away and part of him went with her. A part he feared he'd never get back. The distance he felt between them now was more than the distance when he'd first arrived in Pine Haven.

That day, he'd been a stranger—someone after her business. Today, she saw him as a betrayer of her trust.

His mother had made him feel that way when she'd

confessed to hiding Grump's letters from him. He knew that betrayal had the potential to destroy everything they'd established together.

The *Pine Haven Record* was a stronger paper than when he'd arrived. They'd accomplished that by working together.

The article they would print for the next edition would be one of intrigue and truth. Rescue and justice—if the sheriff would agree to release Andrew. It was a story Mary Lou would write alone. One that she'd earned the right to because she'd put herself at risk by going after the criminal alone.

Jared could claim no part in its success.

And Mary Lou wouldn't want him to.

Mary Lou entered the sheriff's office with Jasmine. Jared was there with both sheriffs and Elmer Finch sat on a bunk in the cell next to Andrew's.

"Gentlemen." She greeted everyone. "Sheriff Braden, this is Jasmine Willis. The cameo was a gift from her father to her mother. Her father gave it to her after her mother passed."

"Thank you, Sheriff Braden. I can't tell you how grateful I am to know the cameo has been found." Jasmine looked at the man in the cell. "I am sorry I was unable to wear it when I was married recently."

Sheriff Collins pulled the cameo from his desk and showed it to Jasmine. "Is this it?"

Jasmine nodded. "May I have it?"

"I need to keep it until after the trial. The judge will return it to you then." He locked the cameo in his desk.

"From what Braden tells me, you owe your thanks to Miss Ellison. Her quick thinking kept this fellow from getting away with your jewelry and all the crimes he's committed."

"Thank you so much. I won't forget what you did for me." Jasmine gave Mary Lou a hug. "I've got to get back to the Circle W. I may be the newest member of the family but, even though I'm in charge now, I still have to do my share of the work." She left and closed the door behind her.

Mary Lou asked, "Sheriff, why is Andrew still here? I thought that bringing Mr. Finch into custody would prove Andrew's innocence."

Sheriff Collins pulled down on the edges of his thick mustache. "There's still the mirror, Miss Ellison. I can't just let him go. The mirror was in Andrew's pocket. I can't ignore that."

Jared added, "Mrs. Croft just left here. She wanted to make certain Andrew was kept until the judge comes to town."

"But that's not right. We all know he's not a thief." Mary Lou had hoped this would all be resolved.

"I can't assign blame to the newsagent for something I found in Andrew's possession."

Mr. Finch stood. "I didn't steal anything. This boy here brought all those things to me. I paid for everything I had. He's your thief."

Mary Lou gasped. "You're lying."

Andrew lurched to his feet. "I did not! I don't even know this man. Only that he buys several copies of the paper on Mondays. That's the only thing I ever sold him." Andrew clung to the bars. "Sheriff, you gotta believe me."

Sheriff Braden said, "That wouldn't explain why Finch had the combs that went missing from my sister's store."

Jared stood in the corner of the room making notes. "Sheriff Collins, have you heard back from any of the other stops on the route?"

"Two. They both confirm a number of small items stolen in each town."

Sheriff Braden added, "I was able to search the car where Finch kept his personal belongings. There's a trunk filled with things I expect we'll discover were stolen."

Elmer Finch groused from his cell. "You had no right to go through my pockets and things."

"You gave up your rights when you broke the law." Sheriff Collins sat in the chair behind his desk.

"I'm innocent, I tell you. This is the second time you've thrown me in this cell without cause. I'm sure the judge will want to hear all about how you people jump to conclusions and put innocent people in jail."

Sheriff Collins snorted. "You go right ahead and tell the judge how you get into trouble in Pine Haven more than anyone who lives here. I still have an idea that you took that poor fellow's money off the table when he accidentally shot himself."

"You've no proof of anything against me."

Mary Lou was exhausted with this turn of events. Poor Andrew stood in the cell, his eyes pleading with her for help. "What happens now, Sheriff Collins?"

"We wait for the judge. He could be here anytime. It depends on how much he has to deal with in the surrounding counties."

Jared asked, "What about Andrew? Can you release him to me until the judge comes? I'll keep a close eye on him."

"Sorry, Mr. Ivy, but I can't." Sheriff Collins stood from his chair. "If I let him out, Mr. Finch might decide he wants to stay at the hotel. Now, if you folks will clear out, me and Sheriff Braden need to take a look at the things in Finch's trunk. There's a lot of work left to do before the judge comes."

Mary Lou thanked the men for their help and made her way toward the newspaper office. The sheriff's announcement that the judge's arrival was imminent reminded her of how soon her life could change. She had little, if any, time to clear Andrew's name and help him land his new job and get settled into the bunkhouse on the Double Star Ranch. She'd been certain that having Mr. Finch in jail would restore Andrew's good reputation and allow him to go to work immediately. She'd have to dig deeper to find out what happened.

She sat at the desk and made a list of what she'd need to do in case the judge gave the paper to Jared. Then she made a list of things she could do to show the judge he should let her keep the *Record*.

The office door opened and Jared entered. He went to the press and studied the plate they'd used for the edition they'd printed on Monday.

"I think we can move things around nicely so you'll have plenty of room for your story about Mr. Finch and his capture." He pointed to the plate. "We can take out the top story and the offer of a reward." He turned to her. "I guess I owe you half of that reward, since you and I were going to pay it to anyone who helped find the real thief."

She slid her pencil over her ear. "You don't owe me any money." She put her lists under the magnifying glass. "I do think we need to talk."

He held up a hand. "Let me go first." At her nod, he continued. "I was wrong to let Braden think I was your boss."

"Yes, you were."

"Wait, I'm not finished." He rubbed his jawline with one hand. "I'm sorry I upset you by worrying about you. It's just that I care about what happens to you."

She toyed with the handle of the magnifying glass. "That's very kind." She looked up at him, "Much like the way your grandfather would have felt about the whole situation."

One corner of his mouth lifted in a half smile, and he sat in a chair opposite the desk. "Do you think we can keep working together?"

He didn't say for how long. The sheriff had declared they had to work together until the judge came. A month had already passed. Was he suggesting they continue the arrangement beyond then?

"I think we can trudge along like we have been." She shrugged her shoulders. "It hasn't been as bad as I thought it would be."

He gave a slight chuckle. "That's true."

"So you think we can plan on this story for the top

of the paper for next Monday, even though Andrew is still in jail?" She walked to the front of the office and stared out the window. She couldn't bear the thought of Andrew in the cell beside Elmer Finch.

"Yes. But I want you to write the entire article. You can use whatever angle you want. Criminal, personal, anything that you think would benefit the paper or the community."

"You've had some say in everything we've printed for weeks. Are you sure?" She turned around to see him sitting at the desk.

"You got this story on your own. You should be able to write it like you want."

"I'll do that now then. I've made a couple of lists of things I need to handle."

"What kind of lists?"

"Some things I need to accomplish in short order."

"Is this the list? He moved the magnifying glass and picked up her notes. She tried to take them from him, but he pulled them out of her reach and read them aloud.

"'Make sure Andrew gets the job on the Double Star.'" He picked up a pencil from the desk and drew a line under that item. "This one is very important. I'd like to help you with it."

She held out her hand, hoping he'd give the paper to her. "That list is for my personal use."

"But there are things about the newspaper on here. So that would make them my business, as well." He pointed at the next item. "'Finish writing the articles for the Christmas Eve social.'" He nodded his head as he read several more things aloud.

"Please give me the lists." Mary Lou reached out again. She didn't want him to read the other page.

Jared handed them to her but he let go before she had a firm grip and the sheets floated to the floor. He bent to pick them up and give them back to her but stopped short when he saw the first item on the second page.

"'Compare my work experience to Jared's.'" He drew his brows together. "What is this list for, Mary Lou?"

She reached for the paper but he held it tight. "It's nothing."

"But it is something. And I feel compelled to continue reading since my name is in the top line." He read the next item. "'Choose potential character witnesses.'"

Mary Lou tore the papers from his hand. "I don't want to talk about it."

"You're preparing for the judge." He sat back in the chair.

Her arms hung at her sides, the offending list in one hand. "Aren't you? Sheriff Collins said he could arrive anytime."

"No. I hadn't thought to do that."

"You think your will is all the evidence you need?" She wasn't angry anymore. She was tired. The emotion of chasing after Mr. Finch and trying in vain to clear Andrew's good name had taken its toll.

"To be honest, most days I don't think about it." He took his watch out and checked the time. "I best be getting out to find a story of my own. I've got to have something good to run alongside your piece."

He left her without another word.

Mary Lou slumped into the desk chair and put her

head down. In her effort to prepare for her future, she'd hurt Jared. She thought about the kiss he'd placed on her forehead. Had they grown so close over time only to lose that closeness now that the judge was coming to town?

Chapter Fourteen

Jared paced outside the sheriff's office on Wednesday morning. He needed to see Sheriff Collins, but he hoped he wouldn't run into Sheriff Braden. Jared had stayed late at the office Tuesday evening thinking Mary Lou might come there to work on her story—if her dinner at the hotel with the sheriff from Gran Colina had been about Mr. Finch. He'd finally given up some time after nine and gone to his rooms above the office. Sleep had eluded him for much of the night.

The door to the office opened and Sheriff Collins came out. "Sheriff, I need your help."

"I'm a busy man, Mr. Ivy. It's not often I have prisoners in both cells. Just making sure they eat and such is an added aggravation." The man headed down the sidewalk at a steady pace and Jared followed.

"That's what I want your help with. You've got to have evidence about Andrew, right?"

"I've got enough for the judge to find him guilty. I know you want to help the boy, but I've got a witness and the mirror. I don't know what can be done to save him."

Jared stepped in front of him. "But what if we find someone who can prove Andrew didn't do it?"

"Then I'd have to say you're a better newspaper man than your grandfather." He stepped off the sidewalk to cross the street. "And I don't know if that's possible. Jacob Ivy was one of the best."

"I need to talk to Andrew."

"Go ahead. He's not going anywhere."

"Not in front of Finch. He'll twist anything we say and use it to make Andrew look worse."

"I'm not pursuing the theory that Andrew sold him all that stuff. It doesn't make sense to me."

"But a judge might believe him. That's why Mary Lou and I need to talk to Andrew alone."

"Mary Lou? Are you trying to clear Andrew's name for his sake or for Miss Ellison's?"

"The truth? Both. They're good people. Andrew would never have been suspected in the first place if I hadn't said anything."

"I'm guessing you aren't going to leave me be until I work this out. What do you have in mind?"

"Let's take Andrew back to every place where something was stolen. I'd like for you to come along. He can tell us what happened at each location. Maybe he'll remember something, or the people in those places will remember something that will help us find the truth."

The sheriff grunted. "We didn't find everything that was stolen in Pine Haven. Finch only had a couple of things."

"He'll just say he bought them from Andrew and sold them. Or that he never had them in the first place."

"Come by tomorrow at ten. We'll do all we can before noon." He stepped onto the sidewalk in front of the land office. "But if we don't find out anything, I won't do it again."

"Thank you." Jared couldn't wait to tell Mary Lou. Maybe they could work together on a plan to ask the right questions at each business.

"Two hours tomorrow. Not a minute more." The sheriff opened the door to the land office.

"That's all we need." Jared pivoted and headed straight for the newspaper office. This was the best way he knew to show Mary Lou he was willing to work with her.

He slowed his pace. How willing was he? The paper could be his in a matter of days if the judge ruled in his favor. On his first day in Pine Haven, he'd entertained no thoughts of Mary Lou's future. That wasn't true anymore. He'd been beside himself with worry when Jasmine had told him of her scheme to follow Mr. Finch. She was safe, and he'd thanked the Lord above for that.

He couldn't imagine the *Record* without her. The daily operations of the paper required more than one person. Andrew would be cleared and go to work on the Double Star. Jared could hire another apprentice, but no one could take Mary Lou's place.

Grump had poured his heart and soul into the *Pine Haven Record* and then into Mary Lou. Jared had to convince her to stay. He'd learned so much from her in the last weeks. If she left now, he wouldn't have the opportunity to absorb all she knew about Grump. More than that, he'd miss her.

He'd lost his father and Grump as a child. Then his mother's death had left him with the prospect of reconciling with Grump. When that hadn't been possible, Jared had immersed himself in Grump's world. With every passing day he grew more connected to the man who'd loved him, paid for his education and wanted to be in his life. Without Jared in Pine Haven, Grump had poured his grandfatherly love into Mary Lou.

But that wasn't why Jared wanted Mary Lou in his life. If she left, she'd take his heart with her. For without his awareness she'd captured the broken part of him and healed it. In a way he never thought possible.

If he won the paper, he could lose Mary Lou. If he hadn't lost her already.

He took the steps up to the sidewalk in front of the newspaper.

Lord, I've wondered in the past if You cared about the little things. Mary Lou has taught me that You do. Show me what to do. Help me to win her heart like she won mine. With Your love.

Mary Lou looked up from the desk. "Good morning. I was surprised to find you out so early."

"It is a good morning. I've just been to see the sheriff."

She put her pencil down and waited.

"He's going to give us some time with Andrew away from the jail tomorrow morning. We'll be able to take him to all the places that had items stolen. We'll interview people with Andrew present and try to find some clue to what happened to all the other items. Sheriff Collins said they found a couple of things from Pine Haven in Finch's trunk. We've got to come up with what happened to the other items."

"That's a good idea. I didn't think the sheriff was going to allow Andrew to leave with us."

"Sheriff Collins is coming with us." Jared sat across from her and leaned his elbows on the desk. "There's one thing."

"What?" Her face froze with caution.

"We only have two hours. After that he said he won't be able to do anything else for Andrew. It will be up to the judge."

"How did you convince him?"

"I told him it wasn't fair to Andrew for Finch to hear everything we said to him. Finch could twist Andrew's words into a lie for his own benefit."

She sat at the desk, nodding her head. "Then we need to be prepared. Let's go over everything we know and come up with any scenario we can think of that would help poor Andrew." Mary Lou pulled a clean piece of paper in front of her and held her pencil at the ready.

This was the response he'd wanted from her. There was no indication that she was still upset with him. But he had to know about Sheriff Braden. "Mary Lou?"

"Yes."

"Did Sheriff Braden tell you anything last night that would help clear Andrew?"

"We didn't come up with anything." She rolled the pencil between her palms. "After we discussed the thefts in Gran Colina, we talked about how the porcelain dish and the cameo connect Finch to the thefts. Sheriff Braden wasn't much help."

"That's good news." She gave him a puzzled look. "About connecting Finch to the thefts." It didn't bother Jared one iota that Mary Lou had been disappointed in Sheriff Braden's assistance.

"There's also no way to refute the claims Finch is asserting about buying everything from Andrew. If he says that someone in each town sold him things, it gives him some sense of credibility. If we can't prove Andrew was innocent, it looks as though both of them will be convicted."

He pulled his chair closer to the desk. "Then we better get to work."

Mary Lou gathered their notes for the interviews. She and Jared had worked into the night going over every possibility.

"Are you ready?" He held the door open for her.

"Do you mind if we pray first?"

"Not at all." He reached for her hand and she didn't hesitate to put it in his. They bowed their heads together and he prayed a simple prayer for their success.

She slipped her hand from his and missed the comfort of his grasp. "Thank you."

The walk to the sheriff's office only took a few minutes. Sheriff Collins was opening Andrew's cell when they arrived.

"Thank you, Sheriff." Andrew stepped out.

Mary Lou couldn't resist giving him a hug. She whispered to him, "It's going to be okay. We're not going to give up on you." She stepped back and patted his cheek with the palm of her hand.

Mr. Finch had been on his bunk with his face to the wall. He rolled over and lumbered to his feet. "What's going on here?"

"Don't reckon that's any of your business," the sheriff answered as he put on his hat.

Once in the street, Jared presented their plan to the sheriff. They'd start at the livery then go to the saloon before heading to the hotel and the general store.

The two hours were almost up when they entered the general store. Liza Croft's exclamation could be heard in the street. "What is he doing in my store? I want him out of here this instant." If Andrew's fate rested in Mrs. Croft's hands, the trial would be over before it began.

Donald Croft came through the stockroom doors, wiping his hands on his apron. "What is going on here, Sheriff?"

Jared addressed his remarks to Mr. Croft. "We'd like you to help us remember anything that happened on the days that items went missing from your store."

The owner looked over his shoulder at his wife. "I don't see what good it will do." He spoke to Andrew. "I liked you, boy, but when they found the mirror in your pocket, it was the end of the matter for me and the missus. We can't trust you to be in here. We work too hard for what we earn."

Andrew said, "I understand, Mr. Croft, but I didn't take that mirror. Or anything else."

Mrs. Croft came up beside her husband. "How did

it get in your pocket then?" She lifted her chin in defiance of anything he might say.

Mary Lou drew on all her patience and everything Mr. Ivy had ever taught her. "Mrs. Croft, on the days when other things were stolen, did you notice anything out of the ordinary?"

The ornery woman punched her finger in Andrew's direction. "I noticed him in here."

She tried another tactic. "What about you, Mr. Croft? Have you ever had cause to be concerned about Andrew before the recent thefts?"

"Can't rightly say. I didn't know he was a thief before."

Like lightning illuminating the night sky, Mary Lou had a bolt of clarity. "Has anything ever gone missing before? What was the first thing you noticed?"

"The brush and comb set," Mrs. Croft answered.

"And when was that?" She had to find out the dates.

Mr. Croft thought a minute. "It was the day Mr. Ivy came in and asked if anything was missing. We didn't notice the brush and comb set were gone until we closed up that night."

She turned to the sheriff. "Is that the first thing that was reported to you?"

"Other than Mrs. Willis's cameo and the porcelain dish, yes. What are you getting at, Miss Ellison?"

"I'm just thinking out loud, Sheriff." She looked beyond Andrew to Jared. He stood between the young man and Mrs. Croft. The slight dip of his head let her know he knew what she was thinking.

Jared snapped his fingers and said, "Mr. Finch was leaving the store that day in a big hurry. I encountered him on the steps when I arrived."

Sheriff Collins raised one thick eyebrow. "Was he carrying anything? Something he could have hidden things in?"

Jared thought for a minute. "Not that I remember."

"I'd need more than knowing the man went shopping on the same day to use it against him." The sheriff thanked the Crofts for their help and led the rest of them onto the porch. "I've done what I could. It's time for me to take Andrew back to the jail."

Mary Lou put a hand on Andrew's arm and pinned him with her stare. "Don't you give up. I'm—" she shot a glance in Jared's direction "—*we're* going to find the truth. And we both know you are not a thief."

"Thank you, Miss Ellison. I pray you will."

"That's what you need to do, Andrew. Pray."

The sheriff tugged on Andrew's arm. "Come on. I've got to get you back, so I can feed the both of you."

Jared came to stand beside Mary Lou and together they watched the sheriff lead Andrew down the street.

He leaned close to her ear. "I can see that mind of yours working in your pretty eyes."

His breath caressed the nape of her neck and she stepped away from him. "Let's go back to the office and compare notes." She had to focus on Andrew right now. Later, when she was alone, she'd take time to savor him standing so near and hearing him say her eyes were pretty.

* * *

On Friday afternoon, Mary Lou finished compositing her article about Mr. Finch's arrest and upcoming trial. She included a paragraph about Andrew being held on a separate theft.

A reward might still bring new information to light about that. She picked up the composing stick and began pulling the type to put the reward back together for the next edition.

Jared came in with a rush of wind and pushed the door closed. He rubbed his hands together and slipped out of his jacket. "I'd say we're getting a taste of fall today." He put another piece of wood in the stove and came to look over her shoulder.

"Do you mind if I put the reward back in? Someone knows the truth."

He put a hand on her shoulder. "If you think it can help, put it back in. Make it a reward for any evidence about any of the thefts, and not just about something that will free Andrew. We can't become so emotionally invested in his innocence that people begin to question the integrity of the paper. You can take the top of the column I'm using for my story."

She tried not to react to the gentle weight of his hand. It was a comfort she sorely needed. Since Mr. Ivy had passed there wasn't anyone for her to share her troubles with. They'd shared many pots of coffee in the years since he'd taken her in. Having someone to listen was a luxury she hadn't taken for granted. She'd been without it for years and had treasured it in Mr. Ivy.

Jared was so like him. Though they'd not spent time

together for two decades, Jared had inherited many of his grandfather's mannerisms.

She lowered her hands to the composing table and held the stick at an angle to prevent the type from sliding out. "Your grandfather would have stood just like you are now, with his hand on my shoulder and a kind word." She felt his hand lift.

He went to the stove and poured himself a cup of coffee. "You seem to be carrying the weight of the world on those shoulders these days."

"Not the entire world." She picked up another letter for the reward. "Only my world."

She saw him lean against the desk. "Do you realize how big your world is, Mary Lou?"

"It's not big at all, Mr. Ivy."

"Mr. Ivy?" He put his coffee on the desk and came to stand by her. "I'm not my grandfather."

"You're everything good that he was." She didn't look up but kept adding the font tiles to the composing stick.

Jared took the stick from her and propped it on the composing table so her work would not be undone. She smiled at the thought of how much he'd learned. His spelling had even improved.

"Thank you for letting me know the ways that I am like Grump." He put his hand on her shoulder again. "But when I do this to comfort you, I am one hundred percent Jared at that moment."

She blushed at his words. The warm-rush-of-color-that-made-her-eyes-widen kind of blushing. The kind of reaction no other man had been able to evoke in her. But she couldn't react to him.

She knew the truth about men. They might be handsome and strong, but none ever stayed when it mattered. Even if they wanted to, the circumstances of life—or even death—could take them away.

Mary Lou put her hand over his. "I know. But I also know that you and I are about to face a challenge that has the potential to destroy any friendship we've built. It will be difficult for me to face having to leave this newspaper." She patted his hand and pulled it from her shoulder, then let it fall through her fingertips to hang at his side. "I don't think I can bear it if we become more than friends and then that happens."

He took a step back. "I see." He put a hand to the side of his neck and pressed against the muscles there. "You think I am being kind to you to prevent there being a problem when we stand before the judge?"

"No." She reached out to touch him, but pulled her hand back at the last moment. "I know you are genuine." She stretched her arms in a wide-sweeping motion. "But this is my life. This paper, the house, telling these stories…it's all I've known for years. If I lose that, I don't know who I'll be. And I won't pretend I'll know how to handle that."

He leaned back against the desk and studied his boots. "I didn't mean to make you uncomfortable."

The sound of breaking glass drew their attention to the street. Two men tumbled out of the front of the saloon.

Mary Lou grabbed her notebook and pencil. "I'll go

see what's happening. You finish your article." She was out the door before he answered.

It was another pointless bar fight. The sheriff and Doc Willis took care of the men after the commotion died down. Mary Lou made notes of names and who was at fault.

"Sheriff, where will you put these men? You've got men in both cells at the jail."

Sheriff Collins grabbed the saloon fighter who wasn't injured by the scruff of his collar. "Looks like they'll be sharing their space tonight, Miss Ellison." He pulled the man along and told the Doc to have someone bring the other one to the jail after he got him bandaged.

She grabbed a handful of her skirts and lifted the hem so she wouldn't trip as she hurried after the sheriff. "But who will you put together?"

"Don't guess it matters." He kept a hand on the arm of the ruffian he escorted up the steps to the sidewalk in front of the jail.

"It does matter." She pushed behind him. Andrew was looking out the window at the back of his cell. Mr. Finch was asleep on his bunk.

Sheriff Collins took the key from the nail by his desk and opened the door to Mr. Finch's cell. He gave a nudge to the angry man and closed the door behind him. As he reached to put the key back on the nail, Jared came in the door with the other man.

"Doc said to bring this one to you."

Andrew backed up as the man was put in his cell. Still under the influence of the drink that no doubt started the fight, the man fell across the bunk with his face to the wall.

Jared stepped close to Andrew and spoke to him in a voice so low no one else could hear. Andrew nodded and sat on the other bunk in the small cell.

Mary Lou couldn't bear the thought of Andrew sharing a cell with such a man. "Sheriff…"

Jared took her by the elbow. "Let's you and I go outside."

She looked over her shoulder as the door closed. "Why did you do that?"

"I saw you scurrying after the sheriff when he left. I stepped outside and Doc told me what happened. I brought the other guy so I could talk to Andrew. The last thing he needs is for one of those men to get the idea he's got a woman protecting him." When she would have argued, he held up one hand. "I know you can protect him. But those men don't know you. And they'll be here overnight with Andrew locked in with them. I told him how to handle himself, and he understands."

She knew he was right. "Will this nightmare never end?"

He took her arm and led her down the steps. "I pray it does. I really do."

Chapter Fifteen

Saturday morning, Jared finished reading the proof of the paper. "I don't see anything amiss." He handed it to Mary Lou, who sat at the desk staring at the lists she'd made.

The whistle blew, announcing the arrival of the train.

"I'll read it in a minute." She pushed the proof to the side of the desk.

"I'm going to meet the train and get the newspaper from Dallas. I'm following a story for the ranchers about the cattle markets."

"Okay. We can print this edition after lunch." She didn't look up when he left.

At the station he met the new man the railroad had taken on as the newsagent. He was a friendly fellow who asked if there was anything in particular that Jared would like him to bring on his regular stops in Pine Haven.

Jared was finishing his business with the man when

he heard the sheriff's voice. "Judge Sawyer, it's good to see you again."

Jared turned to see the judge shake hands with the sheriff. A ball formed in the pit of his gut. Not only would this man decide Andrew's fate, he would also decide who the rightful heir to the paper was. Jared had to tell Mary Lou the judge had arrived before anyone else did. They had hoped he wouldn't come to town for at least another week.

"Mr. Ivy." The station master came out of his office and flagged Jared down. "Henry from the telegraph office said you need to stop in and see him as soon as possible."

"Thanks, Mr. Meadows. I'll go now."

Jared stopped in and got several answers to the telegrams he'd sent on Thursday after they'd gone all over town looking for clues about the thefts. He didn't try to read them all. He had to see Mary Lou before anyone else.

At the crossroads in the center of town, he was about to turn left toward the office when he saw Mary Lou headed into the jailhouse. He looked behind him and didn't see the sheriff or judge coming from the station. Perhaps they'd stopped at the hotel to get the judge a room.

Jared followed Mary Lou to the sheriff's office, opened the door and froze. Mary Lou stood in front of Andrew. The judge and sheriff were deep in conversation at his desk. Jared went to her. "I tried to get to you before you found out from someone else. I heard the sheriff talking to the judge at the train depot."

"We both knew it could be any day. I just hope we can convince the judge of Andrew's innocence."

Jared scanned the two cells and asked, "How are you, Andrew?"

He nodded his head. "Thank you for helping me. I won't forget it. No matter what happens."

Mary Lou said, "Keep praying. God pays attention to the smallest sparrows. He's watching over you, too."

The sheriff stepped around the desk. "Folks, we'll be having the trials Monday morning at nine."

"So soon?" Mary Lou bit her lip.

"The judge needs to be on the train Tuesday morning."

The judge stepped forward. "I want to be home with my family for Thanksgiving next week. And I don't like to work on the Lord's Day, or we'd do it tomorrow."

The sheriff made introductions. "This is Mary Lou Ellison, she took ownership of the *Pine Haven Record* when Jacob Ivy passed a few months ago. This is Ivy's grandson, Jared Ivy. He's come to town with a will saying the paper is his. Their case will be the last one for the day. I figure it will go quick."

A discussion on selecting a jury for the trials ended the meeting.

Jared and Mary Lou left the sheriff's office.

"Would you like to go to the hotel for lunch? I think we need to spend all of our spare time before the trial going over the notes we have." He glanced at her. She'd been quiet most of the day. "My treat."

"We can go. You don't have to buy my meal. I'm as anxious as anyone to see Andrew freed. If you think we might find something we've overlooked in all this time, I'm glad to be there."

"I've prayed for some way to help Andrew. It happened gradually, but I've prayed more since I came to Pine Haven than ever before. I think it may be on account of your influence." It was a change that gave him comfort and peace.

"The Lord never lets us down. Mr. Ivy said to do what you know to do and trust God for the rest."

"That seems wise."

"Your grandfather was a wise man."

Monday would hold many answers. Jared knew that God would see him through whatever those answers were.

And the telegrams in his pocket might contain information that could help, too.

They sat at a table with plates of fried chicken, mashed potatoes and gravy, green beans and biscuits. "We'll be full for the rest of the day."

Mary Lou said grace and they began to eat. "I wish the paper would go out before the trials. If we'd known, we could have put it out today. I'd like people to see the reward offer again before the judge makes his decision."

"I've received several replies to the telegrams I sent Thursday afternoon." He pulled the telegrams from his pocket and put them on the table between them. "I haven't had a chance to read them."

Mary Lou dropped her fork onto her plate and picked them up. "This is wonderful. The company where Mr. Finch worked before fired him because they thought he was stealing from them."

"We'd need more than a suspicion. We'll need proof for the judge."

"Listen to this." She held the second telegram. "Finch fired. Stole jewelry from wife. Spent two years in jail." She handed it to him.

"This is from the Houston area. I'm glad the sheriff recommended making inquiries further afield." He folded the telegram and put it in his pocket. "I'll show this one to Sheriff Collins."

Mary Lou read three more telegrams that were consistent but didn't bring absolute proof. The last one caused her to smile as tears filled her eyes. She passed it to him without comment.

Jared read it. "This is the one we needed. Now we know Finch was a pickpocket and tried to frame someone else before he was caught. We just have to convince the judge that this is what happened to Andrew."

"Oh, Jared, there's hope. Real hope." She blinked the tears away.

"I'm sorry I ever doubted your judgment." He put his hand over hers on the table.

She shrugged her shoulders. "You didn't know me or Andrew. It's difficult to assess someone's character until you know them." She slid her hand from beneath his and picked up her fork again. "Let's pray the judge sees the truth, too."

They finished their meal and returned to the office to print the paper. Operating the press with her today could be the last time they worked together.

What did Monday hold? He wanted time to stand still, so he'd never have to know.

* * *

Mary Lou inked the plate and Jared loaded the paper onto the press. "I'm wondering if a special edition would be in order for next week." As soon as she said the words, she realized she might have no say in the matter. Everything on her list had to be done by Monday or she might never get to do it.

"Let's make that decision on Monday." Jared pulled the lever to print the page. "How are you coming along with the things on your lists?"

She hung a paper to dry. "I thought I was making good progress. To be honest, Judge Sawyer arriving today caught me a bit off guard. Even though the sheriff warned us, I'd hoped for more time."

"At least we have some evidence to help Andrew."

"Yes. I wonder who they will try first."

"That's a good question. I'll see if the sheriff will tell me tomorrow. That could greatly affect Andrew."

Mary Lou had to know what he was thinking about their own situation coming before the judge on Monday. "What do you think will happen with us? And the paper?"

Jared cranked the plate under the press and pulled the lever again. "I think the judge will honor Grump's will." There was no gloating or grandiose tone in his statement. Just the truth as he saw it. Plain and simple.

There was nothing she could say. No way to defend her position to him. She still believed the paper rightly belonged to her.

Jared stopped working. "I have a question that has troubled me since I arrived."

"What?"

"Why didn't you contact me after Grump died?" He stood facing her, with the press between them. The machine they used to inform the community was the thing that held them together and kept them apart.

"I didn't think you cared." She felt it only fair to be as honest as he had been.

"You didn't know me."

"That's the point. I didn't know you. Neither did Mr. Ivy." She gave a hopeless shrug. "You never answered your grandfather's letters. I didn't think you wanted anything to do with him or his life. I never thought you'd want the *Record*."

"I had a right to know."

"He loved you, you know. He built this for you, but he gave it to me." She took a deep breath. It was time to bare her soul to him. As much as she'd grown to care for Jared, Mr. Ivy had wanted her to have the paper—even though no one else heard him tell her so, she knew it. And God knew it. "I can't just give it to you. It's all I have left of the man who taught me everything I know about journalism and life.

"About how people could let you down. And how you could let them down. He said he'd learned his lesson the hard way—when he lost his son, and ultimately his grandson. He didn't want me to do the same thing. I won't let him down."

She stretched her arms wide. "This was his dream. The way he'd hoped to win your favor. He gave himself to it without reservation. I won't let someone who didn't care enough about him to answer his letters take away the only thing he had—his voice."

Jared argued, "I will speak for him. It's my right as his grandson."

"Blood isn't the only thing that makes someone part of a family. No one ever protected me until he did. Even when I declined his offer to adopt me so I'd be a real member of his family, he never stopped protecting me."

"He wanted to adopt you?" Jared didn't sound surprised.

"He did, but I thought I was too old."

"Blood doesn't make you family, either. My mother didn't protect me like family should."

What? His mother, the woman he'd been with all his life, hadn't protected him. "What do you mean?"

"She didn't tell me that Grump wanted to be in my life."

"The letters were mailed to you."

"I never saw them. Not once. She burned them all when they came and never told me." The sadness in his eyes proved the truth of his words to her.

"Jared, I'm so sorry."

"She must have used the money he sent to take care of me and pay for my school, like you said, but I didn't know it. I thought it was her money."

"How did you find out about the letters?"

"When she was dying, she confessed. She told me about how desperate Grump was to see me and get to know me. How she'd kept me away from him to protect me. She blamed him for my father's death. It caused her to be bitter. I can see that now." He came around the press to stand in front of Mary Lou. "She's the reason I mistrusted women. My whole life was a series of deception and lies. Every time I asked about Grump, she avoided a direct answer. Sometimes she lied. But she was always unhappy after I asked. I eventually stopped asking."

It was a tragic tale of a child denied the love of a man who'd wanted to be in his life. But it didn't change the love Mr. Ivy'd had for her. "I loved him. And he loved me. I wasn't his kin, but he loved me. I was here."

"You've said yourself that he loved me in spite of me not being here."

"He did. But in the end, he had to give his legacy to someone he knew would care for it and protect it. He chose me."

Jared put a hand on her arm. "I know you don't understand, but I can't let it go. As much passion as you feel about the *Record*, I feel that way about fulfilling Grump's lifelong dream. The *Pine Haven Record* should always have an Ivy at the helm."

"I guess, in the end, it will be up to Judge Sawyer to decide." She backed away from his touch. "We've bared our hearts to one another without malice. It's a matter of seeing the story from two sides. Only, we are the story. And the paper will record our future when it happens. The only thing left to do is put it in God's hands and wait."

"You're right." He moved to the other side of the press and put another piece of paper in place.

The rhythm of the press was the only sound as they finished printing the paper. He offered to clean the

press, so she bid him good-night and went home to
gather her thoughts and to pray. To pray for Andrew.
For Judge Sawyer. For Jared. And for her broken heart.
Her instinct that they could not surmount their differences had been right.

She'd broken Mr. Ivy's steadfast rule. She'd forgotten to remain objective. Her heart would be safe if she
hadn't fallen in love with a man who embodied everything she admired and respected. But if he took the
paper from her, he would rob her of everything. She
wouldn't be safe—and it would be his fault.

Reverend Dismuke prayed the closing prayer and dismissed the service just after noon on Sunday. He had
announced to the congregation the judge's arrival and
that court would be held the next day. The sheriff's request for them to spread the word and come willing to
serve as jurors if called upon had the people buzzing
with conversation as they dispersed.

Jared sat alone near the back corner of the building.
Mary Lou lifted her hand in acknowledgment of his
presence when she exited the church.

He loved her. More than he ever thought he could
love anyone.

And he couldn't let her know. It would be unfair to
her. She would think he was trying to woo her to protect
his interest in the paper. After a ruling that gave him
ownership of the paper, any attempt to share his feelings
could be construed as pity. She would never stand for
that. If the judge ruled in her favor, she'd think he only
wanted to stay because he felt it was his right. There

was no solution to this problem. What would have happened if he'd never showed her or the sheriff Grump's will? He may have been able to develop a relationship with her that wouldn't have been built around the paper. It was too late for that now.

Doc Willis stopped at the end of the bench where Jared still sat. "You're looking poorly."

"Thanks, Doc." He rose and headed toward the door, alongside the doctor. "The cares of life will do that to a body."

"I heard the judge will be deciding which of you owns the paper tomorrow."

They stepped into the sunlight and Jared put his hat on. "Yep. Everything hangs in the balance for a lot of people tomorrow."

"God always has a way of working things out." The doctor clapped him on the shoulder.

"I know. Thanks for reminding me that He cares about the details. I've done a lot of praying since that day. I may not get my way on everything, but I'm comforted to know that God is in charge of the outcome."

"That's good to know. I'll see you in court tomorrow."

Jared walked toward home, not sure if it would be home tomorrow. There wasn't anything he could do to sway the outcome of the ownership of the *Record*, but he could try to help Andrew. And Mary Lou would want to be involved.

He picked up the pace and caught up to her in front of the hotel.

"Mary Lou, will you go with me to talk to the sheriff and judge about Andrew?"

"What good will it do?"

"I want to see if I can convince the judge to release Andrew without a trial. If we show him all we know about Elmer Finch today, he may decide that Andrew shouldn't be prosecuted."

A sparkle of hope returned to her eyes. "I guess it can't hurt."

They gathered all their information and Jared persuaded the sheriff to meet them in the hotel restaurant to talk to the judge.

The four of them were seated at a table and had placed their order for a meal before the judge asked what new evidence they had that they thought could help Andrew.

Jared placed the telegrams he'd received on the table. "We have several telegrams that, on their own, don't show guilt. Finch has been fired more than once for suspicion of theft."

Judge Sawyer shook his head. "Suspicion won't change facts. I will consider evidence, not suspicion."

Mary Lou pulled a telegram from the middle of the stack and placed it on top of the others. "This telegram is from the Houston area. It shows a history of Finch serving time in jail for theft. He was fired and prosecuted."

The judge tapped the telegram with his finger. "That's the kind of proof that holds up in my court."

The sheriff said, "I think with this and the items we found in Finch's possession, plus the cameo and porcelain dish we know came from this very hotel, there's enough to convict him. The problem is that the only expensive thing we found was the cameo. Most of these items are small and of limited value."

Judge Sawyer clarified his perspective. "The total value is what I'll be looking at. One or two items is petty, but it seems this man has a trunk filled with things and is stealing every time he gets off the train. That makes it a bigger matter."

Jared leaned forward in his chair. "Judge, the thing we want you to consider is the accusation made by Elmer Finch that Andrew sold him these items. We don't believe that. Andrew is a hardworking young man. He holds down three jobs and was meeting with a local foreman about a ranching job when the news began to spread that he might be a thief."

The judge's eyes narrowed. "I understand Sheriff Collins found him in possession of an item that was stolen from the general store."

"Yes, but Andrew says he didn't take it."

"Most folks who go to jail say they didn't do the crime that put them there." The judge wasn't making it easy for him to plead Andrew's case.

Mary Lou sat on the edge of her chair. "Sir, the thefts didn't start until the day Mr. Finch came to Pine Haven. Andrew Nobleson has been under my oversight for two years. I've never had a moment of trouble from him. Nor has anyone else in town."

Sheriff Collins agreed. "He's never been in trouble before. And for an orphan that's saying a lot. Of course, the people of Pine Haven have taken care of him. Given him odd jobs before he was old enough to work steady like he does now."

Mary Lou added, "There's a young boy in town who saw Mr. Finch coming out of the general store at the time the mirror was stolen. We can take you there after we eat and show you where the boy saw him."

"I'll walk by there, but I won't promise it will have a bearing on the case."

Jared pulled the last telegram from the stack and showed it to the judge. "This says Finch was a pickpocket who tried to blame someone else when he thought he would be caught."

The judge read the missive and returned it to the stack. "I'll think on it."

Jared nodded at Mary Lou. They'd done all they could. Now it was in the hands of God.

Naomi brought their food with the help of Josephine, the girl who worked as a maid and waitress at the hotel.

After they were all served, the judge picked up his fork and knife. "This ham looks delicious." He looked up at Jared. "I will tell you both that I'm surprised you didn't come here to try and sway my ruling for the two of you tomorrow. I will keep your compassion for another over yourselves in mind when I'm deciding."

Chapter Sixteen

Mary Lou pinned her watch onto the green vest she wore. She stood before the mirror and fingered the delicate piece, remembering how happy she'd been on the day Mr. Ivy had given it to her. She'd questioned him about the inscription, but he'd only said she'd understand it in time. She wore it every day to remind her of his love. The love of a father who cared for a child he'd found and taken in and protected. She missed him today. More than any day since he'd passed.

Lord, help me to accept Your will for my life today. No matter what happens, help me to honor You. And help me to remember that the love Mr. Ivy showed me was a love he learned from You.

She went to the office like any Monday morning, only today could be the last day she'd go there.

Jared sat at the desk, writing. After all these weeks she'd come to expect him to be there. Today she tried to memorize the sight of him, pen in hand, jotting notes and making lists. She'd learned he wouldn't respond, but couldn't resist greeting him. "Good morning, Jared."

To her surprise he put the pen down and smiled up at her. "Hello, Mary Lou. I was waiting for you. I've got the newspapers stacked and ready to go." They had agreed the night before that it would be best to distribute the papers before they went to court.

"I'm ready." She pulled on the hem of her vest and picked up her pencil and notebook. "We've got time to go together if you'd like."

He stood and gathered a stack of papers. "I'd like that very much." Was he thinking about this being the last day they would be working together, too?

In less than an hour, they'd finished their task. People were milling around town in larger than normal numbers. It seemed everyone would be in court. Mary Lou and Jared stopped by the sheriff's office to see Andrew.

The sheriff had released the two saloon fighters on Sunday morning. Andrew was staring through the back window of the cell when they entered.

Two men stood at the desk talking with the sheriff. Mary Lou recognized them both from previous sessions of court. They traveled into town to serve as lawyers whenever the judge showed up. One acted as prosecutor and the other as a defender. Pine Haven was a growing town, but the citizens were a law-abiding lot. No lawyer could earn a living there by the practice of law alone.

"Andrew." Mary Lou approached the cell. "How are you doing?"

He kept his back to her. "I'm powerful nervous, Miss Ellison."

Jared said, "I can understand that."

"You've got good cause to be scared." Elmer Finch spewed the words from his bunk. "I'm going make sure they know you sold me all those things. I had no idea you were stealing from the people of this fine community."

Sheriff Collins took the cell keys from the wall as the front door opened. "Save it for the judge, Finch. No one in here believes you."

Judge Sawyer entered. "Save what for me?"

The lawyers and the sheriff laughed.

Mr. Finch persisted. "Judge, I was just telling these folks how upset I am to be accused of stealing. This young man sold me those things. I had no way of knowing he was a thief."

The judge held up a hand to stop him. "There'll be time enough for your arguments once we choose a jury." He looked around at everyone. "Are we ready to begin?"

"Yes, sir." The sheriff opened each cell in turn. "I was just about to walk these men to the church."

Mary Lou gave Andrew's hand a squeeze when he walked by her.

Lord, please help him. He doesn't deserve to have his future stolen from him. He's worked so hard. Please bring justice today.

On the street people moved like a herd of lazy cattle in the direction of the church. The shop owners stood in their doorways to watch the processional of prisoners and men representing the law. Children had been dismissed from school for the day so the church could be used for the trials. They ran along the sidewalks, jumping up and down in an effort to see over the heads and shoulders of the adults.

Mary Lou was saddened to see the spectacle, but she'd have been one of the gawkers if Andrew weren't at risk.

Jared walked beside her. As if sensing her pain, he slid his hand under her elbow. The comfort of his support was bittersweet. She needed it, but after today she would no longer have access to it.

"Mr. Ivy!" Reilly Ledford stood on a porch rail, waving and shouting. "That's the man I saw at the general store!" He pointed to Elmer Finch. "See his funny hat!"

Milly Ledford pulled her son by the arm. "Shush, Reilly!"

"But it's him, Momma!" The noise of the crowd covered anything else Reilly may have said.

People jostled along Main Street for the rest of their journey. It was only a matter of minutes, but to Mary Lou it seemed like hours. She knew she was walking into her unknown future.

The church was crowded. Someone had opened the windows to the fresh, fall air. Men stood around the walls of the room while the women were seated on the benches. The first two benches on one side were reserved for the jury.

Sheriff Collins led Andrew and Elmer Finch to the first bench on the opposite side. "Quieten down, everybody." The conversations around the room died down to a whisper.

Judge Sawyer took a seat behind the table that served as the teacher's desk. He thumped his gavel on the table twice. "That'll be enough talking, folks. We've got a lot of work to do today." A ripple of chuckles went through the room. Judge Sawyer was new to their area, and no one knew what to expect from him. He was much more relaxed than the last judge who'd required complete silence before he entered the room and lost all the respect of the people by demanding it.

Mary Lou sat on the end of the bench behind Andrew, and Jared stood against the wall beside her. She glanced up at him and he winked. He winked. She put her hand over her mouth to keep from laughing. In all the tension of this day, he'd known exactly what she needed.

The judge addressed the crowd. "Good morning to you all. I'm Judge Solomon Sawyer. It's my first time to Pine Haven, so we'll have to get to know one another. I don't know what you're accustomed to here, but this is how we're gonna do things.

"We're gonna offer these gentlemen a chance to end these cases before we put a jury together. If we can't make that happen, then some of you will be needed to form that jury. I like to make things run as smooth as possible. It'll bode well for all of us if we can do that today."

Liza Croft spoke out from the other end of the bench where Mary Lou sat. "Your Grace." She waved a hand and sat tall in her seat. "May I ask a question?"

"I think you just did, ma'am," he answered.

Mrs. Croft did not seem to appreciate the laughter that erupted in the room. She stood and clasped her hands together at her waist. "I'd like to know if we'll be able to have the things that were stolen returned to us today. You see, I run the general store." Mr. Croft cleared his throat and she added, "My husband and I run the store, and this thievery has cost us quite a bit of money."

"Take your seat, ma'am. I promise you'll get your stuff back. Seems from the list the sheriff gave me that most of your stuff didn't sell anyway."

The laughter was uncontainable now.

Liza Croft sat down in a huff. "Well, I never!"

The judge had to use his gavel to capture everyone's attention. "If you folks don't mind, we need to move along. Sheriff, please read the charges against these men."

Sheriff Collins stood. "Andrew Nobleson is charged with the theft of a small mirror with a value of less than one dollar. He's been in the jail since Mrs. Croft here sent for me and I found the mirror in Andrew's pocket."

"How long has that been?"

"Ten days."

Judge Sawyer looked at Andrew and motioned for him to stand. "I'd say that's quite a long time for a man your age to be in a cell."

Andrew kept his hands at his sides and met the judge's look with a steady eye. "Yes, sir. It is."

"Tell me what happened."

"I went to the general store and asked Mrs. Croft if I could see a mirror she had on the shelf behind the display case." He pointed to Mrs. Croft. "She let me hold it, but she stood close by the whole time." He pointed to Mary Lou. "Miss Ellison came in while I was there. She saw me with the mirror."

The judge held up a hand. "You're not helping yourself, Mr. Nobleson."

"But it's the truth. I wanted to buy the mirror for Miss Ellison. She's been mighty good to me since my ma died." Nods of agreement went through the room. "You see, I was hoping to get a job on the Double Star Ranch. A good job so I could have a real bunk and not sleep in the livery." He turned to Jim Robbins. "I do appreciate you letting me stay there for the last two years and work for my keep. But I want a real bed and a man's job."

Mrs. Croft's hand shot into the air. "I object!" She was on her feet again. "Is this a court of law, or are you going to listen to this tale of woe from a boy who admits he had the mirror—my mirror—in his hands, with witnesses to prove it?"

The gavel hit the desk again. "Sit down, Mrs. Croft."

Mary Lou could hear laughter coming from the churchyard now. People had gathered close to the open windows to listen to the new judge.

Mrs. Croft looked around the room and sank onto the bench. Mr. Croft sent her a warning glare from his place against the wall.

Judge Sawyer leaned forward and rested his hands on the desk. "This is my court. In it, I seek the truth. If you don't care for the way I do it, you may leave. But I will get to the truth." He pointed at Andrew. "As for this young man, given the limited value of the mirror and the time he's already been in the jail, I'm going to let him go. Ten days is long enough to pay for a trinket."

Mrs. Croft gasped.

"As for you, ma'am. I won't warn you again to be quiet. It seems that's not something you do well, but you'll do it in here or you'll be leaving."

The chuckles settled to quiet. Judge Solomon Sawyer might be relaxed, but he was also serious.

Mary Lou slumped forward in relief that Andrew would be free, and Jared dropped his hand onto her shoulder. But Andrew still had the stigma of theft hanging over him.

"Now, Andrew Nobleson, I want you tell me the rest of your story."

"You're letting me go?"

"I am, but I need to hear what happened. Because if I just let you go, you'll walk out of here with folks wondering if you really stole that mirror. If you did, you'll deserve all the hardship that would bring to you. But if you didn't, we need to know that so we don't let a good man carry a bad reputation out of here."

Mary Lou sat straight again and put her hand over Jared's. They'd worked so hard for the last two weeks to clear Andrew's name. Today, in front of all of Pine Haven, he was getting a chance to prove his innocence.

"Well, I didn't have enough money to buy the mirror that day, so I put it on the counter and left. It was time for me to be at my job at the Pine Haven Hotel. The general store was full of passengers from the train. I guess one of them picked it up."

"Now, now, don't be guessing at anything," Judge

Sawyer admonished him. "That's probably what started this whole mess in the first place. Someone guessed at an answer and got it wrong."

"Yes, sir." Andrew swallowed big. "I left the store and went to the hotel. I'm not sure what happened or how, but a little while later the sheriff came to talk to me." Sheriff Collins nodded when the judge looked to him for confirmation. "He asked me if I'd been to the general store. Said something was missing and Mrs. Croft said I was the one who had it last."

A rumble of murmuring went through the room and carried into the yard beyond the open windows. The judge cleared his throat and brought the room to silence. "Go on."

"I told him I didn't take anything from the store. He said he knew I didn't, but he had to search me to prove it to Mrs. Croft. I told him to go ahead, he wouldn't find nothing." Mary Lou cringed. Andrew was so nervous he'd reverted to speaking as he had before he'd come to work for the paper. She hated the strain he was under.

Andrew dropped his head. "I don't know how that mirror got in my pocket. It was just there. It was so small, I didn't even feel it." His voice faded to silence on the words.

"You told the sheriff to search you?" The judge sat back in his chair.

"I didn't have nothing to hide. I didn't steal it, sir. You've got to believe me."

Judge Sawyer tapped a finger on the desk. "Where is the mirror? I'd like to see how big it is."

Sheriff Collins pulled the mirror from the trunk of

evidence under the window near the front of the room. Reilly Ledford hung on to the windowsill from the outside and peered into the trunk. When the sheriff pulled out the mirror, Reilly exclaimed, "Hey! I seen that before! But it weren't Andrew holdin' it. It was that fella there with the funny hat." The boy pointed to Mr. Finch.

Conversations broke out in hushed tones throughout the crowd.

Judge Sawyer inclined his head to one side. "Who are you?"

Reilly stood tall. He must have been standing on the woodpile to be so tall in the window. "I'm Reilly Ledford. I'm the one who seen that man coming out of the general store the day Andrew got took off to jail." The pride he exuded while he spoke puffed his little chest out.

The judge crooked his pointer finger at Reilly. "Come inside, son."

"Yes, sir." Reilly heaved himself up on his hands and swung his feet over the sill. He landed with a thud beside the trunk and spun to face the judge.

Mary Lou smiled at his exuberance. He was clearly enjoying being in the spotlight. Probably because he had no man at home to show him attention.

A grin creased the judge's face. "Where's your pa, son?"

Reilly dropped his head. "In heaven, sir."

"I'm right sorry about that, Reilly Ledford. What about your ma?"

"I'm here, Judge Sawyer." Everyone turned to see a breathless Milly Ledford come in through the open doors at the end of the aisle. "I'm so sorry Reilly interrupted your court. When I came onto the churchyard, I saw him slipping in the window. I was working and didn't see him leave the house." She sent a stern look in her son's direction. "I promise it will never happen again." She took Reilly by the hand to leave.

"Just a moment, ma'am."

Reilly looked more afraid of facing his mother than the judge. Mary Lou pulled her lips in and clenched them together to keep from laughing. The poor boy was in for a terrible scolding when he got home.

The judge asked, "Is your son one to lie?"

Mrs. Ledford stood straight and held her son's hand. "No, sir. He knows the Lord doesn't tolerate lying."

To Reilly he said, "How did you know it was this exact mirror that this fellow had?" He pointed to Elmer Finch.

A blush crept up Reilly's neck and turned his face pink. "'Cause I seen it in the store. I wanted to buy it for Ma's birthday, but Mrs. Croft said it cost too much money." He leaned in close to the judge. "It was s'posed to be a secret." He put a hand up beside his mouth in an effort to keep his mother from hearing him. "Pink is her favorite color."

This was like no courtroom Mary Lou had ever attended. She smiled at Reilly's boyish charm. The respect she held for Judge Sawyer would make it easy for her to write an article about the events of the day when this was over.

She dropped her hand from Jared's and shifted in her seat.

He released her and tilted his head to see her face. She wouldn't meet his gaze.

Andrew was going home. Reilly just ensured the truth would be known. Mr. Finch would likely go to jail. And at the end of the day, Mary Lou would have no home, nowhere to tell the stories that burned in her to be written, no way to help the people of Pine Haven who had been so good to her.

The judge had Reilly explain how and when he saw the mirror in detail.

"So, Reilly, the last time you saw the mirror, Mr. Finch had it?"

"Yes, sir. And he was walking real close behind Andrew. Andrew was on his way to the hotel. He always goes there when the train comes to town."

"Thank you very much for coming to court today, Reilly Ledford. But next time, you make sure and talk to your ma first."

Reilly nodded his head. Milly Ledford still held his hand. Mary Lou doubted the boy would be allowed out of her sight for some time.

"You may go, Mrs. Ledford." The judge looked at Andrew. "I think we have a clearer picture of what happened that day now, Mr. Nobleson."

To Mr. Finch he said, "I would imagine that a man who is adept at stealing is a man who can reach into someone's pocket and take their things without the person even knowing someone had stolen from them. Especially on a crowded sidewalk with passengers milling around town while the train is in the station for a short stop." He leaned back in his chair again, propped his elbows on the arms and steepled his fingers. "I'd say someone with that skill could slip something into someone's pocket with them none the wiser."

A disgruntled murmur ran among those gathered as they agreed with the judge.

Jared shifted his weight from one foot to the other. Mary Lou wanted to see the end of this matter. But she was loath to move forward to the judge's decision between her and Jared. Everything she'd seen today spoke of his wisdom and fairness. How would he decide?

"Judge Sawyer." The lawyer who would defend Mr. Finch asked to be recognized.

"Wait just a minute, counselor. I'd like to make an offer to Mr. Finch." To the newsagent he said, "You have a choice here. You may move forward to trial and try to convince this room of people, among whom are your potential jurors, of your innocence and Mr. Nobleson's guilt. Or—and I would strongly suggest you consider this option—you may confess to any crimes you have committed and throw yourself on the mercy of this court."

The train whistle blew in the distance.

The judge continued. "These folks may not take kindly to you accusing an orphan they've all banded together to raise. You might get more mercy from me than you would from these jurors. Might."

Mr. Finch resisted. "Why would I—" The judge motioned for him to stand while he was speaking. Mr. Finch grumbled as he stood. "Why would I confess to something I didn't do?"

Henry Hall, the telegraph operator, came in the door.

He took a telegram to the judge and left without saying anything.

The judge silently read the message and then folded it in half. "Mr. Finch, this telegram is from a sheriff near Houston. It is a reply to a query I sent asking for details about you. I needed to confirm some things I'd been told about you for myself. I want you to know that I will use the information it contains should you insist on a trial and a jury finds you guilty."

Mr. Finch's face tightened. He looked from the judge to the sheriff and around at the people in the room. From Mary Lou's perspective he did not encounter one friendly face.

The whistle blew again and the judge added, "If you decide promptly, I may be able to make the train this morning. That would most likely put me in an agreeable mood."

"Judge, that's not fair."

"Do not push me by the margin of fair. I am a fair and just man, who has full authority to call a jury and spend the next several hours listening to the people of this town tell me where and when you have been seen. And there are still the matters in Gran Colina to be settled."

The lawyer leaned in and spoke quietly to Mr. Finch. He shook his head at the first words but nodded at the second communication.

"Judge, I'd like to take the option of throwing myself on the mercy of the court."

"You will have to confess to your crimes and testify to the innocence of Mr. Nobleson."

"The kid didn't have anything to do with it. I slipped

the mirror in his pocket when I saw those two following me." Mr. Finch pointed at Jared and Mary Lou.

The judge looked at them. "Were you following him?"

Jared answered. "We were. He'd been in town every time something went missing. We knew Andrew was innocent."

The judge passed a sentence on Mr. Finch of just a bit under the maximum allowed. It would be a long time before he was out of jail. When the thief protested, the judge reminded him that the leniency he'd received was because he'd cleared Andrew's name and then warned that protesting could change the judge's mind. In the end, Mr. Finch went quietly with the sheriff back to jail.

"Now if the rest of you fine folks would make your way out of the church, I need to settle a private matter between Mr. Ivy and Miss Ellison." Judge Sawyer rapped the gavel on the desk and the room cleared in a matter of minutes. The judge asked the lawyers to have the train wait for him, as he would only be a matter of minutes.

The decision Mary Lou had been dreading was about to be made.

The judge took his watch from his vest pocket. "Tell me what this is about, Mr. Ivy."

Jared hated this. If his mother hadn't hidden Grump's letters, he'd have been here years ago. He could have been Mary Lou's friend—maybe more.

He faced the judge. He couldn't bear to watch Mary Lou's face while he told his side of the story.

"My father and his father built the *Pine Haven Record* as a family legacy when I was four years old. My father died in an accident during the construction of the building. My mother blamed my grandfather for his death and took me back to her home in Maryland, where we lived until she died not long before I came here."

"Is this your knowledge of the events, as well, Miss Ellison?"

Jared turned to see her nod one time.

"What happened next, Mr. Ivy?"

"My mother was very ill at the end. She confessed on her deathbed that my grandfather had written letters to me all of my life. She'd burned them so I would never find them. She told me she'd kept the will he sent leaving the newspaper to me in the event of his death." With a hand, he gestured toward Mary Lou. "Miss Ellison told me that Grump even sent money for my schooling and care."

"Grump?"

Jared smiled at the memory. "To a small boy he had a grumpy voice. It was my name for him."

"Go on."

"When my mother passed, I sold everything except my saddle and came here to connect with my grandfather, but he died two months before I arrived." Jared told the judge about the day he'd arrived and found Mary Lou running the newspaper. He ended with the sheriff's decision to make them work together.

"I'd like to see the will." Jared gave the will to the judge and sat down.

Judge Sawyer put it on the desk and addressed Mary Lou. "What is your claim to the business and property?"

Mary Lou rose and told her story of how Grump took her in and how they bonded like family and loved one another. "Everyone in town knows how special he was to me, and I to him."

"I understand that, Miss Ellison, but did he leave a will establishing you as his heir?" He pointed to the one Jared had given as evidence. "This will is very old, but it is signed by Jacob Ivy and valid unless he made a change later in life to void this."

"All I have is my word that he wanted me to run the *Pine Haven Record* and the deed the land agent made out in my name after Mr. Ivy passed." She looked the judge in the eye and handed him her deed. "Jacob Ivy loved me. I was his family. The fact that Mr. Ivy's mother kept him away doesn't change that. I'm sorry he missed out on knowing his grandfather. He was a fine man. He took me in when I had no one."

"Like you care for Andrew Nobleson?"

She smiled, and Jared's heart started to melt. "Yes, sir. I think it's important to share the kindness he instilled in me with others."

"So that's why you got on a train and went to Gran Colina? To help someone in need?"

She only nodded. Jared felt like a traitor.

"What have you to say about this, Mr. Ivy?"

He stood beside Mary Lou. "I know Miss Ellison is a noble and worthy person. She's a fine journalist and publisher. My grandfather must have loved her dearly because I see her love for him in every aspect of her work. She is a credit to the *Pine Haven Record*, and I'm grateful for all she's done to guard and protect it."

Mary Lou stood there with her hands clasped in front of her skirt, her face forward and no words.

"That will proves my grandfather wanted me to have the *Record*. He signed it and sent it to my mother."

"Why do you have this and nothing else?"

He shook his head. "I have no idea why she kept this and burned everything else. I only know it says that I'm the rightful heir." He turned to Mary Lou. "I'm sorry, Mary Lou. I know how important the paper is to you. And how much you loved Grump. And what a fine person you are. You risked your safety for Andrew and taught me how to run the paper."

She looked up at him then. "But you're still going to take it from me." Her voice was soft and calm. Just like her heart.

"I have to fulfill Grump's wishes. I'm doing this for him. For the legacy he built.

"Judge Sawyer, I don't want to do anything to hurt Miss Ellison, but I have to honor my family's name. I'm the last Ivy in this line. If I don't keep the newspaper, there will be nothing left of my history. I can't let it go."

The train whistle blew a warning and the judge looked at his watch again. "I can see that neither of you wants to hurt the other." He stood to gather his papers and gavel and put them in his valise. "You are both good people. I saw it in the things you said to me during our meal at the hotel and again in what Andrew Nobleson told me today."

Jared stood shoulder to shoulder with Mary Lou and

knew this was the last moment that the two of them would be tied together, bound by the paper they both loved and needed. He reached for her hand and she opened her palm to his. They waited together for the judge's decree.

"As much as it pains me to separate two people who are bound together in so many ways, I have to obey the law. It's not within my power to force either of you to forfeit your interest in order to avoid an official ruling. But my responsibility is to make this difficult decision."

He looked at them and held the will in one hand and his valise in the other. "I declare this will to be valid and rule that the ownership of the *Pine Haven Record* and all properties, furnishings and equipment associated with the business and private residence are the property of Jared Ivy, grandson of Jacob Ivy." He handed the paper to Jared. "Effective immediately."

The judge stepped around the desk and shook Jared's hand. "My advice to you is to perpetuate the legacy of your grandfather—not just his business."

"I'll try, sir."

To Mary Lou he said, "I'm so sorry, Miss Ellison. You are a testament to the goodness of Mr. Ivy. I know the Good Lord will look after you. He always takes care of those who trust Him."

And with those words, Judge Solomon Sawyer walked out the door of the church and left Jared and Mary Lou standing in the rubble of their lives.

Chapter Seventeen

Mary Lou walked into the office and stood in the middle of the room staring. What would she do?

The door opened and closed quietly. She knew it was Jared.

"Will you stay?"

She didn't turn around. "I can't."

"Grump would want me to ask you to stay."

"You don't have to take care of me like your grandfather did, Jared." She put her reticule on the desk. "I'm all grown up now. I know about real life and its challenges." It took all of her effort to speak. The pain in her heart left her weak and sad. Sadder than she'd ever imagined.

Losing the paper was like losing Mr. Ivy all over again. Everywhere she looked there was a memory. She could almost hear the echoes of the laughter they'd shared and the fun they'd had working together.

"Please stay, Mary Lou." There was sadness in his voice, too. Probably because he knew she had nowhere to go. But she couldn't stay because he felt obligated to care for her. That's how she'd ended up with her uncle. Her aunt had wanted her, but when she'd died her uncle had inherited the responsibility for Mary Lou.

She'd been passed down before. She wouldn't be passed along like that again.

Mary Lou turned around and looked at him. "Don't be sad. This should be a happy time for you. You've just inherited your family's legacy." She took his hand in hers. "Thank you for asking. I'm very grateful. You'll never know how much, but I can't stay." She released his hand.

Jared took a step back. "I'm glad you were right about Andrew. Will you do something for me? And for Andrew?"

"Anything." She meant it. The two of them were the most important people in her life. And she was losing them both today. Andrew would be going to work on the Double Star Ranch and she and Jared would be parting ways within the hour.

"Write the story about the thefts."

"Oh, you don't need me to do that. You've gotten so much better. And people respond to you so well. You'll have no trouble with that article or any other in the future. I think it's in your blood."

"I want you to do it. You were here when Andrew came to the paper. It's only fitting for you to write his final chapter here. Andrew is free because of you." He was serious.

"Okay. I'll do that."

The front door banged open and Andrew burst into

the room. "Miss Ellison, you saved me!" He darted around the desk and wrapped her in a hug. "I'll never forget what you've done for me. Never." He lifted her off her feet.

Mary Lou laughed and pushed against Andrew's shoulders. "You need to put me down now."

He dropped her to her feet but held her arms until she found her balance. "You had faith in me when no one else did."

"Ahem…" Jared grunted behind him.

Andrew laughed and nodded his head in Jared's direction. "Well, he had faith in me after you convinced him to."

They all laughed then. Mary Lou put a finger on his chest. "I want to make sure you get that job now."

Andrew grinned. "You don't have to worry about that, either. Mr. Barlow was in the church today. He came by the livery and told me he was going to speak to Señor Morales this afternoon. He wants me to come out to the ranch to start work at first light tomorrow."

Jared clapped Andrew on the back. "Well done, young man."

"Thank you, Mr. Ivy."

"If you need anything, you let me know. I worked on a ranch for several years before I came to Pine Haven. I'll be glad to help any way I can."

The joy of the moment seeped into the brokenness of Mary Lou's heart. "Look at the two of you. I'm so grateful that God has made friends of two men who could so easily have become enemies."

"We owe that to you, Mary Lou." Jared's words were

kind and tender. "You taught me to look deeper than the surface. You were right about Andrew. And so much more."

"Then you owe your gratitude to your grandfather. He taught me that."

Andrew hugged Mary Lou again. "I have to go talk to Mr. Warren. I'm going to work for him this afternoon, but I won't be back after that." He headed for the door and shook Jared's hand. "Thank you for the offer of help. I'll let you know if I need it." He looked over his shoulder at Mary Lou. "You take good care of her now."

Jared smiled at Mary Lou. "I think she'll be all right. She's a strong lady."

"It won't hurt for her to have someone looking after her like she looked after me." He opened the door. "I think Mr. Ivy would have liked for you to take care of her." Andrew waved and closed the door behind him. The happy tune he whistled faded as he walked toward the hotel.

Jared watched Andrew through the front window. "That's one exuberant young man."

"Yes." Mary Lou came to stand beside him. "Your grandfather loved him. He'd be very proud of him today. Andrew didn't take as long as some people do to find his way in life."

"That's true of your relationship with Grump, too. I couldn't see it at first. Please forgive me."

"There's nothing to forgive. You couldn't know what was going on here with Mr. Ivy. Your mother didn't give you that choice."

"She blamed Grump for Pa's death. That's why she didn't want to stay here. She became a bitter woman."

"He thought you blamed him for your father's death."

Jared shook his head. "No. As a rancher you see the cycle of life and death every day. As a boy I may have wondered what happened, but as a man, I know it was no one's fault. My mother should have known that, too. Then maybe she wouldn't have kept me away from Grump."

"You need to forgive your mother. It's the only way to move forward with your life. Hurt and anger, even bitterness, will keep you trapped in the past. Bitterness is a root that chokes the life out of your heart."

"She kept me away from here. From Grump. I might even have gotten to know you without the strife of the inheritance hindering our friendship if she'd been open with me."

"Forgive her and remember the good things. There had to be good things." She watched his face as his mind searched for and found things that made him smile. "No one should only be remembered for the bad they've done."

She sat at the desk. "I'll write the article now, if you don't mind. Then I'll get started clearing out my things."

"There's no rush."

"Just the same, it has to be done." She pulled her pencil from its place over her ear and opened her notes.

Even with her head bowed over the desk, she could see his restlessness as he moved around the office doing one thing and then another.

Unable to focus on the article without her mind wandering to her uncertain future, Mary Lou took a full hour to complete the story. She slid it under the magnifying glass on the desk.

"I've finished." The finality of the words hit her. She was done. Finished. What was next?

Jared came downstairs after lunch to find Mary Lou removing her personal belongings from the desk. Her movements were deliberate and steady. Unlike his heart that quivered in his chest at the thought of her leaving. But there was nothing he could do. He'd known she wouldn't stay, but he'd offered anyway. He couldn't help himself.

"You don't have to do that now." He sat on the front corner of the desk while she sat behind it with the drawers open and papers askew.

"I do." She put more papers on the desktop. "For me. I have to prepare for the next stage of my life." She stopped for a moment. "Whatever that may be."

He caught sight of her lists among the things she stacked. "Did you finish the things on your lists?"

"Most of them."

He pulled them free of the other papers. "You accomplished everything on this one." He held up the list about getting Andrew released and writing the Christmas articles.

"I don't have to finish the other things."

She reached for the paper but he read aloud, "'Find somewhere to live in case the judge gives Jared the paper. Search for a new job. Save money for the time be-

tween jobs. Deep clean the house before moving out.'"
The more he read, the more he hated this day.

"You're embarrassing me." She sat in the chair,
watching him read her deepest fears. The ones he'd
brought into reality.

"You have nothing to be embarrassed about. I'm the
one who put you in this position."

Mary Lou shook her head. "What else could you
do?"

He didn't know what he could have done differently,
but he wanted her to know he'd tried to find a way to
keep from hurting her. He went to the composing table
and got his journal. He put it in her hand.

"Open that to any page and read. I've read your deepest concerns. You should read mine."

"I don't want to." She pushed the book back at him.

"I'll read them to you."

"You don't have to."

"'Find a way to make Mary Lou smile. Practice spelling. Ask Tucker Barlow about hiring Andrew even if
he isn't cleared. Find a way to kiss Mary Lou again.'"

"Stop, Jared. We can't go back there. I told you it
would tear us both apart." She pulled a key from her
reticule and opened the locked drawer on the left side
of the desk. Another stack of papers from the drawer
joined the ones teetering on the desk next to a rolled
parchment tied with string.

"Why do you still have that?" He toyed with the
string that held her copy of the deed to the *Record*.

Mary Lou sat back in the chair. There it was again—
the fresh sadness of loss. "It's not valid anymore, but

Judge Sawyer left it on the desk. I want to keep it as a memento of what can be achieved by hard work." She pulled several of her notebooks from the drawer and held them in her lap, seemingly trapped in the memories they held.

"Can I help you?" He stood. Watching her felt so awkward, not helping seemed unkind, and offering to help seemed heartless. There was no good answer.

"No, thank you. I'll have it all out of your way in a few minutes." She swooped her hands across the desk to rake the piles of paper into some sort of order. One handful at a time, she added them to a small crate by the desk. She reached out again and the deed rolled onto the floor and under the desk.

"Let me get it." Before he had time to bend, she was on her knees under the desk. She grabbed the deed and banged her head on her way out from under the desk. "Ouch!"

Jared knelt beside her to see if she was injured. "Let me see."

"You don't have to help me." She sat on the floor, bent over under the desk and holding the crown of her head.

"Please, Mary Lou—" He tried again but she cut him off.

"What is this?"

He twisted to see what she was pointing at under the top of the desk. "It looks like a drawer." He leaned out to look at the drawer side of the desk. "There is no front for this compartment."

She ran her hands along the edges of the small box-like shape. On the third side she stopped and reversed direction. "I think I found a keyhole."

"Let me see."

She laughed. "Really? There's not enough room for me under here, and you're already pushing in too close."

He didn't want to, but he backed away. "Do you have a key for that?"

"I didn't know this existed." She fumbled with the key that opened the drawer on the front of the desk. "This one doesn't work."

"Let me try." He held out his hand.

"I'll let you look at the key, but I promise you it doesn't work." She showed him the key in her open palm.

"Try the other end." It was intricate and much smaller than the opposite end.

"Why?"

"Just try it. Trust me."

It took a bit of maneuvering, but she got the key into the lock. "You were right." She tugged on the box and it dropped into her hands. She passed it out to him.

He left her under the desk and sat in the chair to explore the contents of the secret compartment. "There are several things in here. Photos of my parents. And Grump." He became absorbed in the treasures she'd found until she came out from under the desk on her knees.

He offered his hand to help her up but she refused. "I'm fine." She pivoted to use the desk to pull up to her feet, and then he saw it. She was trying to tuck something into the pocket of her skirt.

"What is that?"

"It's nothing." She faced him and held something behind her back.

"What did you tell me about always being honest?"

"This is something, but it's mine. It was wedged between the box and the desk. It's private, and I don't wish to share it."

He pointed at his journal where it lay across her lists. "We've already shared our private thoughts."

"This is different." She went to step around him and her skirt snagged on the crate that held her papers, tripping her.

Jared caught her in his arms and the paper she held fell to the floor. He made sure she was steady on her feet and bent to pick up the document. As if drawn by a force he couldn't resist, his eyes fell on the words at the top of the page.

Last Will and Testament.

He looked up at her.

"Don't read it. It doesn't matter."

He unfolded the paper to see his grandfather's name and last wishes. The wording of the document was much like the will he'd given to Judge Sawyer. The signature was the same. He was certain of it. And according to the date, it was only three years old.

"Mary Lou, Grump gave the paper to you." A weight like none he'd ever known lifted from him. He took a deep breath. The first one since the judge had ruled in his favor.

"It doesn't matter. Mr. Ivy wanted you to have it. I

was only a second choice to a man who had no one else."
She shrugged one shoulder. "He'd rather have had you."

"There's a condition on your inheriting. 'Mary Lou
Ellison as sole heir to all my earthly possessions, including the *Pine Haven Record*, conditioned upon the
inclusion of my grandson, Jared Benjamin Ivy, as joint
heir should he ever return to Pine Haven.'"

Jared placed the will on the desk and stepped close
to her. He put his hands on her elbows and grazed the
outside of her arms with his palms coming to rest on
her shoulders. "I'm glad he had you. You are sunshine
and joy. Spunky and fun. A man with you in his life
will always be a happy man. No sorrow can live in
your presence."

Her breath caught in her throat and he took a step
nearer to her. "Don't you see what this means, Mary
Lou?" He moved his fingertips up the curve of her neck
to her cheeks. "Grump wanted us both to have the *Record*." He laughed. A warm laugh that came from his
heart. "He knew we needed to be together. By leaving his legacy to both of us, he bound us to each other
with his love." Jared raised his eyebrows. "He knew
the two people he loved most in the world were meant
to be together."

Her words were barely more than a whisper and her
eyes glistened in the afternoon light. "How could he
know that?"

"Maybe he thought that as much as he loved you, I
would love you, too. He was right. I do love you, Mary
Lou."

"You do? I don't know how he could have known I

would love you—but I do." She reinforced her words with a nod and her eyes grew wide.

Jared smiled. "Doc Willis reminded me that God is in the details." He leaned closer still. "I'm very glad He is."

He met her lips with his and she wrapped her hands around his shoulders.

The kiss she shared with him was filled with her side of the story. A story the two of them would share for a lifetime. A story not meant for the *Pine Haven Record* but sure to be told to their grandchildren. A story of how Grump played matchmaker.

Epilogue

Mary Lou and Jared arrived at the Christmas Eve social about a half hour before it was scheduled to begin.

She found it hard to believe it had been over a month since they'd settled the ownership of the *Pine Haven Record*. The afternoon she'd found the second will, the sheriff had come by the paper and told them that Judge Sawyer had missed the train. It seemed the conductor had been more concerned about his schedule than an unhappy judge. The delay had allowed Judge Sawyer to amend his decree. He'd met them at the land office and ensured the new deed was drawn up to reflect their joint ownership.

Jared left Mary Lou just inside the door and went to interview Mr. Willis, the owner of the barn, for the article they would write about the social.

She made notes about the decorations Peggy Dismuke and a group of ladies from the church had used to turn the Circle W barn into a festive setting for the town to celebrate Christmas.

Large wreaths of green adorned with red bows hung over the doors at the front and back of the barn. The children of Pine Haven had made paper chains and cut out stars that hung between the beams that supported the loft. Lanterns lit the interior with a soft, warm glow. Pinecones and berries were nestled in lush greenery on the serving tables.

Jasmine Willis stood at the bottom of a ladder and handed Doc Willis a sprig of mistletoe tied with ribbon. He hung it on a nail on the beam that crossed the center of the barn.

Mary Lou stood by the punch table and swayed to the cheerful music as the band practiced one final time before the guests would arrive. She jumped when Jared came up behind her and whispered in her ear, "You look lovely tonight, Miss Ellison."

"You really shouldn't startle me like that, Jared."

"Well, the only way I know for you to stop being startled is for you to get used to having me near."

He led her to a chair. "I'd like to talk to you about something important."

"You would?" She strained to look up at him. "Then why don't you come down here where we'll be eye to eye."

He nodded. "I think I can manage that." He knelt on one knee in front of her. The music slowed and faded to silence as the musicians saw what he was doing. The few workers who were putting the finishing touches on the decor turned to watch.

Mary Lou couldn't breathe. He took her left hand in his and held up a beautiful ring with an oval emerald at its peak pinched between the thumb and forefinger of his other hand.

"Mary Lou, would you like to wear this?" He slid it on her finger. "For the rest of our lives?"

She wrapped him in a hug. "Yes! Yes!" She didn't loosen her grip when he stood and lifted her to her feet.

Andrew arrived just in time to witness the moment and called out from the doorway of the barn. "It's about time you kept your promise to take care of her!"

Everyone laughed and resumed their work as the band played a lively tune.

Mary Lou relaxed her arms enough to look into Jared's face, but she didn't release him.

He winked at her. "Were you surprised?"

"You have my permission to surprise me anytime you want to, Mr. Ivy."

He got punch for both of them and they sat close, talking for ages about the best time for a wedding. He kept saying New Year's Eve, while she extoled the romance of a Valentine wedding.

She had every intention of letting him have his way. But she wouldn't tell him just yet.

Several people stopped by during the course of the evening to congratulate Jared and offer her their best wishes.

Darkness had fallen outside and Mary Lou checked her watch for the time. She was about to close the cover when Jared reached for it. "May I?"

"What is it? You've seen this watch every day since you moved to Pine Haven."

"Where did you get it?" He ran his finger across the

carving on the outside of the pendant where it hung at shoulder height, pinned to her cape.

"Your grandfather gave it to me on my twenty-first birthday."

Jared smiled that smile that told her he was discovering something deeper than a surface story. "Is it engraved?"

She was puzzled now. "Yes."

He pulled his watch from his pocket and opened it. "My mother gave this to me when she was dying. She said Grump had sent it for my twenty-first birthday but she'd hidden it." He held it out for her to see. "Does yours have the same inscription as mine?"

She almost cried when she read, *A broken heart is an open heart.*

Unable to speak, she nodded.

"So when I said Grump knew we needed to be together, I think he knew our hearts would be broken in the process."

"He must have." She was amazed at how God had taken her on a journey from being a young girl no one wanted to the happiest of women with a heart that had to be broken so it could expand enough to hold all the love that would come into her life.

"Would you care to dance, Miss Ellison?" He could still make her blush with his charm.

"I would like that very much."

As they twirled around the barn floor on the Circle W Ranch with almost everyone in Pine Haven, Mary Lou felt wrapped up in a world all her own. Jared led them to the center of the floor and looked up at the mistletoe. She followed his gaze and at her smile he dropped a tender kiss on her lips.

He looked into her eyes, with one hand on her waist and the other holding her hand aloft. "We got off to such a rocky start. When did you decide you might be able to like me?"

"You may not believe it." She let him spin her and came back into his arms.

"Try me."

"When I saw you weeping at Mr. Ivy's grave. I knew then what a caring man you are."

"It was so hard to come here and find that he was gone. I wanted to know him and share his legacy with him."

Mary Lou smiled up at Jared. "His legacy is in good hands."

* * * * *

If you enjoyed THE RIGHTFUL HEIR, look for these other Love Inspired Historical titles by Angel Moore.

CONVENIENTLY WED
THE MARRIAGE BARGAIN

Find more great reads at www.LoveInspired.com

Dear Reader,

Life can turn suddenly and present an uncertain future.

Without Grump's love for Jared and Mary Lou, they would never have met. The tapestry of God's plan is bigger than we can see from our finite perspective. Grump's commitment to build the newspaper to provide for the people he loved ultimately became a legacy bigger than he'd ever imagined.

Thank you for reading *The Rightful Heir*. I hope you enjoyed the characters' journey from suspicion and mistrust to faith and commitment—and to their happily-ever-after.

Please look for another Pine Haven story soon.

I'd love to hear from you. You can reach me through my website at angelmoorebooks.com You'll find the latest news and links to connect with me on social media.

May God bless and guide you through life's situations with His wisdom and peace.

Angel Moore

REQUEST YOUR FREE BOOKS!

2 FREE INSPIRATIONAL NOVELS
PLUS 2 *FREE* MYSTERY GIFTS

Love Inspired® H I S T O R I C A L

YES! Please send me 2 FREE Love Inspired® Historical novels and my 2 FREE mystery gifts (gifts are worth about $10). After receiving them, if I don't wish to receive any more books, I can return the shipping statement marked "cancel." If I don't cancel, I will receive 4 brand-new novels every month and be billed just $4.99 per book in the U.S. or $5.49 per book in Canada. That's a saving of at least 17% off the cover price. It's quite a bargain! Shipping and handling is just 50¢ per book in the U.S. and 75¢ per book in Canada.* I understand that accepting the 2 free books and gifts places me under no obligation to buy anything. I can always return a shipment and cancel at any time. Even if I never buy another book, the two free books and gifts are mine to keep forever.

102/302 IDN GH6Z

Name	(PLEASE PRINT)	
Address		Apt. #
City	State/Prov.	Zip/Postal Code

Signature (if under 18, a parent or guardian must sign)

Mail to the **Reader Service:**
IN U.S.A.: P.O. Box 1867, Buffalo, NY 14240-1867
IN CANADA: P.O. Box 609, Fort Erie, Ontario L2A 5X3

Want to try two free books from another series?
Call 1-800-873-8635 or visit www.ReaderService.com.

* Terms and prices subject to change without notice. Prices do not include applicable taxes. Sales tax applicable in N.Y. Canadian residents will be charged applicable taxes. Offer not valid in Quebec. This offer is limited to one order per household. Not valid for current subscribers to Love Inspired Historical books. All orders subject to credit approval. Credit or debit balances in a customer's account(s) may be offset by any other outstanding balance owed by or to the customer. Please allow 4 to 6 weeks for delivery. Offer available while quantities last.

Your Privacy—The Reader Service is committed to protecting your privacy. Our Privacy Policy is available online at www.ReaderService.com or upon request from the Reader Service.

We make a portion of our mailing list available to reputable third parties that offer products we believe may interest you. If you prefer that we not exchange your name with third parties, or if you wish to clarify or modify your communication preferences, please visit us at www.ReaderService.com/consumerschoice or write to us at Reader Service Preference Service, P.O. Box 9062, Buffalo, NY 14240-9062. Include your complete name and address.

LIH15

SPECIAL EXCERPT FROM

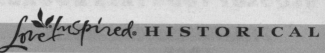 HISTORICAL

Nora Underhill needs a husband to fend off her overbearing family, and Simon Wallin wants the farmland he'd earn by marrying her. Their marriage of convenience seems like the perfect bargain...as long as love isn't part of the deal.

Read on for a sneak preview of
CONVENIENT CHRISTMAS WEDDING,
by Regina Scott, available November 2016
from Love Inspired Historical!

"There's the land office," Simon said, nodding to a whitewashed building ahead. He strode to it, shifted Nora's case under one arm and held the door open for her, then followed her inside with his brothers in his wake.

The long, narrow office was bisected by a counter. Chairs against the white-paneled walls told of lengthy waits, but today the only person in the room was a slender man behind the counter. He was shrugging into a coat as if getting ready to close up for the day.

Handing Nora's case to his brother John, Simon hurried forward. "I need to file a claim."

The fellow paused, eyed him and then glanced at Nora, who came to stand beside Simon. The clerk smoothed down his lank brown hair and stepped up to the counter. "Do you have the necessary application and fee?"

Simon drew out the ten-dollar fee, then pulled the papers from his coat and laid them on the counter. The clerk took his time reading them, glancing now and then at Nora, who bowed her head as if looking at the shoes peeping out from under her scalloped hem.

"And this is your wife?" he asked at last.

Simon nodded. "I brought witnesses to the fact, as required."

John and Levi stepped closer. The clerk's gaze returned to Nora. "Are you Mrs. Wallin?"

She glanced at Simon as if wondering the same thing, and for a moment he thought they were all doomed. Had she decided he wasn't the man she'd thought him? Had he married for nothing?

Nora turned and held out her hand to the clerk. "Yes, I'm Mrs. Simon Wallin. No need to wish me happy, for I find I have happiness to spare."

The clerk's smile appeared, brightening his lean face. "Mr. Wallin is one fortunate fellow." He turned to pull a heavy leather-bound book from his desk, thumped it down on the counter and opened it to a page to begin recording the claim.

Simon knew he ought to feel blessed indeed as he accepted the receipt from the clerk. He had just earned his family the farmland they so badly needed. The acreage would serve the Wallins for years to come and support the town that had been his father's dream. Yet something nagged at him, warned him that he had miscalculated.

He never miscalculated.

Don't miss
CONVENIENT CHRISTMAS WEDDING
by Regina Scott, available November 2016 wherever
Love Inspired® Historical books and ebooks are sold.

www.LoveInspired.com